SONS FROM AFAR

I0891625

Books by Cynthia Voigt

THE BAD GIRLS SERIES

Bad Girls

Bad, Badder, Baddest

It's Not Easy Being Bad

Bad Girls in Love

Bad Girls, Bad Girls, Whatcha Gonna Do?

THE TILLERMAN SERIES

Homecoming

Dicey's Song

A Solitary Blue

The Runner

Come a Stranger

Sons from Afar

Seventeen Against the Dealer

THE KINGDOM SERIES

Jackaroo

On Fortune's Wheel

The Wings of a Falcon

Elske

OTHER BOOKS

Building Blocks

The Callender Papers

David and Jonathan

Izzy, Willy-Nilly

Orfe

Tell Me if the Lovers Are Losers

Tree by Leaf

The Vandemark Mummy

When She Hollers

SONS FROM AFAR

CYNTHIA VOIGT

ATHENEUM BOOKS FOR YOUNG READERS
New York London Toronto Sydney New Delhi

ATHENEUM BOOKS FOR YOUNG READERS
An imprint of Simon & Schuster Children's Publishing Division
1230 Avenue of the Americas, New York, New York 10020
This book is a work of fiction. Any references to historical events, real people, or real locales are used fictitiously. Other names, characters, places, and incidents are products of the author's imagination, and any resemblance to actual events or locales or persons, living or dead, is entirely coincidental.
Copyright © 1987 by Cynthia Voigt
The stories about Daedalus and Icarus and about Apollo and Phaëton are derived from *Bulfinch's Mythology*.
ATHENEUM BOOKS FOR YOUNG READERS is a registered trademark of Simon & Schuster, Inc.
For information about special discounts for bulk purchases, please contact Simon & Schuster Special Sales at 1-866-506-1949 or business@simonandschuster.com.
The Simon & Schuster Speakers Bureau can bring authors to your live event. For more information or to book an event, contact the Simon & Schuster Speakers Bureau at 1-866-248-3049 or visit our website at www.simonspeakers.com.
Also available in an Atheneum Books for Young Readers hardcover edition
Book design by Debra Sfetsios-Conover
The text for this book is set in Baskerville.
Manufactured in the United States of America
First Atheneum Books for Young Readers paperback edition July 2012
2 4 6 8 10 9 7 5 3
The Library of Congress has cataloged the hardcover edition as follows:
Voigt, Cynthia.
Sons from afar.
Summary: Six years after coming to live with their grandmother, James and Sammy Tillerman go in search of their long-lost father.
ISBN 978-0-689-31349-3
[1. Fathers—Fiction. 2. Brothers—Fiction.] I. Title.
PZ7.V874Sp 1987
[Fic] 87-1857
ISBN 978-1-4424-5065-3 (hc)
ISBN 978-1-4424-2883-6 (pbk)

SONS FROM AFAR

She didn't know about those boys, Gram thought, watching them through the kitchen window. She'd sent them down to bail the boat, which Sammy didn't mind—but James was dawdling on behind his brother. Who knew what went on inside James's head, who ever knew, she thought. Her attention went back to the dinner plates she was washing off in a sink full of warm, soapy water. When she lifted her eyes again, she could see only the big vegetable patch, waiting to be planted, soon now, and the stand of pines melting away into the hazy evening.

At the unforgotten emptiness of that scene the smile she had felt, thinking about those two boys, faded. Her hands rested quiet in the water. She got her hands moving again, soaping off the last plates, piling them up on the counter. Twilight was a bad time for remembering: It was the loneliness of things lost, lost and gone, that twilight recalled. There were seasons of your life, she knew, when remembering lay like winter on your spirit; but there were also seasons when remembering rose in your heart like a summer sun. Her busy hands splashed among the cutlery, bringing it up to the foamy surface; she sponged over forks and big serving spoons, then set them down with a clatter on top of the plates. She didn't know how those boys would manage the chore she'd given them, but she thought she could make a good guess about who would actually do the work, and who would sit there thinking about nobody could imagine what. That thought made her smile.

She pulled the plug on the sink and the water gurgled out, down the drain. She could barely hear the notes from the piano while the water was draining.

Then, when she turned on the tap to rinse off the glasses, plates, and forks, she couldn't hear the piano at all. But she knew it was there, all the same, as she ran the washed dishes under scorching hot water, the way Dicey said dishes should be rinsed. If you rinsed them with really hot water, Dicey had told her, they practically dried themselves. In this house, with her three grandchildren living there and the fourth away at college, there wasn't much danger of loneliness cozying up close to you. From the first day Dicey had walked up on her from she didn't know where, from the end of that day when the four of them sat at her table for the first time and she'd been trying to tell herself it wouldn't be right to let them stay, however much they needed a home, because the kind of home she'd offer wouldn't be right for them; from the first, they had crowded up against her loneliness and crowded it out.

They hadn't given her half a chance. They'd steamrollered her, outfaced her, tricked her; they'd tied her up in knots until she'd known there wasn't any way she was going to let go of this second chance. You're a foolish old woman, she had told herself, not knowing which choice was the greater foolishness. I'm not so old, she had answered herself. Avoiding the question, as she well knew. All she had known, then—and at that thought she laughed out loud—was which was the cowardly choice. So she made the other one.

Almost six years ago, that was. Six years and how many of these scouring pads, she thought, watching the blue suds foam up around the inside of the stew pot, the fine woolly steel scraping away at crusted bits of meat and potatoes. Carefully, she squeezed the extra water out of the pad and set it into the soap holder Jeff Greene had given her a few Christmases back. Over the years, almost six years now, a whole second life given to her, it wasn't only her grandchildren who had crowded away at her. It was people attached to them as well, like Jeff who'd made up his mind years ago about Dicey. If making up your mind was what you did about love, she thought; personally she'd say love had a way of grabbing you by the throat and shaking you until you cooperated. This soap dish Jeff had given her—china painted a midnight blue with the moon on the bottom and the stars sprayed all around. Gram suspected that it was valuable, though Jeff—who knew how to give presents—would never say so; whatever her suspicions, she knew that it was something lovely, and she valued it. Dicey knew Jeff's value, she suspected, but Dicey—like some other people she could name—got her mind made up over things.

Gram could shake Dicey up, she knew that, and Jeff, if ever he wanted to, would be able to. Mina too, Mina Smiths never took any guff off of Dicey. Those two could stand up to one another, and they stood up beside one another most of the time. Mina crowded in on her too, and not only because of Dicey. Mina had taken Sammy out to the tennis courts, saying she needed someone to play with and guessing, quite rightly, that Sammy was the one who'd make a real opponent for her. The person who introduced Sammy to tennis did him a favor. Mina was that person, and Jeff helped her out. It was Jeff who'd found the tennis racquet to put into Sammy's hands, because the Tillermans didn't have money for anything extra in their lives. Gram was willing to bet she knew where Jeff had found that racquet, and it wasn't in his closet, but Jeff knew what presents needed giving. Gram had learned, she thought, turning off the faucet, how to receive. Or she hoped she had. If she hadn't, she thought, it was sheer stubborn stupidity on her part.

With the water turned off, the piano notes were back in the room with her, accompanied now by Maybeth singing. The dishes dripped away onto the draining rack. Gram used the drip-dry method for dishes. Maybeth liked to dry them right away, and stack them back in their proper places. Maybeth's voice made Gram take the towel up and start rubbing at glasses. If she dried, then she could stay out in the kitchen, listening.

She supposed she ought to worry about Maybeth, but somehow she never could. Maybeth was singing one of her songs for school chorus. The song was about coral being made, and pearls, but Maybeth's voice was like gold. Six years ago, when those four bedraggled children had sat down at her table, Gram might have worried most about Maybeth, with her silences and her slowness of speech, with her angelic face and fearful eyes. Now she knew better, although she'd have been right enough then. Even more than the rest of them, Maybeth had grown, like some sapling planted down into the right place. Dicey might have been the one who took charge and led her brothers and sister all that long distance to plunk them down at Gram's table, but it was Maybeth who was home. Home in both senses—at home here, and the home itself for the rest of them. Maybeth's golden voice floated across the quiet kitchen and wrapped itself around her grandmother.

Maybeth had her mother's voice, Liza's voice, and that was a pain and a joy so mixed together Gram couldn't sort them out. But Maybeth wouldn't have Liza's life, the life that had taken all the weakness in Gram's daughter and blown it up until she couldn't stay alive any longer. That life wasn't going to happen to Maybeth.

That, Gram thought, putting the glasses back onto their shelf and beginning on the plates, that she was sure of. The other three she might worry about—when she wasn't too busy, if she found the time—but Maybeth was home, in both senses, home for good. The other three now—those boys, she thought, looking out the window at the gathering darkness, wondering what it was they thought they wanted from one another but didn't know to ask for.

There was so much she didn't know, and learning what she could kept her busy. Maybe she'd learn enough—the Lord willing and the creek don't rise, she thought. She didn't know what it was all for, what it was all about, or even how it was she'd been given this second chance for her life, but she knew enough to be grateful. She'd be of no more use to anybody than a flea's eyeball, if she didn't know that. Although who knew if fleas had eyeballs.

James would know, if he'd ever read it in some book, sometime. Or Sammy, he was the kind who might be curious enough to put a flea under a microscope. The trick would be to catch the flea first. Catching the flea was the hard part, the way fleas jumped around. Sammy would take a try at that trick, if he ever thought of it, and James would know what book to look in and he'd remember the answer, too. So if Gram wanted to know about the eyeballs on fleas—which she didn't—she knew who to ask.

CHAPTER 1

James Tillerman watched his brother, Sammy, who was bailing two inches of rain water from their boat. It had rained all the previous night—a cold slanting March rain—and most of the morning, too. Then, Marchlike, the wind had shifted in the afternoon to the southwest, blowing the heavy clouds away, blowing warm. In the twilight, the boys had come down to bail the boat.

Sammy sat on the narrow gunwales, using his weight to tilt the boat and bring the water within it into easy reach. He bent and straightened, rhythmically, bailing the boat. The bailer was an empty bleach jug with the top cut off; it poured water into the bay with a wet, rushing sound. Sammy, whatever he did, moved as if he would never get tired. James, sitting cross-legged on the dock, his arms resting on his thighs, his fingers laced together, watched his brother.

"Do you ever wonder—?" James started.

"No." Sammy bent, straightened, poured water out into water.

Irritated, James looked at his own hands, jealous, too. He moved the fourth finger of his right hand beneath the fingers of his left hand, then moved over the little finger to conceal the gap. In the growing darkness, you could fool someone, they might not notice that one finger was apparently missing. Things were so simple for Sammy, clear and simple. But he had wanted to ask Sammy. He didn't like being just cut off like that, didn't like it one bit.

Sammy broke the rhythm of bailing to look at his brother, sitting there on the dock above, just sitting there looking at his own hands. He could have asked James to help out. If he asked James, James would probably get down into the boat and help. But it seemed to Sammy that James shouldn't be waiting around to be asked, shouldn't just sit there, a pale blob in the dim air. There was another bailer. The job wouldn't take so long if James helped, and Sammy wouldn't have minded getting his hands into the cold water only half as many times. The air was warm enough, but the water held a winter chill longer than the air, long into spring, just the way it held summer's warmth long into fall.

Sammy bent to work again, enjoying it actually. It was good to feel the muscles along his back and shoulders, the way they worked. It was good to feel the balance of his body, the way his legs kept his own weight and the water's weight and the boat's buoyant weight all in the right balance. His body knew how to do that, without any thinking. James would have to think it out, and he'd probably have gotten both of them wet before he figured out how to sit right. James was always thinking about something, wondering about something; it was almost as if he was always trying to make Sammy feel stupid, showing off a busier, smarter brain. Sammy smiled to himself, remembering how long it had taken him to figure out that there was no way he'd ever catch up the three years between him and James. But he was catching up in height—at five five he was only an inch shorter, and he weighed more, too, because of his muscular build. Sammy looked, he knew, older than twelve, while James looked younger than fifteen-almost-sixteen. Sammy didn't mind that, not one bit.

"Seriously," James said. "Wonder about our father. Do you ever?"

"Cripes, no." When Sammy emptied the bailer, the water splashed up from the dark bay. "Why would I wonder about him? He never even saw me."

"I do."

"Not even once."

"He did me, I guess. I don't remember. Dicey remembers—but even Dicey was just a little kid the last time she probably saw him. I might as well never have had a father."

"Considering that he blew the scene before I was born, I'd say I didn't have one. So, why worry about him?"

"Haven't you ever heard of genes and chromosomes? Heredity?"

"Don't talk to me like I'm stupid."

"Look," James began, leaning forward.

"I can't look. I'm working," Sammy pointed out. "It's too dark to see anyway."

"We all have the same eyes," James went on, ignoring what Sammy said, because it wasn't to the point. The point was heredity. "The particular tones and colors vary, but they're all hazel, because of dominant genes. We've got Tillerman eyes, that's the way genetics work. Have you heard of Mendel's laws of heredity?"

James didn't think Sammy would have, but he waited a minute, anyway, before going on, in case his brother had anything to say.

"Mendel discovered genetics. He worked with beans. To discover what laws inherited characteristics are governed by."

"What kind of beans? Green beans or pole beans? Lima beans?"

"Don't be ridiculous. What does it matter what kind of beans?"

"I don't know what any of it matters."

"Because of the law of dominance," James explained patiently. "Because you get one gene—for eye color, for example—from each one of your parents. So there are two genes for eye color. If they're different, one of them will be dominant, and that's the color eyes you'll have."

"Very educational." Sammy shifted his position, sliding into the boat and hunkering down low next to the backseat, careful to not clunk his shoulder on the motor. The bottom of the bailer scraped along the wooden floor of the boat. Sammy was almost done, which was lucky because it was almost full dark. James continued explaining genetics to his brother.

"So all of our physical characteristics are inherited, according to Mendel's laws. But it's not just physical characteristics. Maybe. That's one thing I'm wondering about. It's like—mental characteristics, too. You know, intelligence, right or left brain dominance, maybe even aptitudes."

Sammy was looking at him, but he wasn't really listening.

"Integrity, aggression, whether you're an extrovert or an introvert, whether you're psychologically stable or have a tendency to mental disease, like schizophrenia, maybe that kind of thing too," James went on. "Nobody knows for sure just how much is encoded in DNA, they keep finding out more about it, so it could be that character traits as well are inherited."

"So what?" Sammy stood up. He dropped the bailer into the bottom of the boat. Reaching up, because the boat sat low on a low tide, he hauled himself onto the dock.

James gave up trying to explain to Sammy, who didn't care about anything that wasn't right under his nose. Intellectual curiosity, that was what Sammy didn't have.

"Thanks for all the help," Sammy said, sarcastic. He stood next to James, but looking out to where the dark bay moved under the dark sky.

James kept his mind on the important thing. "I mean, we don't even know what color his eyes were. Or are."

"Whose?"

"Our father's."

"What does the color of his eyes matter?"

"We don't know anything. We might even be orphans."

"Come on, James," Sammy turned to him. "How can we be orphans? We had Momma. And—cripes—we've got mothers coming out our ears, between Gram and Dicey and even Maybeth." That idea made him laugh and James had to smile, too, in the darkness.

"Yeah, I know, but—"

"Why are you getting hung up on that now?" Sammy asked.

"I don't know," James said truthfully. "I've just been wondering about him."

"Seems to me the last thing we need is a father." Sammy sat down. His legs hung over the edge of the dock. "Besides, I thought you had a big algebra test tomorrow, and a history report to work on."

James didn't answer. Sammy didn't mind. He lay back and looked at the sky. The stars were coming out, little pale pinpricks of light. He knew they weren't really coming out, that they'd been burning away out in the darkness of space all day long; but it looked like they were coming out, like flowers coming into bloom. Sammy had his head against the stiff splintery boards of the dock, and he was looking out into space so deep it might as well be endless. He thought it would be great to explore space: sailing out among the stars, discovering . . . you couldn't even begin to imagine what you might discover. If there were huge winds that blew across the vast empty reaches, and your ship had a big metal sail . . . but he didn't think there were space winds. He could ask James, but he didn't want to. "I'm good at math and science, I could be an astronaut," he said to the stars.

"I thought you were going to play tennis," James answered.

"I'll do both," Sammy said. The sky turned darker, and darker still. The stars burned white, making the sky look crowded. You could put a tennis court in a spaceship; the ship would have to be large, anyway, and people would have to have something to do, to fill in the vast stretches of time, and to keep in shape. "Why shouldn't I do both?"

"Because they're both careers for young men—too short-lived," James's voice informed him. "Be practical."

That was pretty funny, coming from James, Sammy thought. Now James was getting going on being a lawyer and Sammy was letting his brother's words blow away on the wind. He'd heard it all before, about a 4.0 average so you could get a scholarship to a good college; about the right major, something to do with history or political science, to prepare you for the three-year course in law school; about the best schools and the scholarships they offered to the best students. After that, the voice went on—Sammy had heard it all before—you just chose how you wanted to make your money. Government work was secure but paid the least. If you did corporate law, working for a big corporation, you earned big bucks but the job wasn't that secure. Or you could work for a law firm, criminal law or property law, or handling wills and estates. You could do whatever you wanted, whatever you were good at, in a law firm, as you worked your way up to being a partner and taking a percentage of the firm's earnings. With a law degree you could even go into politics—although Sammy couldn't see anybody voting for James. He didn't think *he* would.

"International law, international banking law," James's voice said. "I think I'd be good at that."

"I wouldn't," Sammy said. "I wouldn't like something where you didn't do anything."

James sputtered and Sammy was afraid he'd start explaining about how important banking was, but he didn't.

James had heard the boredom in Sammy's voice and reminded himself that Sammy was still young, still just a kid, only twelve. "What about *your* homework?" he asked.

"What I don't get done tonight I can finish on the bus."

James shrugged: Sammy just didn't care about grades. He just didn't know how important they were; he didn't care about knowing things either.

"You know," Sammy's voice said, "it always looks like the stars are coming out, even though they aren't."

"They're really suns," James told him. He looked up at the sky then. It was black, silky black, with no moon yet so the suns burned clear out there. James picked out the constellations he knew: Orion, by his belt, he could always always find Orion; the big dipper, like a geometric figure, like a rhomboid; the little dipper, a smaller rhomboid, his eyes searched it out. Then the North Star, Polaris. The Pleiades, the sisters, crowded together, the seventh sister burning faintly. "Every one of them is a sun, a mass of burning gases. Do you know how hot the sun burns?"

"So what," Sammy's uninterested voice said.

"Neither do I," James admitted. He used to know, but he'd forgotten. Sammy's laugh sounded friendly. "Tell you a story," James offered. "You want to hear a story?" Sammy always liked being told stories.

"Good-o."

James identified the story's source, first. "This is from Greek mythology. There was an inventor, named Daedalus, a famous inventor. Everybody knew about him. So when King Minos of Crete wanted a labyrinth built—a maze—where he'd keep his son, the Minotaur, in the middle—"

"I remember the Minotaur," Sammy interrupted. "It was in my book of monsters. It was half man, half bull."

"Yeah. So Minos hired Daedalus to design and build this

labyrinth. Daedalus took his son Icarus with him to Crete. But when the job was finished, Minos kept them prisoners in a high tower."

"Why?"

"Because they knew how to get out of the maze and Minos wanted that to be a secret. In the tower, they had to haul their food up in baskets, and they had candles for light. The only things that could get into the tower were birds. They were prisoners there for a long time. There was no way to escape, but Daedalus figured out a way. See, when the birds flew in they'd shed their feathers. So he and Icarus collected the feathers. They stuck them together with wax, to make huge wings. When they had enough—it must have taken years—they were ready to fly out, away, to fly free. Before they left, Daedalus warned Icarus that he shouldn't fly too close to the sun, because the heat of it would melt the wax that was holding the wings together. But Icarus didn't pay attention. Or he forgot, maybe. Because when they were out and flying, he went up, and up, until the heat was too great. His wings fell apart and he fell—he fell out of the sky into the ocean. He drowned." James never could tell a story the way it should be told; when he told it, he could hear it sound like a series of facts, like a history book, not like a story.

"I can see why he did that," Sammy said. "If you could really fly, you'd always want to go higher, once you started flying. Wouldn't you?"

Not if he'd been warned against it he wouldn't, James thought, and explained why. "He should have listened to his father. His father knew."

"That's an interesting story, even if the air actually gets colder as you go higher, even if they'd need more than wax. Even if—" Sammy sat up suddenly. "Okay, James, what is it? You figure that if we had a father he could tell us what we should do?"

"We have a father," James said. Now that Sammy was willing to talk about it, and they were facing one another, James wasn't sure he really wanted to talk. He looked over Sammy's shoulder to the night sky.

"You know what I mean," Sammy said. James guessed he did. "What would a father do, anyway?"

"Fathers are—like a constant," James tried to explain. "They're always there, they don't change, they know how things go, they have experience, or knowledge, anyway, they're pretty wise—so they can help you decide."

"Not ours. Not our father."

"You sound angry." James thought maybe he shouldn't have brought the subject up.

"When I think about him, I am," Sammy said. "I mean, you don't go around just starting babies and—ignoring them. Abandoning them. Or their mother, either."

"That's what our father did," James pointed out. "We don't know anything about him. Not anything. We should know about him."

"We do," Sammy's voice insisted.

"No, we don't. We don't *know*—although, if fathers take responsibility—you know, keep you safe?—because they're bigger and stronger like 'my-daddy-can-beat-up-your-daddy'—and help you out of trouble." James made himself draw the logical conclusion: "If that's what fathers do, ours is pretty much of a bust."

"You can say that again."

"But maybe he didn't have a chance, or something. We don't know."

"You mean maybe he died?"

"He could have. We don't know anything about him. Nobody would even know to tell us if he was dead and couldn't have taken care of us anyway."

"But what difference would that make?" Sammy asked. James waited while Sammy worked it out. "Do you mean a father would be on your side? Like the Professor and Jeff, like the Professor is on Jeff's side? Like, the way the Professor knows what Jeff means, or what he wants."

"Or what you needed, and he'd want you to have that."

"Do you think Momma might not have died, if we'd had one?" That thought got Sammy up onto his feet.

"I dunno about that, Sammy." James kept emotion out of his voice. The trouble with Sammy was, when he did care, he never stopped. He cared too much. "It doesn't do any good to think about that. You can't change what's happened."

They didn't say anything then, for a while. Sammy lay down on his back again. James moved down the dock, lifting his backside carefully to be sure not to get splinters, and tried his brother's position. His calves dangled down over the water and the boards were uncomfortable against the shoulder bones in his back. That was the place where wings would be attached, if you had a pair of huge wings attached to you, if your father had designed a pair of wings made out of feathers and wax so you could escape. The wind flowed over the water, over the two of them, over the marsh grasses and into the pine trees. The noises of the wind rippling the water and echoing in James's ears, the wind running along the tops of the grass and then tangling itself up in the thick-growing pines—sometimes, what really scared James was the sense that he was being blown along on some wind, and he couldn't do anything about it.

"I thought, maybe we could try to find him. Or find out something about him," James said.

"Why?"

"Aren't you even curious? I mean, especially if they're right about how much we inherit from our parents, what Mendel discovered about dominant and recessive genes—don't you want to know?"

"No," said Sammy.

"I do." He wasn't about to try to explain to Sammy how true that was.

"Well, if you do find out, don't come telling me about it."

James guessed he wouldn't. He guessed he was sorry he'd even asked Sammy about it. He guessed—it was a pretty stupid thing, anyway, and impossible anyway, since none of them knew anything about their father, except Gram, who had actually met him. And he couldn't ask Gram about his father because—she wouldn't understand. James didn't know what it was his grandmother wouldn't understand, but he knew she wouldn't understand it. Not because she didn't want to, but because she couldn't. Because she wasn't a teenage boy who needed to have a father. Or, if he couldn't have one, at least needed to know about the one he didn't have. Even Sammy didn't understand.

James sat up. He guessed the whole idea was pretty useless, so he thought he'd go take a look at the three chapters they were going to be tested on in algebra. He didn't think there was anything he didn't understand, but it never hurt to review. It was better to forget about his father and concentrate on his grades.

"There's only one reason I'd ever want to find him," Sammy said.

"Yeah? What?" James stood by his brother's head, waiting.

"To hurt him."

"That's weird." Sometimes, James just didn't know about Sammy.

"Well, it's true," Sammy said.

James left Sammy to the wind-filled silence of earth and space and went alone up the path to the house. The long path from the dock to the farmhouse wound like a black ribbon. The marsh grasses spread dark and restless on both sides. The pines that grew in a mass between the marsh and the garden waited ahead, in deeper darkness. The night lay around James as dark and uneasy as his own life. James wasn't used to dreading the school days, but because they ended in baseball practice, he did. He'd been dreading them ever since baseball practice began, in late February.

James knew why he'd gone out for baseball, but he didn't know whether he was right in his analysis of the problem. He hated making himself run laps and do exercises; he did it, of course, but really because he was afraid of the coach noticing him and making him an object of scorn for everybody to enjoy. He knew he'd just sit on the bench all season long. In fact, he was pretty much counting on that. When he was in the outfield, playing, all he could think about was how much he hoped nothing would come his way. He didn't like playing, or even drills; he spent all his time afraid of messing up. James had gone out for baseball because he wasn't about to try lacrosse—and get his teeth knocked out or his bones broken, or something. He went out for baseball because he really wanted to sing with the chorus. Because only dorks sang in chorus.

That was the problem. James thought people thought he was one of the dorks—a wimp, a nerd—whatever—a jerk. A lot of the things he liked were dorky things to like—math and Shakespeare, thinking, and singing stuff like Handel's *Messiah* the way the chorus did at the Christmas assembly. And he was so afraid—name it and he'd get anxious about it, war, any disease, death, people seeing how dorky he really was. He did his best, he did what he could, but what could you do when you were weak and skinny and didn't look cool, and couldn't ever say what you were thinking because people would think you were showing off. He'd learned how to get A's without people minding, or labeling him a brain, without being the kind of student teachers paid special attention to. Teacher's pet, there was the kiss of death. He knew how to say just so much, and no more, of what he was thinking. A real dork wouldn't figure out how to do that, would he?

James had tried to think things out, figure out why, what there was about him. He knew he didn't fit in. He was wrong, somehow, and he wanted to be all right, but it was almost as if there was some secret nobody would tell him, so he was always going to be stuck outside. For a second, the image of Celie Anderson's face floated in front of him, but it was too painful and he pushed her away; but if he could just once, just for one second, get her to look at him as if he were a human being . . . not the way she did and had done for the two years she'd lived in town, looking through him as if he were invisible, or not even there, the way people looked at dorks. Didn't look at them, that was more accurate.

In the denser air of the belt of pines, James admitted to himself that they might be right about him; if that was true, it wouldn't do much good to try to change their minds. He stopped walking and let the darkness come up over him like water. He was so embarrassed about himself, so ashamed. When he thought about it, there wasn't much he was proud of in his life. One thing was the way he'd always helped Maybeth with school, first reading and then math, too, whatever she needed. He did a good job of helping his younger sister, he knew that. He should probably be a teacher, or something, some no-money job where it didn't matter if you were a wimp. Also, he sometimes had good ideas, like when he suggested to Gram that she rent out the acreage of the farm, so the land would earn them some money. Now the fields were planted every spring, with soybeans, and Gram and James had negotiated a deal with Mr. Hitchins, the farmer, to take some of the rent in cash in the spring, and the rest in a percentage of the net profit. So James wasn't a total loss. He thought.

But he really didn't understand—they'd been here for five years, now, five and a half, and all the rest of them had done all right. Even Dicey, who was the most different of all the Tillermans, had a couple of friends; Dicey didn't care much about people, what they thought, but she had Jeff who probably wanted to marry her, and Mina, who was popular with everyone because she was such a terrific person. James figured that Dicey was probably out there at college right now, finding one or two really good friends. Maybeth, for all that she was so slow at school, which usually guaranteed unpopularity, was always getting phone calls, getting invited to parties or to do things. People liked Maybeth. She was like their Momma had been, just a good person, and when you heard her singing around the house it made the whole day better. That was another reason James couldn't sign up for chorus, because Maybeth was in it, and nobody was as good as Maybeth. Then Sammy, who was—if anybody thought about it—almost as stubborn and cranky as Dicey; everybody thought Sammy was cool, a cool dude. He was a natural athlete, and good-looking, and he didn't care about people so people cared about him.

Which left James. A real lunch-pail. Maybe, he thought, making his feet start moving again, knowing it did no good to hang around in the darkness thinking about himself, maybe he'd end up like Gram, the way she lived before they all dropped down on her, all the Tillermans. Maybe that was the way he'd end up living—everybody thinking he was crazy and leaving him alone—except he would go to law school and get a good job, and make money. He wasn't the kind of person who got physical work done, he knew that, but he'd get his scholarships and his education, he'd make good money.

His father had been the kind of man who just—had these children and then disappeared, not even giving them his name, not even marrying Momma. And his grandfather, on his mother's side, had read all of the books on the shelves in the living room, read Aristotle and Gibbon and just about everything and he'd just—stayed there on the farm, maybe trapped, but to hear Gram talk it sounded like he'd choked to death on his own life, or his own brains, or something. Gram might be weird, but she was nobody's fool, and she had courage. James almost wished he'd gotten his grandmother's courage instead of his grandfather's brains.

James heard running footsteps and waited in the middle of the garden for Sammy to catch up with him. The house, a black square with light the color of melted butter pouring out of its windows, lay ahead of him. Sammy was running fast, but easily—How did the kid get the energy, James wondered.

"Good, you waited," Sammy said. He wasn't even breathing heavily. "I figured, we should go in together, because we went out together. Or Gram might worry."

James hadn't even thought of that, and he was supposed to be so smart.

"With Dicey away," Sammy explained, "Gram does the worrying for both of them. I liked it better when they split it up, didn't you? Sometimes they overlooked things that way."

They walked together back to the house. Sometimes, James really liked the way Sammy saw things.

"I wish Dicey was here," Sammy said.

"I kind of like not having her telling me how to run my life," James admitted.

Sammy ignored that. "Anyway, how would you go about finding him, tracking him down?" he asked.

"I don't know," James said, as if he wasn't interested.

"Yes you do. You always have ideas. And some of them are even good ones." Sammy seemed to catch on that James didn't think his teasing was any too funny. He ran ahead, up the steps and into the kitchen.

James came more slowly, watching. Maybeth sat at the wooden table, reading something, a textbook, her lips moving the way they still did when the material was confusing to her, her finger pointing under the words. She looked up at Sammy, and smiled. "Hi. Where's James?" Pretty, she was pretty, as pretty as Momma, James thought, stepping into the doorway.

"Hey," Sammy said. "Is there anything to eat?"

"Cookies," Maybeth told him, her voice soft and low; even when she was just talking, Maybeth sounded like she was singing. "There was a phone call for you, a girl. She didn't leave her name. She said she'll call back later maybe."

"I hope she doesn't," Sammy answered, taking the top off the glass jar where they kept cookies. "Girls are a pain."

James stood by the door. Those two, they'd gotten their Momma's good looks, her golden good looks, and he'd gotten—he didn't know what he'd gotten. He'd gotten lost and helpless and confused. He'd gotten the bad differences. No wonder he was such a dork. But maybe he would do it, anyway, maybe he *would* try to trace their father and find out something about him. Maybe he'd just go ahead and do it.

CHAPTER 2

James did know that they had all been born in the same place, the hospital back in Provincetown, Massachusetts, where they used to live. He sat down that night and wrote a letter to the hospital, saying who he was, the date of his birth, and who his mother was. He asked for a copy of his birth certificate. Birth certificates had both the mother's and the father's names on them. When he was satisfied with it, he typed up a copy of his letter on the old office-style manual typewriter Gram had gotten for them. He didn't remember the name of the hospital, or its street address, although he had a vague memory of a building he knew was the hospital where he'd been born. He figured Provincetown was small enough so the letter would get there addressed to Provincetown Hospital, Provincetown, Mass.

When he had folded his letter and sealed it into the envelope, he spent some time sitting back, trying to remember the place where he had spent the first ten years of his life. The pictures his memory came up with were blurry at the edges, and faded quickly into one another—he remembered the children's room at the library, the way it filled with sunlight, the way motes of dust floated in that sunlight; he remembered the way their little house was hidden among sand dunes with long sparse beach grass to cut at your bare feet; he remembered the store where Momma had worked, and being given chunks of fried bread by the owner's wife, thick, hot, chewy chunks of sweet dough, dusted over with confectioner's sugar. He remembered a map of the original thirteen colonies he'd done in third grade. His mother—with a terrible rush like a wind rising up suddenly across the night, he remembered the kind of worry he'd lived with that last year or so with Momma, not knowing what to say because you never knew what she'd answer, because her answers didn't make any sense to him. He remembered pretending not to hear the other kids calling him names, espccially bastard, even though he had no idea of what the word really meant then, he just knew it was a name they said to hurt him. He remembered sitting there at a blue desk, pretending he was deaf, and the way they got bolder because he didn't dare get up and look at them. Dicey had always hit out at anyone trying to pick on her, like Sammy did, but James didn't know how to fight. He'd seen the bloody noses and swollen faces, the cut knuckles, after fights; he could imagine how that felt, he could almost see how bad the flesh and bones looked, under the bruised skin. He remembered—he stopped remembering because it hurt him, the confusion of feelings toward his Momma, he'd felt so sorry for her and been so angry, and he didn't know how to do anything more than be as smart as he could in school. What they would have done without Dicey, he didn't know. She had herded them all down to Gram's house that summer, when Momma left; no matter what got in their way she kept on going. And then James remembered—as if it was just happening—how it felt when Gram said they could stay, stay here, stay home with her. It had felt as if the sun was rising up inside of him, as if magic had happened, better than magic, a miracle. Sitting at his desk in his bedroom on the second story of the old farmhouse, with the wind whispering outside his open windows, remembering, James felt again the sudden joy when Gram said it was okay for them to stay. Like the whole school chorus singing out the "Hallelujah Chorus," it was that kind of feeling.

James looked out of the window at the night, where he couldn't see anything. He'd used to think that Maybeth was the one who might, like Momma, slip away into depression and quiet lunacy. But now he thought, probably he was the one who might, because he was the one who was so different from the rest of them. Dicey and Sammy never seemed to be afraid. James was the one it was so easy to make afraid, who could make himself afraid by just thinking. Even Maybeth, who was the shy one, timid, could withdraw into herself, and not be afraid. James had thought about them: Maybeth was almost exactly like Momma, and not just in her looks; Sammy and Dicey, for all they looked so different, were a similar mix of Tillerman and whoever their father was. James figured, he was probably the exact opposite of Maybeth, so he was probably like his father. Whoever that was.

Gram had said their father was the kind of man who sailed close to the wind, James remembered that, and she'd said he was the kind of man who'd gamble, and probably cheat, too. That was great, just great. Wasn't that great? Another reason not to ask Gram about him. James pushed the typewriter to the back of the desk and opened his history book.

The next morning, James put his letter into the mailbox. He pulled up the flag, to let the postman know there was outgoing mail, and closed the little metal door. Maybeth either didn't notice or assumed he'd written to Dicey. She didn't ask him any questions; Maybeth wouldn't ever ask, if she thought you didn't want to say. Sammy had gone off on his bike twenty minutes earlier. James—looking around at the moist brown fields and the pale sky filled up with filmy clouds—regretted not having ridden his bike in to school.

He crossed the road to stand next to Maybeth. She was dressed almost exactly like him, in jeans, shirt, and sweater, but you'd never mistake Maybeth for a boy. It wasn't just her figure, although she had a really good figure. It was the way her hair curled around her head, too, the way her eyes looked at you, something about the way she held her shoulders and when she moved—feminine. "It's warm," James said to her.

"Yes," she said, her mouth turned up in a not-quite smile, her hazel eyes peaceful.

"You okay for school today, and all?" James asked.

She nodded. She'd tell him if there was something she didn't understand, in math or English or science. Maybeth didn't need any help in home ec—she got B's in the course, her first B's ever in school, and they'd probably have been A's if there hadn't been some written tests she had to take. Chorus, too, when she was in ninth grade next year and got grades in chorus, that would be an A, James was willing to bet. He was honestly glad there were things Maybeth was good at. She earned her C's and D's with hard work, and he never could see how she just kept on trying, working, not being discouraged by the grades. He couldn't see how she did it, but he sure respected her for it.

"There's a unit test in science on Thursday," she told him.

"We'll start on it tonight," he assured her.

The school bus lumbered around the big curve and drew up in front of them, filling the quiet morning with the noise of its engine and the smell of gasoline. They climbed on. Maybeth went to sit with friends, a bunch of girls who called down the length of the bus to her. James slid into an empty seat. As soon as his backside was settled on the stiff plastic, and his bookbag was at his feet, he felt the mix of dread and anticipation he couldn't seem to get used to. He'd have to go to practice at the end of the day, for a couple of hours. There was no getting out of that. If it rained, they had chalk talks, where James couldn't understand what the coach was saying and just sat there hoping nobody would ask him any questions, watching the clock tick the minutes away, trying to push the hands faster with his mind. But before the day ended in practice, it would begin with French. French was the only class he had with Celie Anderson.

Mr. Norton had the twenty-four students in French II-A sit in alphabetical order, so James could watch Celie Anderson from the middle of the third row; he could start off each day with his eyes filled with Celie Anderson. He never got tired of looking at her. Her hair, which he had finally decided was mahogany-colored, was cut shoulder length and hung thick, straight, and heavy. When she moved her head, her hair brushed across her shoulders, brushed against her cheeks. She had dark eyebrows, with almost no curve to them, and dark eyelashes that set off her greenish eyes as perfectly as black velvet sets off diamonds. Her nose was straight, narrow, and just the right length. Her face was almost heart-shaped and her skin, whether creamy pale in the winter or tanned from summer sun, was smooth and clear. All the makeup she ever wore was just the faintest lipstick on her mouth. She didn't need anything to make her look better. Celie Anderson almost always wore skirts, with a light blouse in warm weather, with sweaters for cold seasons. She wore fall colors, mostly, rusts and brown, gold, but she had one black turtleneck sweater that was James's favorite. In her black turtleneck, she looked like a New York actress, dramatic, and full of passions. He thought Celie Anderson was about the same height as Maybeth, but they looked entirely different. Maybeth was really pretty, round and strong looking; Celie Anderson looked delicate, beautiful. James watched Celie Anderson that March morning. She bent her head over the French book and her mahogany hair moved, like a curtain, brushing against her cheek.

She was popular, of course, but he didn't think she was going steady with anyone. She'd come to Crisfield in ninth grade; he'd first seen her the first day of French I-A. All of James's classes were A, the most advanced. Celie was only in the advanced French because, he found out by listening to what she told the teacher, she'd lived for two years in France. Her parents were divorced, he found out by listening from his corner of lunch tables in the cafeteria. She lived with her mother, who worked in a real-estate office and wanted to be a painter. That was how Celie had gotten to live in France, because when her parents were divorced her mother went off to France to study painting, taking Celie along with her.

So, James thought, they had in common a lack of father, he and Celie Anderson. He loved to hear her speak French, say anything in French, even something as commonplace as conjugations or putting the right pronoun into a sentence. She made the language sound graceful and quick, the way she spoke it. Mr. Norton enjoyed it too, James could see that in the expression on the teacher's face. Celie wasn't that good with grammar; she just had a broad vocabulary, which probably came from having actually used the language.

Some days, James said good morning to her—but never *bonjour*—he had a terrible accent—and sometimes she lifted her face to answer hi, looking right through him. "Good morning," he said, that morning.

"Hi," she answered, not seeing him.

James minded, but he guessed he didn't mind as much as if she'd absolutely ignored him. He went right back to his seat beside Andy Walker. He opened his notebook and took out the homework. He watched, out of the corner of his eye, the way Andy checked his own homework paper against James's, changing things when they didn't agree with what James had written.

This had been going on all year, and Andy had never said a word to James except now, on the baseball squad, occasionally Andy would grunt in James's direction. James figured, Andy *had* to know James knew that Andy was copying, if only from the way James always hunched his shoulders and angled his body so Andy could never copy from him during tests. Sixty-four was the highest Andy had ever gotten on a test. James knew that from watching papers returned. That made him laugh, inside himself. Andy would never say a word, but he needed James in order to get the C he had to have to go on in French. James didn't know how Andy had ever gotten into this A section, except he must have sat next to somebody smart last year too. Mr. Norton seemed to think that Andy tensed up on tests, and Andy didn't contradict the teacher. During tests, Andy did a lot of rustling around in his seat and throat clearing, a lot of erasing and writing over; he always kept his paper until the last minute. That was one of the games students played, to convince a teacher they were really trying, so the teacher would be a little easier on them when it came to grades. In James's experience, the game usually worked. It worked for Andy anyway.

James wished he could figure out some game for getting through baseball. Or at least, he wished he could figure out some way of not always looking like the worst, slowest, weakest, stupidest, when they stood in rows and did warm-up exercises. The coach, a big burly man with a big voice that could carry across the whole diamond, had no interest in James except every now and then to say, "Come on, Tillerman, a little sweat never hurt anyone." Andy Walker, of course, was up in the front row, his light brown hair damp at the hairline, his body perfectly coordinated. James jumped and ran, did sit-ups and stretches, making himself keep on, hating it. To avoid thinking about how he looked, and what everyone was probably thinking of him, he kept his mind busy. That March day, he concentrated on the letter he'd mailed, figuring out how long it would take to get an answer. If you figured it would leave Crisfield in the evening, go up to Baltimore probably, then Boston, then it would be three or four days to Provincetown. Maybe two or three days to be answered there. Three or four days back. He should hear during the first week of April. That allowed for a couple of weekends, when nobody worked and mail wasn't delivered. So he'd know in the first week of April what his father's name was. Then he could start figuring out how to track him down.

Besides, James reminded himself, standing at the end of a line of boys that faced another line for the throwing and catching drill, not looking at any of the faces opposite him for fear of what he'd see if they were looking at him, it looked good on a college application if you played a sport. Colleges wanted well-rounded people, not just brainy types. Brainy types, if they didn't do anything else, colleges figured they were liable to be dorks. Colleges didn't want dorks any more than anybody else did.

The ball, which was going quickly down the lines, thrown and caught, back and forth, came closer to James. He nerved his body, and tensed his arms, getting ready. He hoped it wouldn't burn into his glove the way it sometimes did, coming in so fast that it stung his fingers even through the leather, and hurt, causing him to fumble it. You could break fingers catching wrong, he was willing to bet. Nobody else seemed bothered by the ball coming at them fast, coming too fast, coming at their faces. They'd probably all had fathers playing catch with them from the time they could stand up alone, showing them how to catch and how to throw. He wouldn't have had anyone to do that with, even if he'd wanted to waste his time throwing a little round object around, catching it.

When James finally got back home, the daylight was fading

and hunger was like a knife in his stomach. If he'd had the strength, he would have jogged up the driveway from the bus, just to get to the kitchen sooner, but he was too worn down to hustle. He walked up the driveway, enduring hunger, then around to the back. Inside, he dropped his books on the table and grunted hello at his grandmother. Gram barely turned around to look at him from where she was peeling the skins off carrots. He was glad she ignored him. He was too hungry even to talk. He poured himself a glass of milk, drank it, ate a banana and then a handful of cookies. The hunger faded, dulled by food, and he turned around to face the room. Something smelled good, some kind of pot roast.

"You know, you come in here like you haven't eaten for a week," Gram said.

"I feel like maybe I haven't," James said. "Anything I can do?" She had a pot of peeled potatoes in water on the stove.

"Nope. It's all been done."

James took the pitcher and mixed up more milk, because he'd finished what was made. They used dried milk, which was thirty percent cheaper than regular. Gram made their bread, too, which saved about seventy percent of the cost. She bought flour in hundred-pound sacks from Tydings grocery store. Maybeth's piano teacher, Mr. Lingerle, brought out the sacks for them, when they ran out, or Jeff Greene loaded one into his station wagon, if he was home from school. Gram's bread was about three hundred percent better than anything you could buy in a store, even the fancy brands which they would never have bought anyway because of the cost. Dried milk was only about fifty percent worse than regular, so James figured they came out well ahead. He stirred the milk and water with a wooden spoon until all the granules had been absorbed, then put it into the refrigerator to chill.

Gram was watching him. "You look to be growing again."

At her tone of voice, James laughed inside himself. Baseball was over for the day and his stomach wasn't empty, and Gram said he was growing as if she'd discovered mealworms in her flour. Gram thought he was smart and easy to handle, he knew that; she liked him, and she knew him too. He didn't worry about what she thought of him, because he knew. "I sure hope so," he said and let his laughter leak out.

"I hope you're properly grateful to your sister," Gram reminded him, because Maybeth would be the one to let down the hems on his khakis and jeans, and make whatever adjustments were possible in his shirts. "You don't laugh enough," Gram said, unexpectedly.

"There's not much funny," James told her.

"Sometimes, I know what you mean. Are you going to start on your homework before supper?"

"Are you going to make gravy?" James answered, as if he was negotiating a deal.

"Go away," was all she answered. She didn't need to say more. He always started his homework before supper. She always made gravy with pot roast.

James took his books into the living room, where the big desk was set out in front of tall bookcases. Maybeth was practicing piano. James moved quietly behind her into the room, even though he knew how hard she was to disturb when she was playing. He set out the algebra book and his papers. This was one of the times he liked best: Maybeth playing the piano (Mozart, he thought; the quick melodic symmetry of the music was probably Mozart) while he did homework, math for preference. The music constructed its design in the air and the equations marched out onto his paper, the music and the math, matched up together somehow.

Maybeth sat straight-backed at the piano, wearing an old brown sweater Gram had knitted for James years ago. Her head, curls the color of yellow corn ripened in the sunlight, bent forward a little, and her hands moved over the piano keys. The music tumbled out, filling the room, generous. Her hands were what made the music, her hands and Mozart and the piano. James sometimes wondered how it was that Maybeth, who was so slow at everything else, even the cooking and sewing she had a natural ability for, could be so quick and sure with music. He never wondered why everybody liked Maybeth so much. One look at her face, with the mouth that turned up a little at the ends, ready to be happy, and you knew Maybeth would never hurt anyone. He reminded himself to set aside a couple of hours after the dishes for studying science with her, and went back to the algebra problems, graphing parabolas.

By the time the first week of waiting for an answer from Provincetown was behind James, March had turned cold again. Dark winds and dark rains rattled at the windows all night long. On days when it wasn't actually raining, a thick mist rose up, shrouding the landscape, as if the clouds had sunk down out of the sky and settled onto the flat land. Shapes came up at you out of the mist, spiny fingers of trees, squat thick squares of buildings. Even when it was daylight, it felt like night. At the end of the second week of waiting, James figured that his letter was going to be ignored, because it came from a kid. He should have had an answer by now, he thought. He began to calculate how long he should wait before he sent a second letter. He began to wonder how to write a letter that sounded like he was a grown-up, so they'd have to answer it. Maybe he'd write in Gram's name. It wouldn't be a crime to forge her signature on a letter, would it?

When the sun finally came out, Sammy could get out of the house again, which made life easier for all of them. It was the first of spring and, if you looked, you could see little pale green buds coming out on the trees. In town, on sheltered corners of lawns, crocuses poked up, purple, yellow, and white, nestling up close to bushes, keeping low to the ground. Spring seemed to cheer everybody, give everybody things to do. Everyone, that is, except James, who found himself more and more oppressed by baseball. He wanted to quit the team, badly, but if he did—well, they'd say he was a quitter, and maybe he was, but he didn't want to be—and besides, you could stand anything for a few months, couldn't you? Other people could. So James should be able to. Anyway, if he couldn't, he didn't want anybody finding that out about him.

On the last Friday in March, even hunger couldn't make him hurry up the driveway home. Not on a day that had begun with the sight of Celie Anderson walking down the corridor with Andy Walker, leaning toward him a little as she said something, smiling up at him, wanting him to smile back at her. Not a day that ended with a hard, low hit to the right outfield, a hit that James had seen coming at him and still jumped back from at the last minute. He didn't trust his glove to catch the ball, to protect his face, and he could imagine how it would feel to be smashed in the face by a ball going that fast. Nobody had said anything to him, and that was worse than if they had. He almost wished, when he thought about it, that they'd cussed him out, even though, at the time, he'd only been hoping maybe nobody had seen what happened.

It would be, he thought, a good day to get a letter from Provincetown. He made his feet move along the dirt driveway. He needed something good to happen.

But there was no letter, of course. And at supper Gram started out reminding them that Dicey would be home next week for spring break. Dicey got two weeks, while the public schools only had a long weekend around Easter, a long weekend followed by a string of baseball games. Maybeth and Sammy went on and on about the things they wanted to do when Dicey was home; they wondered if Jeff and Mina would be around as well, and when Dicey would want to get her boat into the water. James ate away at macaroni and cheese, almost without tasting the food. He moved his fork steadily, filling his mouth, swallowing, filling his stomach. Thinking: they'd probably insist on coming to see the games.

As if she could read his mind, Gram looked down the table at him and asked, "When do the baseball games start?"

"I'm not sure," James said carefully. She just looked at him and looked at him. "Second week in April?" he guessed.

"Pah," she said, an exasperated noise made by blowing air out through pursed lips. "You can do better than that."

No, he couldn't, James thought. Gram was staring at him, waiting, impatient, but James looked across at Maybeth, who was looking at him too. But Maybeth looked at him as if she knew how much he hated it, as if she understood how, every day, he had to make himself do it.

"Will you be playing in the games?" Gram asked.

"I doubt it," James told her truthfully. That was a more cheerful thought. "Pass me the vegetables?" he asked. In the fall, Gram put up jars of zucchini mixed with tomatoes. When she heated them, she added fresh-cooked onions, which made it like a vegetable stew. James emptied the serving bowl onto his plate.

"Don't you want to play?" Sammy asked. He was serious.

"Don't be ridiculous," James answered, then filled his mouth with food. Sammy honestly thought everybody liked playing sports. He had no imagination.

"I got a seventy-one on the science test," Maybeth said.

For once, Gram had no opinion. "Well," she said. "Well."

"Good-o," Sammy said.

Maybeth always did that, brought her good news to the table and held it out, like a little kid holding out her hand, then unwrapping her fingers to show some treasure, some stone or flower. She held her good news out to them all, giving it to them.

James was pleased. He just went ahead and let the smile he was feeling spread over his face. If James hadn't known that his heart was just an organ designed to pump blood around his body, he'd have thought that smile began way down in his heart and blossomed upward. He was just so proud of his sister, and himself, too, as proud as he was of any of his own A's. They let Maybeth's news rest in front of them for a couple of minutes. Everybody else had finished eating, and James scraped the last of the vegetables off of his plate. Then Gram turned back to him. "What are we reading next?"

"Macbeth," he told her. "Shakespeare."

"Good," she said. Gram had started when he was in seventh grade, reading along with what he was reading. She didn't read textbooks, except history, although she looked them all over, but she did all the English reading and the outside reading in any course that had outside reading lists, like science and history. She said that when Dicey was going through the grades she hadn't been settled enough in their life together to keep up, but with James she felt ready. "You're getting all this stuff put into your heads," she explained, "and I'm your grandmother." Whatever she said she was doing, what Gram actually did was get started on something and then read along her own route. When James had read *Romeo and Juliet* last year, she'd started on that and then hauled down the big Shakespeare books from the shelves and read on through all of them, tragedies, histories, comedies. She would get started with James and then she'd go off in her own direction. He didn't mind. It meant that if he had any questions, he could always talk things over with her, try out his ideas or listen to hers.

"I liked *Macbeth* all right," Gram said now. "I was thinking—" she started, then she stopped herself. "You won't want to hear my ideas until you've got some of your own ready to match up with."

James no longer wondered how she knew things about him. He just kept silent.

"I think I'm getting too old to enjoy tragedies anyway," Gram said.

"You're not old," Sammy said.

"Sixty-four," she answered.

"You had a birthday? You know what that means," Sammy warned her.

"I know exactly what it means, young man. It means I'm a year older."

"C'mon, Gram. You know what I mean. Because the last time, you said you were sixty-three, and that was in September, on my birthday. So your birthday has to be between September and March."

"Inclusive," Gram reminded him.

Sammy laughed. He was leaning toward his grandmother, teasing her. Gram leaned back, away. James didn't know why she kept her birthday such a big secret—it wasn't that she was trying to keep her age a secret—but she had always refused to tell them.

"Not *all* inclusive," Sammy pointed his finger at her. "Because you said the first year we were here, you said there'd never been a Tillerman until Maybeth who was born in February. So, it can't be February either."

"Unless," Gram countered, her eyes snapping with laughter she wouldn't let out onto her face, "I don't count myself a Tillerman because I wasn't born one."

"But you can't do that," Sammy protested. "It's not true anyway, is it? Because you belong with us," he explained.

"I'm afraid so," Gram agreed.

Sammy watched her silently for a little while. "So, February is out, too, isn't it. That narrows it down."

Sammy could always make Gram laugh. James got up to clear the table, while Maybeth served plates of pie, apple pie made from the apples Gram and Maybeth had put up in the fall. Preserved apples made a juicier pie than fresh apples, so you could soak up juice with the flaky crust. James had two pieces, then a third after they had finished doing the dishes.

James still hadn't heard from the hospital in Provincetown by the time Dicey came home. Dicey came home and took over again. After a couple of days, it was as if she'd never been away. She was out in the barn, scraping the sailboat and repainting its bottom; she was charging around the house emptying all the drawers in James's room and washing them out, spring cleaning. She didn't talk much, and never about college. Gram asked her about this over supper, Dicey's third night home.

"I wouldn't call your mood exactly ebullient," Gram said.

Dicey shrugged. "I'm okay." She would be too, James knew, whatever her life was like. At college, she lived with a professor's family, exchanging room and board for babysitting and household chores, because it was all they could do to scrape up the $2,500 a year for tuition and books. But Dicey was stubborn. She wouldn't even think of getting a student loan, wouldn't borrow money from anyone; instead she worked out a way to work off expenses. James guessed—looking at her sharp-featured face, the narrow head and dark hair, noticing how her eyes looked darker than the rest of theirs except Gram's—he guessed there was nobody he admired as much as Dicey, even though she always made him feel that he wasn't doing enough, wasn't doing his life well enough, so he didn't like her all that much.

"I'd rather hear the truth," Gram asked.

At that, Dicey smiled, and Gram smiled back at her, both smiles flashing across as sudden and brief as falling stars. Those two really were alike, James thought; he saw Sammy and Maybeth, side-by-side listening, and thought, So are those two.

"Okay," Dicey said. She leaned forward, elbows resting on the table, ignoring the fried chicken on her plate. "It just—seems like such a waste, my being there. A waste of money. Money that we could put to better use. And a waste of time, too, a waste of my time."

"The courses aren't too hard?" Gram asked.

"No, it's nothing like that. I'm getting B's and A's. Maybe they're too easy, but they're certainly not too hard."

"You always are cocksure about things," Gram remarked.

"They're not teaching me anything I need to learn," Dicey said.

"*Want* to learn, maybe. Certainly you can't speak to need. Not at your age."

Dicey took a minute over that one. "But that doesn't matter. We should be saving that money."

"What for?"

"For James and Sammy, when they go to school," Dicey said. James approved of that. He wouldn't mind any money that was available to send him to college with.

Gram picked up a chicken breast in her fingers, forgetting that she had started eating it with a knife and fork. She took a big bite out of it. While she was thinking, Sammy announced that he didn't need to go to college if he was going to play tennis, and Dicey started to argue with him then gave it up. James ate and waited.

"There's that new expression I keep hearing now. Sexist," Gram finally said.

Dicey laughed out loud. "It's not new," she pointed out. "What I want to do is build boats," she told Gram. "That doesn't take a college degree. It takes—doing it."

"I told you, girl, I want you to go to college." Gram's mouth set in a stubborn line and her dark eyes looked right at Dicey.

"Well I am, aren't I," Dicey said, looking right back at her grandmother. Gram was the only one who could make Dicey do things, James thought. She was the only one strong and bossy enough to tell Dicey what to do. And vice versa too. He wondered, for a minute, what it would be like to live in a house where the man was the boss. A house with a father.

He wished the hospital would write to him. Or that he had some memory of his father. It would make a big difference if he had some memory of his own.

Dicey, being the oldest, did remember. Once, she'd even talked about him. With that idea in his mind, James knocked on the door to her room when he'd finished his homework. Dicey was sitting at her desk, reading an open book, writing down notes. "What do you want?" she asked, still writing.

"What are you doing?" James wasn't so sure now that he wanted to ask her to tell him anything, if that was the way she was feeling.

"Papers, I've got two papers. One for English, on symbolism in *The Old Man and the Sea*—"

"But that's an easy book. I did a book report on that. What are you going to talk about?"

"And one for history, on Hobbes."

"What's Hobbes?"

"A man who wrote a book," Dicey dismissed the subject. "So what is it?"

Sammy, wearing just pajama bottoms on his way back from his final trip to the bathroom, stood in the doorway. "What're you two talking about?" he asked.

"Ask James. He won't tell me."

"Nothing," James told Sammy. "We're not talking about anything." That was true. He tried to think of some excuse for having come in, but he couldn't. He couldn't even think up any excuse, and besides, what did it matter if Dicey didn't think much of him anyway. She didn't think much of most people. Since it didn't matter and she'd never tell him anyway, he went ahead and asked. "Remember in Bridgeport? I was wondering. Because you talked to the police there, didn't you? When they were trying to find Momma." He got his words out fast because Dicey's impatience was about to shut off his question. "Did they tell you anything about our father?"

"For pete's sake, James," Dicey said. "What kind of a flea have you got up your nose now? How am I supposed to remember something that wasn't even important then?"

Defeated, James went past Sammy and back to his own room, where he turned out the light and got into bed. He lay there in the darkness, with his eyes open. He couldn't see anything.

CHAPTER 3

Sammy watched James leave the room. He listened to the way James's feet scuffed along the hall floor and the careful way he closed his bedroom door. Poor old James. Sammy leaned his naked shoulder against the doorframe. Dicey was ignoring him. He folded his arms and waited. James just didn't know how to deal with Dicey.

She was leaning back in her chair, with her legs stretched out on the desk. Her bare feet were crossed at the ankles. She didn't look at Sammy.

Sammy grinned. She'd get the message pretty soon.

He watched her face get the message, until she couldn't stop herself from smiling and turned to look at him. "Okay. What do you want?"

"Why didn't you tell him? He only wanted to know."

"Because I don't feel like talking about it. I don't feel like talking. I've got these two stupid papers to write."

"So what," Sammy said, "But—"

"But what?"

Sammy didn't want to say what he was thinking. He was thinking, *But what about poor old James?* He didn't know why James was suddenly so interested in this father of theirs, but there was no way for him to find out anything. If Dicey did know something, Sammy didn't think she ought to just brush James off like that. If she stopped to think about it, she wouldn't think she ought to either. Sammy went across the room and sat on the bed. Dicey pulled her feet down and turned around in her chair. She sat backward in it, with her arms resting along the top, her chin resting on her arms. "I've got papers to write, Sammy."

"I don't care," Sammy said. "Just telling me won't take long, and then I'll go away. That would be the quickest way."

She chewed on her lower lip, deciding whether to be angry with him. He didn't let any expression onto his face. He figured she'd see the sense of it and tell him. He knew she'd rather talk than work on her papers anyway, which was why she was trying to get out of talking. That was the way Dicey treated herself. "Oh, all right," she said. "Give me a minute to remember."

Sammy gave her all the time she wanted. She was looking at him but not seeing him, remembering. He looked at his sister, at Dicey: He knew she wasn't perfect, but there wasn't anything he'd change about her. Most people wouldn't agree, but he thought she was fine looking; he liked the way her eyes saw things and reacted, he liked the way she held her chin high, he liked the way her body looked, lots of angles. Her desk was set right below a window that faced east, so that in daylight she could look over to the pines, beyond which the water lay. He liked the way Dicey liked the water.

On one wall, she had a big bulletin board. Before she went away to college, that bulletin board had been filled, with notes and reminders from Dicey to herself—about what hours she was supposed to work at Millie Tydings's grocery store, what schoolwork was due, things she wanted to be sure not to forget. There were also pictures on it: a photograph Jeff had taken of her moored sailboat; a couple of magazine pictures of big ocean-racing yachts, their sails trimmed against an ocean wind; and an old cartoon Jeff had given to her, years ago, its paper turning brown with age, as if it had coffee stains on it. In the cartoon, there was a maze built in a box, but the mouse that was supposed to run around the maze to find food, or something, had chewed a hole in the floor and was busy tunneling its way to freedom. Sammy liked that cartoon. There were no pictures of people on Dicey's bulletin board. Sammy knew why, whatever other people might think. He knew that Dicey carried her people close in her heart, and didn't need any photographs to remind her. He looked back at her face. It was good to have Dicey home again.

"And what's so funny?" she asked him.

"Nothing, I'm just feeling good," he said.

"Yeah. It's so good to be here—" and her quick smile washed over her face. "I think, it feels so good I'm trying to make it feel bad with these papers. You know?"

"That's really stupid," he said.

"Tell me about it," she said, and he laughed. "Okay, here's what I know. It isn't much. His name was Francis Verricker. He was a sailor, a merchant seaman."

"We knew that. They probably called him Frank, don't you think?"

"The policeman in Bridgeport—you never met him, did you?"

"You kept sneaking around," Sammy reminded her. "You kept putting me to bed, and things."

"Cripes, Sammy, you were only six years old. The policeman said, when they were trying to trace him, that he was wanted. By the police. I don't know what for, but I remember once, in Provincetown, when you were maybe not even born yet or just a baby, some policeman came and asked Momma questions."

"What do you think he did?"

"I never thought about it," Dicey said. "I never thought about him much, if you want the truth. I never wanted to because—

well, it wouldn't do any good, would it? And if I did . . . it made me angry."

"What he did to Momma?" Sammy knew that feeling.

"He must have been pretty rotten to just—leave her."

Sammy agreed. It didn't bother him, it didn't have anything to do with him, but he asked, "So you think it's something James doesn't really want to know about?"

"Is there anything James doesn't want to know? What's got into him, anyway?"

Sammy had no idea. "It just came up one night. He brought it up. Maybe it's been bothering him. Something's bothering him."

"And baseball," Dicey said. "Who'd ever have thought of James playing baseball. Or going out for any sport."

"Sometimes, I think he's just weird," Sammy said.

"With all his life mapped out that way?"

"No, it's not that, so much. It's—" As he spoke, Sammy heard what he was saying, and realized what he had been thinking without really admitting it to himself. "It's as if he was embarrassed."

"Embarrassed? What about?"

"I dunno. Embarrassed at himself."

Now he had Dicey's full attention. Her dark hazel eyes were fixed on his face. Dicey's full attention was pretty fierce, but he didn't mind; he gave her his own full attention back.

"By embarrassed, do you mean ashamed?" she asked.

"I don't know. Maybe. I hope not. I dunno, Dicey. I don't understand him at all, much."

"Me neither, after a point. What does Gram think?"

"She hasn't said. She doesn't trust book learning, she always says that, but—"

"I should *be* here. I shouldn't be away at school."

Sammy knew what she meant. But Gram was right, he thought. "No, you should go to college."

"Why?"

"Because you're smart."

Dicey shook her head; that wasn't reason enough.

"And because Gram wants you to," Sammy said.

"Yeah," Dicey admitted. "Look, will you keep an eye on James? I shouldn't have just dismissed him like that, should I have?"

"No," Sammy said.

"I'll tell him in the morning," Dicey said. "He'll be asleep now. Eating and sleeping, James can always do those."

"Me too," Sammy said.

"Then why don't you do that," his sister said. "And I'll knock off one of these horrible papers. In peace and quiet. Without being interrupted. Without any little brother here asking me questions."

Sammy was giggling as he got up from the bed. "I can take a hint. But Dicey—"

She was turning herself around again and didn't want to be interrupted. "What is it now?"

"Is Mina going to be home?"

"In a week. Why, what is it, are you looking for some tennis?"

"She'll be so much better than I am."

"You know that doesn't matter. She likes playing with you."

"Yeah," Sammy said. "She taught me how, didn't she. Good night."

"Good *night*."

He turned at the doorway, to say "See you" because he would, for almost two weeks, and that felt good.

Dicey would tell James. Like Sammy, she did what she said she'd do. So Sammy forgot about it. He got on with his own life, which he liked just fine. Mina did come home, and after a couple of days Sammy could give her a good game. He went to school, which he didn't mind. The classes were easy, and never gave him any trouble. During recesses, he played soccer, a pickup game run by his friend Custer. Custer played center forward on one team, and Sammy played center half on the other. As seventh graders, the biggest kids in the school, they claimed the wide center section of the playground. Sammy liked the running in soccer, because he was fast. He liked having the ball at his foot, under control, trapping it, moving it around the opposition, shooting off a pass. Every now and then, when he felt like it, he'd take it on down the field himself and score the goal. Ernie, whom he'd known as long as Custer, since second grade, played goalie. Ernie wasn't a friend. He'd been a big second grader, a sneak and a bully too; he'd gotten away with that in second grade. But they'd caught up with him in size, most of them, anyway Sammy had, and now Ernie was just an overweight sneak. He pretended to like Sammy, and they hadn't had any fights since fourth grade. The last time, Sammy had rolled Ernie around in the dirt, had sat on his back and pounded on his shoulders until he quit, almost crying. Ernie never came close to an argument with him after that. Sammy couldn't even remember what that last fight had been about.

One Friday noon, a couple of days before Dicey had to go back to school, Sammy drifted out to the playground after lunch. Sunlight washed over the scene—the little kids digging in the sandbox or riding on the swings or just running around after each other, some older girls walking and talking, as if they were already ladies going shopping, the soccer game at the center. Off against the cyclone fence, behind the tall swings, a few kids worked with lacrosse sticks. Sammy didn't feel like soccer, so he drifted over to watch the lacrosse. The sun felt warm on the top of his head, and the fence was hung with bright sweaters kids had peeled off in the warm noon air. With the sweaters hung over it, or tied through it, the fence looked like some kind of cartoon clothesline.

"Hi, Sammy, how are you," some girl's voice called behind him, but he ignored that. There were maybe ten seventh graders playing with the long-handled lacrosse sticks, scooping up the ball and then cradling it before making a pass. Sammy moved up beside another kid who stood watching, holding a stick. Sammy didn't even look at the kid, because he was interested in the game. There didn't seem to be any positions. People ran around, crashed into one another, caught and cradled, and swung their sticks almost like broadswords to knock the ball out of the shallow net of an opponent's stick. "Where are the goals?" Sammy asked, his eyes on the moving figures.

"That bush," the kid waved a hand to the right, then to the left, "and they've got a sweatshirt on the ground."

Sammy turned to look at the boy. He was a skinny kid, with brown hair flat on his head, and brown eyes that kept looking at Sammy and then away, as if he was nervous. "Are you using that stick?" Sammy asked.

"Not right now," the boy said. He'd come new to school in February, Sammy remembered, but he wasn't in any of Sammy's classes so Sammy had no idea what his name was.

"Could I try it for a minute?" Sammy asked.

The kid didn't want to give it to him but didn't know how to say no. He handed it over without a word.

Sammy held the stick in his hands for a minute, getting the feel of it, getting the balance of it. He wrapped his hands around the long octagonal handle, imitating the way the players held theirs. He practiced cradling the empty pocket, elbows in, shoulders moving. "Looks easier than it is," he remarked to the kid.

"Umnnh," the boy answered, the way you do when you know you have to say something but don't know what the right thing to say is.

There was a lull in the scrimmage. "Hey!" Sammy called over. He picked out Tom Childress to ask. "Can I come in?"

Tom was breathing hard, and sweat ran down his chocolate-colored skin. "Yeah, sure. Make it fast."

"I never played before," Sammy told them.

They didn't mind. Tom said he should play defense, told him what team he was on, and the game started up again. Sammy missed a couple of catches before he figured out how to handle the stick, how to hold it out and scoop up a rolling ball, how to swoop it sideways to pick up a pass and be already cradling when the ball came into the pocket. He played back, at first, and then—the ball safely held—he charged up the center, watching for someone to break free to receive a pass. "Move up!" he called to Tom. Tom started moving, while Sammy twisted around an attacker. He brought his stick around to his right, to toss the ball to Tom, but there was a cracking sound before he could throw it. The stick was jerked out of his hands at the same time that he careened into somebody. Sammy fell pretty hard, fell over sideways, scraping his face into the ground. As soon as he hit, he rolled over and jumped up, bending down to pick up the stick. The play had gone on back toward the sweatshirt, which was their goal. While he ran back to try and stop the attack, Sammy wiped dirt off his cheek with his left hand. His right hand held the stick up, and ready. The goal was scored before he got there.

As play started again, Sammy watched the way the sticks could be used to check an opponent's progress, crashing down from behind to dislodge the ball, as had happened to him, or swinging straight across someone's chest. Three of the opponents charged toward him, passing the ball back and forth, making another run down the field. They didn't run in a straight line, but wavered back and forth. Tom Childress moved in to stop their progress, using his body and his stick.

This game was like wild Indians, Sammy thought, flexing his legs, getting ready, watching. Tom fell behind the rushing trio, reeling a little from an impact. Sammy moved up, watching for their pass, ready to intercept. They came at him bunched and he went right for them. He slammed his stick down on the stick that had the ball, at the same time shoving his shoulder into the second player, who might be in a position to scoop the ball up from the ground. Somebody's hip jammed into him, but he had his eye on the ball, rolling along the ground, and he just kept on after it. Running, he scooped it up, cradling it, and fired it off up to Tom, who was back on balance, holding his stick up high, ready. Sammy knew it was a bad pass; he could feel it. He took time to check behind himself, winded by the impact of the body that had flung itself at him. Two of the three attackers were on the ground, scrabbling for their sticks. Sammy watched Tom shoot the ball directly into the bush, making a goal. The buzzer sounded to end recess.

Sammy rested his stick on the ground like a lance, and laughed. He felt the sweat he'd worked up, and an ache on the side of his face. His knuckles, too, on his right hand; somebody had cracked a stick down across Sammy's knuckles. He didn't mind, he thought, flexing his fingers. This lacrosse was great, it was—like wild Indians. He laughed aloud, with his face raised to the sunny sky.

Then he ran back to the kid whose stick he'd borrowed. "Thanks," he said.

"I didn't know you were going to keep it so long," the boy said.

"Neither did I, but it was great," Sammy answered. The kid

wanted to complain. But Sammy Tillerman played to his own rules, and everybody knew that. Sammy knew that about himself, and he liked it. However, this boy, whose name he couldn't remember, was looking at him out of brown eyes that made Sammy feel bad about having kept the kid's stick so long. "I'm sorry," he said, handing it back. People were moving into the building. You only had five minutes after the bell to get to class.

The brown eyes looked at him, just the way James used to look standing at the edge of the playground, watching.

"C'mon with me while I wash up my face," Sammy said, "or they'll think I've been in a fight or something."

"All right."

"Does it look pretty bad?"

"Yeah." The boy fell into step beside him.

"My name's Sammy. Tillerman."

"I know."

Sammy jostled through the big doors and the boy trailed along. "So," Sammy said, while he examined the damage to his face in the mirror over the sink in the boy's bathroom, with the usual bathroom noises echoing around him. "What's yours?"

"My what?"

"Name."

"Oh. Robin."

He thought Sammy was going to make some crack, and he was waiting not to notice it. Sammy, using warm water to rinse the dirt off his cheek and leaning forward to study the damage close up, didn't say anything.

"My mother named me that," Robin apologized. "Like Robin Hood," he explained.

"I'm named after my uncle," Sammy said. These were just bruises and scrapes. He didn't look too bad. He'd looked a lot worse. "He was killed in Vietnam, but they called him Bullet."

"Bullet?"

Sammy nodded, turning around. The kid, Robin, stood there, clutching his lacrosse stick.

"That's pretty weird," Robin said.

"So what," Sammy said. He walked away, leaving the kid and his lacrosse stick behind.

Sammy was the one who brought James's answer from the Provincetown hospital up from the mailbox, after school. He noticed the return address and figured out what James had probably done. He couldn't figure out why, after what Dicey had told him, James had gone writing off to the hospital, but who knew what went on in James's mind. He left the rest of the mail on the kitchen table; he put James's letter on the desk in his bedroom so he could find it in private, with no questions from Gram.

Sammy waited for James to say something to him about the letter—through dinner, and the long evening, through the next day's dinner too. It wasn't like James not to say anything. Sammy waited for a while and then, finally, he interrupted James at his homework. Maybeth was playing and singing at the piano, music from chorus, he thought. She sounded good, as always, but he didn't like the kinds of songs the chorus sang nearly as much as real songs. The songs chorus sang were either from Broadway musicals, with smooth smooth melodies and smooth smooth lyrics, or odd old-fashioned songs, filled with true-loves and laralaralus. Sammy ignored the music and words and just listened to his sister's honey-colored voice. Then he sat on top of the big desk and put his hand down over the paper James was covering with neat handwriting. It looked like a lab report.

"Cut it out," James said, looking up, annoyed. He picked up Sammy's hand and set it down off of the paper.

Sammy kept his voice low, although when Maybeth was singing she didn't hear much of anything else going on. He had his back to her and his voice low, so he just asked James outright, "What was in that letter from Provincetown?"

James's eyes were medium hazel, like creeks muddy after spring rains. They flickered at the question, as if Sammy had just pasted James a good one, in the belly. "What letter?"

"C'mon, James." Sammy didn't like this kind of lying. If he hadn't known about the letter, he wouldn't have known to ask what it said. James was too smart not to figure that out. "Who do you think put it on your desk?" He pointed out the favor he'd done James: "So nobody else would see it and ask questions."

"Oh. Thanks." James turned his attention back to his paper. "It didn't say anything."

James was about the worst liar Sammy had ever seen. But he was also behaving strangely, strange even for James which was strange enough at the best of times. Usually, if James had an idea he was working on, and you gave him any hint that you were willing to listen, he was off and away talking, as if he had to get everything said at once, as if, if he didn't get it said the world would end, or something. But this time—it wasn't like James. "What anything didn't it say?" Sammy asked.

"I told you, nothing."

Because Dicey had asked him to keep an eye on James, Sammy insisted. "I figured out, you probably wrote for your birth certificate." James looked up again, surprised. Which was pretty insulting, if you thought about it. "That makes sense, it's the only reason you'd write. So what did they say?"

"Just a form letter. You have to send in four dollars to get a copy."

"Have you done that?"

"I don't have four dollars."

"Why not?" Sammy asked. He had twenty-one dollars left of the hundred dollars he'd started off what James called their fiscal year with. They had a summer crabbing business, he and James, and Jeff helped out when he wanted to, which was pretty regularly. They kept the first money they made for themselves, for a year's allowances, a hundred dollars apiece. Jeff didn't keep any, but James and Sammy did. At first, Jeff had agreed to split the earnings three ways, for the days he worked along with them, but then he'd stopped, refusing to take his share. He'd told them to put his share into a college fund, or get something they needed. Usually, Jeff did what he thought you wanted him to do, but about the money he wouldn't budge. So James and Sammy started out the summer with a hundred dollars and the rest of the profits they gave to Gram. It wasn't a fortune, but it helped. "You had twenty dollars after Christmas," Sammy reminded his brother.

"I had to buy a glove."

Sammy opened his mouth to ask what James was doing playing baseball anyway. Then he closed it. "I'll give you the money."

"Never mind. Dicey already told me anyway. What his name is. So I didn't need to write."

"Is that all a birth certificate tells you, just someone's name?"

"How should I know?" James asked. "I never saw one. I'd think so, though. I mean, sometimes there isn't even any father's name at all, if the father doesn't want to acknowledge the baby. I bet. Or if he says it isn't his."

Sammy grinned. "I guess there's never any mistake about who the mother is."

"That strikes you as funny?" James asked him. Sammy cleared all expression from his face. "I wonder why she named me James though."

"You wouldn't want to be Francis, would you?"

"I dunno. It would be something, at least. Unless that wasn't his real name."

"Do you think he would have lied to Momma about his name?" Sammy hadn't ever thought of that.

"If he had, she never would have caught him. She'd have been easy to lie to. Like Maybeth."

They looked at their sister, at her straight back and her golden hair. Her voice wound around the room. Sammy kept his voice pitched under the music.

"But that's just why you don't ever lie to people like that," Sammy argued. "Because they are so easy."

"That's why *you* might not," James countered. "So—" He waved his hand, dismissing Sammy, giving up. When he smiled, his eyes looked hungry.

"I'm going to ask Gram," Sammy decided, sliding off the desktop.

"Ask her what? Don't you do that," James warned him.

But James couldn't stop Sammy. "Don't worry, I know how to keep a secret." Even if it wasn't a secret he thought was worth keeping, he'd keep it. "When she adopted us, maybe they found out something more, because they'd be so cautious about letting her adopt us. The lawyers."

"I never thought of that," James said. "How'd you think of that?"

"It just makes sense," Sammy told him. "Go back to work, I'll take care of it. Do your lab, or whatever it is. Otherwise, how'll you keep your perfect grade-point average?" He felt so good, he stood behind Maybeth with his hand on her shoulder for a minute, to say, without interrupting her, that he liked the way she played and sang. Because he did.

Gram was sitting at the kitchen table, studying an old notebook that was filled with pale brown writing. Sammy sat down across from her. He waited until she looked up.

"I'm not going to tell you," she said, figuring she knew what he was after.

"So you've said. Over and over," he answered. "I'm not asking," he told her.

"That's what I figured." He waited for her smile before he let himself laugh, the way he wanted to. He'd find out when her birthday was. She'd get careless again sometime. He'd keep narrowing it down, she'd forget and let something slip: but he'd remember.

"What is it then," she asked.

"What're you reading?"

"An old recipe book. I am bored with what we've been eating. Bored stupid. But I can't find anything new that doesn't make my stomach turn. Barley soup with sliced hotdogs floating in it? Feeds ten for fifty cents a person. Did you ever think how many dinners I've cooked?"

"No," he said. He hadn't. Now he did. "A lot," he suggested.

"A lot."

"Too many?"

"Maybeth helps me out, and frequently."

"Dicey did too, when she had to. We wash the dishes," he reminded her.

"Yes. That's all true. Then what is it you want?" She knew there was something.

"If I knew when your birthday was, I could give you a cookbook for your birthday."

That made her smile again. "Yes, you could," she agreed again, but didn't say anything more, which made him smile.

"You have my birth certificate, don't you?" he asked her.

"Your birth certificate?" It wasn't often anybody surprised Gram, and he enjoyed having done it. "I guess I do at that. It's in with all the papers the lawyers collected."

"Where?"

"In the desk, of course." He watched her face, as she decided whether or not she needed to ask him why he was asking. He knew what he'd answer, if she did: I just want to see it. But he didn't want to answer that, because it wasn't entirely true. He would answer that, if he had to, but he didn't want to have to. But he didn't think Gram would ask him why, and he was right.

"Thanks," he said, getting up from the table. "Does the library have cookbooks?"

"How would I know that?"

"Ask James. I bet he'll know. Because you could get some from the library. But I'm not bored," he told her, leaving the room.

It was so simple, Sammy thought, going back down the hallway to the living room. He didn't know why James found things so difficult when they were so simple. He suspected that James manufactured difficulties, that he did it because he liked things more complicated than they were. He heard the piano playing softly, and two voices singing. James's voice had settled to a light baritone, which made a good contrast to Maybeth's full soprano, like a thin gold chain.

Sammy stood in the doorway, watching James standing there beside the piano bench, bent over to read the music and pick out his part from the piano background. "Full fathom five thy father lies," they sang. "Of his bones are coral made." Maybeth's voice sang to the melody, but James sang to the words. "Those are pearls that were his eyes. Nothing of him that doth change." When they got to the ding-dong bell chorus, they needed another voice, so Sammy stepped up and put one in. He couldn't read the music, but he could hear in the chords the notes he was supposed to sing, the tenor part. "So sea-nymphs hourly ring his knell," he read, because Maybeth started on the refrain again when he joined in. "Hourly ring, hourly ring" the line repeated, in that irritating way old-fashioned songs had. Sammy sang along, getting impatient for it to finish. "Ding-dong bell, ding-dong bell."

Ding-dong bell, he thought, *kitty's in the well.* He knew James didn't care about the ding-dong bell part of the song; James liked the father part, the bones turned to coral and pearls for eyes, the water-changes.

"Let's sing a real song," Sammy said when they'd finished.

"This is Shakespeare," James protested.

"So what."

Maybeth just waited for them to be through arguing.

"The Tempest."

"Never heard of it," Sammy said. "Sing something I like. That was for chorus, wasn't it?"

"Yes," Maybeth said. Then, taking her hands off the piano, she started. "Oft I sing for my friends." That was more like it. James and Sammy joined in. Sammy didn't feel like singing the loneliness of that song, although he knew why he liked hearing it, why they all liked it. In the kitchen, Gram would have lifted her head, to listen too. "When I come to the cross of that silent sea, Who will sing for me?" James and Maybeth sang. The sad and lonely song reminded Sammy of Momma; it was a simple melody that flowed along, a good singing song. When they sang it, he always thought they were singing it for Momma, answering her question, if she was wondering who would sing for her. They would. He would.

Sammy went to the desk. James didn't even notice. With his face turned up, he was singing away as if he was sending his song out among the stars. His eyes were closed and he looked happy enough, listening to his sister's voice, listening to his own. Sammy opened the side drawer, just humming now.

The birth certificates were in a manila envelope, with medical records and old report cards. He emptied the envelope out onto the desk. The birth certificates were big sheets of paper, with a red wax seal at the bottom right-hand corner. They were pretty fancy. Each one, except for the name of the baby and the date of birth, was the same. Sammy picked James's out and folded the rest. He put all the papers back into the envelope, put the envelope back into the drawer. James was sure going to be surprised.

Sammy just stepped up beside James and put the folded thick paper into his brother's hand. Then he sat down on the bench beside Maybeth and, before she could start another song, he sang in her ear: "There's a hole in the bucket, Maria, Maria." While he finished his lines, she turned around to face him, happy because she knew how much he liked this song. He could never sing his part of the last verse of the duet, without breaking out laughing. That about ruined the joke of the song, but he couldn't keep from laughing, at the step-by-step logic of the verses, at the patient, plodding Henry character and the quick-tongued, impatient Maria. He liked it best when he could talk Dicey into singing the song with Jeff, because Jeff had a way of waiting, as if Henry were thinking and thinking, scratching his head and wondering why Maria had forgotten, before he started in on that last verse. "There's a hole in the bucket, Maria, Maria."

Sammy deliberately didn't pay any attention to James, but when they finished singing, he turned around. James was back at the desk, just staring at the paper. He held the paper flat, with one hand at each side of it. The desk light fell on his dark narrow head as he studied the writing on the paper.

Sammy got worried. But it was just a birth certificate. What was there that would be on a birth certificate that would bother James? Maybeth went back to the Shakespeare song and Sammy went back to his brother. "What's the matter?"

James didn't look up, didn't answer. He just pointed with his finger to one of the boxes where information was filled in, in black ink. Occupation of parent, Sammy read, Merchant Seaman.

Name, surname, and birthplace of father, he read. Francis Verricker, Cambridge, Maryland. He read on beyond the finger. Name, maiden name, and birthplace of mother. Elizabeth Tillerman, Crisfield, Maryland. His mother might have been born right here, in this house.

"Cambridge is just an hour from here," James said, his voice a whisper.

"That probably explains how they met," Sammy deduced.

"No it doesn't," James said. "Not necessarily. We could go there."

"Why?"

"To find out things about him."

There were a lot of things Sammy thought of saying. He thought of reminding James that would have been years and years ago, that their father had only been born in Cambridge so there might not be anything to find out. He thought of asking James how he intended to get to Cambridge. Without letting Gram know what he was doing, too. But all he said was, "Like what?"

"I dunno. Like—where he lived, and maybe there would be some family? Or maybe, we could find someone who knew him, some old friend who could tell us what he's like. Or might even know where he is right now. That's not impossible."

If the police in Connecticut couldn't find him how can we? Sammy wanted to ask, but didn't. He didn't say anything.

"Not absolutely impossible," James whispered.

Sammy didn't argue. "Yeah, we found the birth certificate."

"That was you. You did that," James said, looking up. In the shade behind the lamp's light, his eyes looked sad.

"Maybe so, but you're the one who's going to have to cook up a way to get us to Cambridge," Sammy told his brother. "You're the one who's supposed to have all the ideas, so get going on that one. Okay?"

"Okay," James said. "O-K." He folded up the birth certificate and gave it to Sammy. Sammy showed him where the envelope was in the drawer. "How much money do you have?" James asked. "Twenty-one dollars?"

Sammy nodded. What was James thinking of, taking a taxi?

"Okay," James muttered to himself, getting up from the desk and wandering out of the room, thinking hard. Sammy hoped the idea he came up with wouldn't be too complicated. He hoped when they got there, if they got there, there would be something for James to find out. James needed to find out something, he thought; although he couldn't imagine what James thought that was.

It didn't matter to him if they found out anything or not. He'd never been to Cambridge and he never minded seeing new places, that was a good enough reason for going along. He could always find something to do, to amuse himself while James detected. And maybe he'd have a week or two of quiet while James tried to figure out a way to get where he wanted to be going to.

CHAPTER 4

He should have known better, Sammy told himself. He *knew* that once James's mind got going on something, it worked fast. Dicey was barely packed into Mr. Lingerle's car, heading back to College Park, with Gram going along for the change of scenery. "We have to go to Cambridge," James said.

"If you say so." Sammy didn't care; he wished Dicey didn't go away to school, hadn't gone away. They were standing under the big paper mulberry tree in the front yard. The mulberry came into leaf later than any of the others. It spent all spring dropping seed pods around the yard, and you had to rake them up or they'd all sprout into saplings that would take over everything if you let them. Whenever Sammy stood under the tree he thought of Momma, and not just because her ashes were buried among its deep roots. The ground was littered with squishy seed pods, and the branches of the tree spread overhead, the long new leaves still curled up tight. The tree, Momma, Dicey, and yard work, all those things washed up around his mind, like waves flowing back and forth from side to side, running into one another and getting added together and cancelling each other out.

"Listen, will you?" James insisted. "Cambridge is our only lead. In Cambridge we can check the hospital, and schools, the library or the town hall. We can look at their records. It has to be on a school day though, and I can't figure how to do that."

"Why a school day? The library is open on Saturdays, and they don't close hospitals."

"Because most offices close on Saturday."

"What about summer?" Sammy wouldn't mind waiting.

"The schools will be closed."

"Why schools, anyway?" James always thought he knew everything. Sammy kind of enjoyed asking him questions and then asking him more questions. It drove James crazy.

"Because they have records. Like—in the gym, at school, there are some trophies that Bullet won. He was a runner. I've seen them."

"You never told me that." Sammy didn't know that his uncle had won trophies. He'd go check it out, next year, when he was in the high school. It would be his own name, Samuel Tillerman, he'd see on those trophies, because Bullet had lived here, because Momma had liked her brother so much she'd named Sammy after him. He didn't know why James was getting so het up about their father. Sammy felt the land, farmland and marshland, spreading out from the deep-rooted paper mulberry tree; he felt how his feet stood on that land. He could almost believe that the land felt him standing there, and liked him being there. He didn't see why, with the farm, they needed any father. He'd go along with James, but not because he expected to find anything out.

"Ask Mina to take us up there, okay?" James asked.

"Why me? Why don't you?"

"Because she's your friend. She'll say yes to you. You can ask her the next time you play tennis."

"Mina hasn't been playing much tennis at college, so I've gotten better and she hasn't," Sammy told James, who didn't care about that. He only cared about his ideas, Sammy thought. It wasn't up to Sammy to find a ride; this was James's project, not his.

* * *

Sammy did ask Mina, however, because it was no trouble, and she said she couldn't take them because she had to go back to school early, because of the singing group she'd joined. But Mina's father, Sammy reported to James, often went up to Cambridge to talk with other ministers. "Ask Reverend Smiths then," James said.

"Why don't you do that?"

"You know them better."

"Yeah, but there's no reason for me to be the one to ask."

"Does it bother you to ask?" James asked.

"No. Why should it? Does it bother you?"

James wanted to say no, but he couldn't. "Maybe. Sometimes. It's easier for you."

There he was, getting Sammy to feel sorry for him again. They were standing waiting for the school bus, with rain dripping down James's thin face. Sammy could tell, from the way James's eyes wouldn't meet his, that James didn't like that about himself—things being harder—and making Sammy feel sorry. "Okay," Sammy said. Anyway, James might be right. Sammy did get a lot of yesses from people, and pretty easily. He didn't mind that.

"It isn't that I don't like the Smiths family," James went on, proving something, Sammy didn't know what. "I wouldn't mind at all having a father like him."

So Sammy went on over to the Smiths house, which was right next to Rev. Smiths's church, and he asked Mina's father if they could hitch a ride up to Cambridge with him. It worried Rev. Smiths that they wanted to go on a school day, that they'd be missing school, even though when Sammy explained about James having this idea about finding out about their father, he understood that. Sammy wasn't sure the minister would keep the secret from Gram, but since those two almost never met up he didn't see any problem. He tried to explain why James hadn't asked Gram about their father. Mrs. Smiths fed him lemonade and oatmeal cookies while this conversation went on. Finally, Rev. Smiths said that *if* they had their grandmother's permission to miss a day of school, then he'd be happy to take them up the next time he went. He went the last Wednesday of the month. "If she'll agree, then I will. She's not careless, so if she says yes all you have to do is call me up."

"Thanks," Sammy said. "James'll be pleased."

"What about you?" Rev. Smiths wasn't being nosy, he was just asking.

"This is really bothering James," Sammy explained.

He tried to get James to ask Gram for permission to miss the day of school, but James refused. She'd say no, she'd ask him to explain, she'd say yes to Sammy. Sammy knew that Gram was one person who said an awful lot of noes to him, but he also knew that somehow he did a better job of asking people for things than James did. It was funny the ways James expected people to say no to him.

When Sammy asked Gram about cutting school and going up to Cambridge with Rev. Smiths, she asked him: "Why?"

"I can't say," Sammy said. He looked at her and she looked at him. He was just waiting, while her mind turned over a lot of things.

"All right," she finally decided. "I won't tell them you're sick, though. I won't lie. But I'll tell them you're out with my permission and knowledge."

"Good-o," Sammy answered. He was looking forward to missing a day of school, now that he thought about it.

"But you didn't have to ask. You could have just gone ahead and done it, skipped school."

"I could have," Sammy agreed, turning back at the door. "But James is no good at lying."

"And you are?"

"I can, yeah," Sammy told her, as if she didn't already know that. "But I don't need to lie to you."

"That," Gram said, "is just what I'm trying to figure out."

"Don't worry, I don't. I don't even want to," Sammy said, running off to find James.

He heard Gram's voice asking behind him: "Why not?"

Rev. Smiths picked them up at the end of their driveway, at quarter after eight. James had made Sammy wear good khaki pants and a button-down shirt, because he didn't want them to look like just kids. Sammy thought since they were kids, there was no reason to pretend they weren't. James was all spruced up, his hair slicked down from having been combed with water, even wearing one of the old striped ties Gram had brought down from the attic. If his arms hadn't been too long for the sleeves, he probably would have worn his jacket.

When Rev. Smiths's car stopped for them, Sammy got into the front seat and belted himself in. The Smithses had an old black car they seemed to have had for about a hundred years, but they'd had seat belts put in. James got into the backseat.

After they had greeted one another, they all kept quiet. Sammy looked out the window, all along the road up through Princess Anne to Salisbury. This was farmland, flat under a broad blue sky, lowland, with shallow ditches dug at the edges of the fields to drain off water. The highway was ditched at its edges too. Sammy knew the car was moving, but it looked like it was the scenery that moved. He breathed deeply. It was a plump spring morning, the air swollen with warmth. Not heat. Heat would start coming in about the end of May, but now, in late April, it was spring. Spring was about the most perfect season in Maryland, with everything bursting into flowers and little green shoots just pushing up out of the dark fields. Light shone from a blue sky that wasn't dark at all, just deep, pale blue. Light glowed over the land. It was almost as if it was the earth giving off the light, the air was so full of soft brightness. Sammy felt at home in spring—his whole body felt like one of those sprouts, swelling up and pushing out to be . . . whatever he wanted. The only advantage summer had over spring was that school was out in the summer.

After Rev. Smiths had made the turn onto Route 50, he broke the silence in his car. "Sammy? What did you think of the new Mina?"

"You mean her haircut? I guess her hair's not much longer than yours, now."

"Not much, if any," Mina's father agreed. "How do you like it?"

"I thought she looked—strong," Sammy said. He liked the haircut a lot.

"I guess she is that. But it doesn't look like a woman's hairstyle to me. Well, it's of a piece with those caftans she's wearing these days. I guess, she wants to tell those people up North she's not ashamed to be who she is."

"Mina does what she wants," Sammy told Mina's father, who should already know that, better than anyone.

"It's just that she's so different from her brothers and sisters." Rev. Smiths wasn't really worried about Mina, Sammy could tell. He was just finding out what Sammy thought.

"All brothers and sisters are different," Sammy explained. "Aren't we, James?" he asked, looking over his shoulder. James nodded. "And Louis," Sammy added, "Louis isn't a bit like Mina."

"About the last thing Louis would want to do is walk out into some courtroom and argue," Rev. Smiths agreed. "Mina's going to be a lawyer, and nothing will stop her, not money, not color, not sex—I wonder sometimes what she expects of herself. That girl is always surprising me." He didn't sound like he minded that; he sounded proud. "I ask her," he smiled to himself, "if she's ever thought about the Pharisees."

Sammy had no idea what Rev. Smiths was talking about. But James entered the conversation at that. "You think all lawyers are Pharisees? Do you have something against lawyers? I'm probably going to go into law."

"Are you going to right all the wrongs of the world, too?"

"I doubt that. All I hope is to make a good income, probably in business. I don't think I'd be much good in a courtroom."

"So you see law as a business—not as—what shapes society?" Rev. Smiths looked at James in the rearview mirror.

"Do you mean shaping society like the Ten Commandments do?" James asked, leaning forward.

Sammy looked out of the window at the day around him, and didn't pay much attention as they talked and talked. James had forgotten that Sammy was the one who was more at ease with people, Sammy thought. Sometimes, smart as he was, it looked like James didn't know beans about himself.

Rev. Smiths parked behind a church, the chunky gray stones of which looked warmed by sunlight. It had a steeple that pointed up into the deep sky. Sammy waited for James to get started on his agenda for the day. He was pretty sure James had an agenda. And he was right.

They started off at the hospital, where a friendly woman with big glasses, wearing a bright red smock, sat behind the reception counter and tried to help them. She talked to James between answering the phone, receiving flowers, and directing visitors which way to go. But she didn't know about records of birth, especially since they don't know what year they were looking for. "All the old records are at the state archives, in Annapolis," she told them. "They're kept at the Hall of Records. Or the Department of Health and Mental Hygiene in Baltimore." She was sorry, because she really did want to be able to help them out. "The hospital only keeps records on file for a limited number of years. The doctor who delivered the child might remember, but . . . maybe this person wasn't even born in a hospital. A few decades ago many women still had their babies at home. I'm sorry, boys, I just can't think of anything else. Unless you want to go to Annapolis and look at the records there."

"But—" James said.

"Thank you," Sammy interrupted. Couldn't James figure out there was nothing more to be learned here? He went back outside, knowing James would follow. Before James could begin to say whatever he was thinking of complaining at Sammy about, Sammy asked him, "What's next?"

"Next?"

"You have a plan, don't you? What was next, if the hospital didn't know anything?" Sammy made himself speak patiently. He didn't remind James that they didn't have all day. They had to meet Rev. Smiths by three.

"The school, but—"

"Where's that?" Sammy interrupted again. James had made a photocopy of a map of Cambridge. Their school library had maps, and for a dime you could make a copy. James pulled the map out of his pocket and unfolded it carefully.

"We have to go back downtown, then out this Glasgow Street." James showed Sammy on the map. "But it's going to be just like the hospital, and I never thought of that. He'd have to be born about forty years ago, don't you think?" Sammy hadn't thought, but James wasn't really asking the question. "Probably, at that time, the elementary school wouldn't have been so far out of town, if he was even living here when he went to school. I mean, he could have just been born here, then moved away. I never thought of that. Did you?"

Sammy hadn't thought of anything.

"I'm going to have to get to Annapolis somehow." James stood there on the sidewalk and let the people coming and going move around him, hurrying into the hospital, hurrying out of it.

"Isn't there a school trip in May? To see the Colonial buildings or something? Maybe they go to this Hall of Records."

"You have to stay with the group. Besides, it costs money."

"I've got some money left, I told you. So, what do we do now?"

"I don't know. I guess, we might as well try the school."

Sammy could have laughed, but he thought James would mind being laughed at. They walked back toward the center of town, across the little bridge that went over the town creek. A railroad used to run right down there. The tracks were still set in the ground, and an old station house, just one low room, stood at the end of the tracks, its roof dull and windows boarded over, its faded wooden paint covered with graffiti. The tracks stopped there too, with only the broad Choptank River ahead. They turned onto High Street, the main street, long and broad, stretching away from them. The buildings were big and square, with big square glass windows lining the sidewalks. Cambridge was a small city. Sammy liked the walking, and looking around at stores and people. Most of the people they saw were women, because it was a school day and a workday. Some of the women were wheeling babies in strollers, some of them carried shopping bags, and some just sauntered along studying the store windows. None of them paid any attention to Sammy and James.

Once they turned off the main street, they were back in a

residential district, and had the sidewalks to themselves. They walked on down toward a redbrick building, with a short square tower for its front entry, like a kid's castle built out of blocks. "There it is," Sammy said, in case James had missed it. The way the building sat back from the road on a generous spread of lawn, and something about the long, many-paned windows, told him it was a school.

"That can't be it. The map shows it much farther out of town. Unless I've gotten the scale all wrong. And there isn't any playground."

"It looks like a school to me," Sammy said.

When they approached the front of the building, a sign set on the grass announced that this was the Board of Education. "I told you," James told Sammy.

Sammy just pointed to the white concrete slab over the doorway. Set into the concrete, like letters cut into a tombstone, were the words CAMBRIDGE ELEMENTARY SCHOOL. So it used to be a school. Sammy didn't say I told you, but he was thinking it. He waited for James to lead on out to the new school building, wherever it was. But James turned up onto the sidewalk that led to the front door.

"What're you doing?" Sammy hurried along behind his brother.

"It was a long time ago, so the school records are likely not to be in a new school, but they might be here," James said. He sounded excited. "This was lucky, our finding this."

Inside, it was more obvious that the building had been built as a school. Three broad steps led up to a small foyer; two long hallways went off, one to the right and one to the left; the floors were dark brown linoleum squares; the doors that lined the hallways were closed. One door had a little black sign sticking out into the hall. RECEPTION, it said. James moved toward it.

"I have to go to the bathroom," Sammy said.

"I don't," James told him. "You don't even know where it is. Can't you wait?"

No, Sammy couldn't and didn't see why he should. There was bound to be a bathroom along the corridors. Schools had lots of bathrooms. "You go ahead, I won't be long, I'll find you."

"I'll wait," James told him.

Sammy went down the hall, past the door to reception, where a woman sat at a desk piled with papers and file folders, talking on one phone while another rang. He found a men's room, and was as quick as he could be. The long mirrors over the sinks reflected his own face back to him: he looked like he was having a good time. Well, he was. He figured they'd spend all day chasing their own tails, but he didn't mind. It was a kind of adventure, and it made James happy; besides, Sammy wasn't sitting at a desk in a classroom looking out at the sunny day through a window. He went to find his brother.

As soon as James saw Sammy coming, he stepped into the reception office. Sammy guessed James was feeling impatient. When he got there, James was already in the middle of a conversation, so he just stayed by the door, not interfering.

"I think so," James was saying. "I'm looking for—"

"Of course," the woman interrupted. She stood up and came around the desk, holding her hand out to shake, as if she had been expecting James. She wore a khaki cotton suit, belted at the waist with a belt made from rope. When she got up from her chair she tugged down at the skirt with one hand, the one she wasn't holding out to James. She banged her leg into the corner of the desk. "I'm Mrs. Wylie," she said, rubbing at her bruised thigh. Her glasses slid down her long nose and fell off.

Luckily, they were held around her neck by a metal chain. Sammy stood in the doorway, enjoying this. Mrs. Wylie looked frazzled. Her skirt was rumpled and her blouse pulled out at the waist a little. Her light brown hair curled wispily up all around her head and down below her ears. She put her glasses back on and ran her fingers through her hair, as if she knew it was messy and wished it wasn't but didn't expect to be able to do much about that. When she did that, her white blouse pulled up still further, so she pulled it down again, pushing it into the belt of the skirt with her fingers, which didn't work very well to keep it tucked in. She never did get James's hand shook.

"I'm so glad to see you. You don't have any idea. I guess Marietta told you how desperate I am. Well, you can see for yourself, can't you? I assume you know how to file. All you need is to know the alphabet. Do you know the alphabet?"

"Yes," James said. He was trying to figure out how to take the conversation back to where he'd started it.

"That was stupid of me. I know a college student has to—" Mrs. Wylie stood in front of James and smiled up at him. She was a little woman, little height, little hands and feet. She giggled, as if she were a seventh-grade girl, Sammy thought. Her pale skin was scattered with freckles. She hadn't paid any attention to him at all; she probably hadn't even seen him.

"I didn't even ask your name. You must think I've no manners at all."

"James Tillerman," James said, "but—"

"How do you do?" Then she did shake James's hand.

"Hello," James answered politely. "I was wondering—"

"Do you type?" she asked.

"Not too quickly, but I'm accurate," James answered.

Sammy stood in the doorway trying not to laugh out loud. She wasn't listening to James and James couldn't figure out what she was talking about. Mrs. Wylie noticed him, then.

"You'll have to wait a moment," she told Sammy. "We have a

crisis here. I won't be a moment." She turned back to James: "Because I don't know if Marietta told you that there is typing to be done, too, it's really general office work more than simply clerical."

"But you haven't—" James started.

"Oh," She put her hand back into her hair. "I'm so sorry. I never mentioned the pay, I just assumed you'd take the job." She giggled. "I'm not usually this foolish. I'm a little rattled today, as you must have noticed. I am sorry. It's not much," she told him. "It's only three dollars and ten cents an hour. That's below minimum wage, I know."

"That wouldn't be bad," James said, "if—"

"No benefits either. It's only a temporary position. But Marietta was supposed to explain all that to you." Mrs. Wylie went back behind her desk and sat down again, more businesslike now that she was cross. Sammy just grinned. She put her glasses back up on her nose and picked up the phone. "You look awfully young anyway."

James just stood there, in front of the desk. He didn't say a thing. Sammy would have butted in and explained, but he was busy keeping his laughter down.

"Well—?" Mrs. Wylie asked James. She held the phone in her hand, her fingers ready to dial it. She looked at him over the top of her glasses, which were already slipping back down her nose.

"I didn't come about a job," James said, finally spitting it out.

She put the phone back in its cradle. Her cheeks stained pink. She covered her face with her hands, and giggled behind them. Then she sat up straight and secretarial, looking right at James. "You shouldn't have let me think you had," she told him. "This job is enough to drive me crazy without your help. You'd probably have been a big help, too, you have that look about you. I hope somebody shows up. What is it you want then?"

"I'm wondering how to find out if somebody went to school in Cambridge," James said. "It's sort of—a genealogy project. This is my brother who came with me."

"Ah," she said, her eyes going back to Sammy. He nodded at her to say hello. She nodded back. "Now I see," she said. "I've made a mistake." She was ready to enjoy her mistake, but James didn't give her any time.

"I was wondering if you could show me any records from—I'm not sure, about forty years ago."

"Oh no," she said. Her glasses dropped down to the end of their chain. "If you had any idea of what state those records are in, in the first place, after years and years of understaffing—but you can't just go through school records. It's not allowed. They're confidential."

James just turned away as soon as she said that, giving up right away.

"Don't you even know a name?" Mrs. Wylie asked, half getting up from her chair. She looked at Sammy, as if she were apologizing: "He didn't even tell me a name."

"Verricker," Sammy answered. "Francis Verricker."

"I've never heard of him."

James had turned back. "What about any family with that name?"

"Not that I've heard of. But then, you see, this is the Board of Education and I wouldn't have the local names to mind the way the schools would, or teachers. You said it was forty years ago?"

"That's an estimate," James told her. Sammy could see that James was hoping again.

"Probably, then, you'd do better to talk to someone who was here at that time, in the schools—exactly how old is this person you're trying to trace?"

"We don't know. We think he'd have been in grade school

thirty or more years ago. If he went to grade school here. Is there anybody left from that long ago?" Sometimes Sammy worried about James. He hoped so hard and gave up so easy.

Mrs. Wylie pushed her glasses back up her nose. "It doesn't seem such a long time to me, young man."

"Oh. I'm sorry," James said. "I didn't mean that." Sammy grinned.

"It sounds like an imaginative project," Mrs. Wylie took pity on James, ignoring his embarrassment. "I never had anything so interesting to do in school, not that I remember. Almost a detective story, isn't it?"

"I guess," James agreed.

"Mrs. Rottman—wait—I just thought of her—Mrs. Rottman might remember him. I wonder why I didn't think of her right away." Mrs. Wylie's hands moved eagerly to a Rolodex file and she toppled over a tall stack of papers. She caught the papers before they fell to the floor, and stacked them neatly. "She taught grade school for years, and then she was the principal, for twenty years. I've only lived here for five years, but—if this Francis Verricker went to school in Cambridge she'd remember him. I could call her and ask. Shall I? She's retired now, of course, but she's as sharp as ever. She's only been retired for the last two or three years. The board gave her a rather fine ormolu clock. Do you want me to call her and ask if she knows of Francis Verricker?"

"I'd—" James began, but she cut him off again.

"If she does, she'll be able to tell you about him. Unless—it wasn't Franc-es, was it? Oh dear, have I gotten it wrong? It's so hard when you don't see the name written out."

"No," James told her. "He's a male. That's no problem. I'd be grateful if you would call," he hinted. He tried to glare at Sammy, because Sammy was in serious danger of getting an attack of the giggles. Mrs. Wylie's mind ran around like a chicken in a coop, pecking after corn, running after something else, clucking away. Sammy liked chickens.

Listening, Sammy expected her to say something that would tell them that this Mrs. Rottman never heard of Francis Verricker, but he heard instead, "They'll be very pleased, I'm sure. Yes, I'll send them right over. They look like nice boys, Mrs. Rottman."

James shot Sammy a look filled with triumph. "See?" he would have said, "See, I told you so," if he could have said anything; Sammy didn't respond. He listened as Mrs. Wylie explained how to find Two Water Street, even though he needn't have bothered, with James paying such careful attention. "Good-bye," she said to them. "I'm sorry you weren't here about the clerking job."

"I'm only fifteen anyway. I'm too young."

"You could get work papers. But, there's no need, if you don't want a job, is there?" Her phone rang and she picked it up. "Board of Education, Mrs. Wylie speaking." Her phone voice sounded as if nothing ever confused or upset her.

"Thank you," James said from the doorway. "Really, thank you."

She smiled and raised her free hand in farewell. "He's in a meeting at the moment. May I take a message?" her smooth voice asked. Her fingers scrabbled around the littered surface of the desk for a piece of paper; her glasses slid down her nose and tinged against the telephone receiver. "Yes, of course," she said calmly, tipping over a container of pencils.

Outside, the boys turned down the sidewalk. Two blocks west, then four or five north would bring them to the end of Water Street. "That was lucky, wasn't it?" James said. "But it makes sense. A place like this, where a lot of people stay in the places where they were born, there was bound to be somebody who was around then. It makes sense. We were smart to come up here."

He walked on silently for a while, then stopped, dead. He

turned to face Sammy. Now what? Sammy wondered.

"She knew him. Our father. This Mrs. Rottman, she actually knew him."

"I was there," Sammy reminded him.

James started moving off again. Weird. His brother was weird, Sammy thought. That wasn't his problem, though, so he didn't mind. This was a nice street, neat houses set on bright green lawns, the trees spreading out green branches and a big old magnolia with thick, bushy, black-green leaves. The leaves were green overhead. The air smelled fine, green and sunny. Sammy felt good. Let James worry about where they were going and whatever it was he thought he'd find out. Sammy concentrated on feeling good. "You should have taken that job," he teased James.

James ignored him, so Sammy argued about it.

"Really. I mean, what you don't like about most jobs is the hard physical work, but filing and typing, you'd be really good at those. Think of it James, if you'd stayed there, you'd have earned maybe fourteen dollars before we had to go home."

James shook his head.

"And only gotten your hands dusty," Sammy went on.

"There would have been papers to fill out, so she'd have found out right away, or at least by the time I left, so it wouldn't have worked," James said. "I'd have done whatever, all those hours, and I wouldn't even get any money, because it's illegal to hire people under sixteen, without the right papers. And a board of education is practically a government office. So I'd have just lost the time entirely."

Sammy shook his head. "They have to pay you for the work you've done. Even if you couldn't keep the job. When you do the work, they have to pay you."

CHAPTER 5

The houses on Water Street were older, three-story clapboard buildings mostly painted white, with porches on the second stories. The street ended at the Choptank River, broad here, the distant shore a low smudged line of trees. Sammy would have liked to go sit on the thick concrete wall that ended the street, to watch the sunlight glimmer along the water, but James turned in at a white wrought-iron gate. The short walk was edged with neat little mounds of flowering plants; the grass of the lawn stretched green and neatly trimmed along to the river.

Mrs. Rottman opened the door before James even raised his hand to knock. "You must be the two boys," her gentle voice said. "It was nice of you to come by. Come in, come on up. I have the second floor apartment."

She led them up a flight of stairs, down a narrow hall past a living room filled with fat chairs and a fat sofa, all covered with brightly flowered materials, and out onto the second-story porch. She sat them down on white wrought-iron chairs. The iron flowers and leaves cut into Sammy's backside and thighs. No matter how he shifted his weight, he couldn't get comfortable. James frowned at him, but Sammy couldn't see why he had to sit there, and be so uncomfortable, and sit still.

James was sitting still, with his arms on the hard armrests, as if the sharp pointed design of the seat was perfectly comfortable.

Sammy didn't believe that for a minute. The chairs even looked as if they'd be bad to sit on—he couldn't figure out why anyone would want to buy them, unless they liked being uncomfortable.

Mrs. Rottman had set out a tray on the table the chairs were grouped around. It was a round tray, with a pitcher of orange juice and three glasses on it, and a plate of store-bought cookies, the expensive kind that came in little paper sacks. She sat down in the chair between them and poured glasses of juice. "It's been some time since I had children come to call on me. You can imagine that this is quite a treat for me."

Her voice didn't sound like what she looked like. She looked, with her short gray-white hair cut straight and held to one side by a metal barrette, with a square face and square mouth and little blue eyes behind square glasses, with her square sensible dark suit and square sensible low-heeled shoes, like an army sergeant. But her voice sounded soft, gentle, pillowy. "I never had children of my own," she said, handing around the glasses of juice. Sammy shifted in his seat. "Because I was widowed so young. The children I taught have been my children. Mr. Rottman was killed in the war, in North Africa. That broke my heart, but I had my work, and my children."

She looked back and forth at them. Sammy, holding the glass in one hand, tried to find a comfortable position.

"Don't squirm so. Have a cookie? These chocolate ones are my favorites. Try a chocolate one."

Sammy didn't want anything but to be standing up, which he couldn't. James, however, scarfed up a handful of cookies and smiled at Mrs. Rottman. The whole thing was already enough to make Sammy sick.

"Now, we can get down to business, can't we?" Mrs. Rottman said, as if she were talking to little kids who wouldn't know what business really was. "Why would you want to know about Francis

Verricker?" She smiled at Sammy. He didn't smile back. "Frankie is what I called him. You can't call an eight year old Francis, can you? He was in my third-grade class, the very first year I ever taught school. But why are you asking about him?"

Sammy just looked at James: let James answer that.

"Well, we're—actually, it's me, and Sammy just came along to keep me company—I'm doing a genealogy report. For school," James added, when she didn't respond.

"I'm afraid I don't think that's true," Mrs. Rottman said. Sammy could have laughed. "But I've always said, and told my teachers this, children need to be able to keep things private. Children need to have secrets. So I'll let you keep this one. I'll tell you what I remember about Frankie, but I don't want you to think you've fooled me."

"Yes, ma'am," James said.

She bowed her head at him, like some queen of England. "Your name is Tillerman, not Verricker, so I can only assume it's something to do with adoption, something to do with finding your true parents. One hears so much of such things, these days. I think, myself, it was better when the adopted children knew nothing about it. Children need protection—at least until they're old enough, and strong enough, to take care of themselves. Don't you agree? How can we expect children to understand what the world is like?"

She seemed to expect them to answer that, but even James couldn't think of anything. He munched down a couple of cookies and looked serious. He finished off his glass of orange juice. Finally, "Yes," he said. Mrs. Rottman didn't say anything. "I wonder," James said, "can you tell us when it was that Francis Verricker was in third grade? We don't even know when he was born."

"That was 1938. My first year. He'd have known me as Miss

Rowan—isn't that a pretty name? I was sorry to lose my maiden name, even though the initial is the same, which helps. It wasn't until my second year of teaching that I married. So I was Miss Rowan to Frankie, and he—he was special to me. I couldn't have said so at the time, it doesn't do to play favorites—but he was very dear to me. He was such a bright little boy, you see, and he looked like an angel, big eyes and curly hair and such a sweet face. Not a goody-goody angel, but the kind of little angel God would especially care for, a mischievous little angel who could make God laugh. Frankie was naughty, a very naughty boy, and he was often disobedient, but I could understand why. His behavior never bothered me the way it did some other people. Bright children, especially boys, have such a hard time behaving in school. The other children are so much slower, and you can't ask an energetic little boy to sit patiently by all day long, day after day, can you? Frankie—why he'd remember everything he ever heard or read, and he was so curious about everything—there wasn't anything that got by that child. He was a natural leader, too, and the other children would do anything he told them. Sometimes, what he told them to do wasn't very nice. But you couldn't help loving him. He had such a bright little face, such a happy laugh—even when I had to scold him, or punish him, he didn't hold it against me. I often felt so sorry for him."

"Why did you feel sorry for him?" James asked.

"There was something sad about Frankie—as if he didn't belong—something lost—I could see it in his eyes. He was the youngest, you see, and the only boy. It's always hard being the youngest."

"Why?" Sammy asked.

"Everybody else is quicker, and more clever, and does things for you, I saw this over and over again in my classroom. You get to feeling helpless and you get to like that feeling. It's hard for youngest children to *do* anything with their lives. They seem to give up more quickly."

She didn't know what she was talking about, Sammy thought, and she was making him angry. Let James talk to her.

"Besides which, I suspect Frankie's older sisters babied him. Oh, it was a perfectly nice family, very respectable. They were plagued by the bad luck of the times, but everyone was. They owned a confectionary. Verrickers made good candies, I remember them. The parents had started it when they were newly married—and they were hardworking people. Well, you had to be, to keep going through those hard years, especially with a business of your own, a small business. Frankie was like a changeling in that family. He used to make up stories, about himself, about his real family—wealthy, of course, and his father was a war hero, his mother a beauty, Frankie the only child. He had a vivid imagination, Frankie did; he could write stories I'd have sworn were the truth if I hadn't known better. I tried to help him understand, I'd try to tell him how hard his father worked, and his mother and sisters too, and how lucky he was to have them. But he thought they were stupid—he said that and, in a way, I could understand why he thought that because he was so quick and clever and imaginative, which they weren't. You could say he lived in a dream world, or an imaginary world, but he had a streak of realism that almost frightened me. He would tell me that it didn't make any difference how hard they worked and the terrible thing was that he was right. The family barely scraped by."

What was so bad about that? Sammy wondered.

"Of course Frankie was always in trouble at home, of one kind or another. I'm sure he was provocative at times—he was a terrible liar and sometimes—well, once, I'm pretty certain, he was the one who took a dollar bill I'd left in my coat pocket.

He said he wouldn't ever do that, not to me, but I wasn't sure I could believe him. And I'm not sure I can blame him, either. Life was harder on Frankie than on the rest of us, because he had so much imagination and so many dreams. He was always telling me about what he'd do, what he was going to do, how rich he would be—I was a great favorite of his, you see, and he often came back to visit my classroom, until he graduated into the high school. We had a particular relationship. I thought, sometimes, that I should have asked if he could come live with me. I didn't know then that I wouldn't ever have children of my own, so I never thought seriously about it, but we had such a particular relationship. I could control him, more than anyone else. His family couldn't understand such an intelligent boy, such a spirited little boy. I always wondered what Frankie would do in his life. After he was expelled I lost track of him, although I sometimes still think I'll see his name in the papers, as a scientific discoverer, or one of those entrepreneur businessmen. The kind who take huge risks and amass huge fortunes. He seemed such a sad, intelligent little boy. He'd have been in the gifted program, if we'd had one then. Are you boys in gifted programs?"

Not on your life, Sammy thought. James was, but James didn't say anything about that.

"You said he was expelled," James asked Mrs. Rottman.

"Yes, from the high school."

"Does his family still live in Cambridge?" James asked.

"Goodness no. They went bankrupt, in the late forties. I think Mr. Verricker had died by then, and his wife, too, and the daughters were trying to run the business. It's sad, really, because they'd hung on through the Depression and they'd hung on through the war years, with all the shortages, and then—just as times were getting better—they went bankrupt. They moved out of the area years ago. But Frankie had already left home by then, as I understand it."

"What was he expelled for?" James asked, as if he wanted to hear everything bad that he could, Sammy thought.

"Nobody told mc, except that it was something serious. Well, it would have had to be, wouldn't it? Perhaps they wanted to spare my feelings. I'd like to think so. People sometimes want to be kind." Her hand reached out for a chocolate cookie, which she bit into thoughtfully. "I hadn't seen him since he was in sixth grade, at that time."

Sammy figured she was finished, and he tried to catch James's eye so they could leave. James just took some more cookies, and kept on eating.

"Is there anyone who might have known him in the high school? Anyone like you, who has been a teacher here all their lives?" James asked.

"All his life," Mrs. Rottman corrected.

"Yes, all his life."

"No, I can't think of anyone, personally. There are lines drawn, you see, between the elementary and high school teachers. Quite a gulf lies between us. High school teachers do look down on those who teach in elementary school."

"I never thought of that," James answered, as if that was something worth caring about.

Sammy was glad that James seemed to know what to say to this woman. He squirmed in his seat and thought about this little boy Frankie. It sounded like Frankie could have been anything he wanted to be, in his life, if he was so smart, and a natural leader. A liar, too, Sammy thought, and probably a thief—this Frankie reminded Sammy of himself.

"I don't want you worrying about Frankie, if he is your father," Mrs. Rottman told them. "Sometimes, in a family, there's one child who is just different. Like a changeling child. Frankie was like that—he had so much potential, bright, imaginative, he never seemed to run out of energy and he looked just like an angel. He was the most beautiful child I ever taught, in all my years. He simply didn't fit in among the Verrickers. There's Mr. Ferguson, of course, but he's always been in administration. He never taught in a classroom, except for occasional substitution. He came to the high school as assistant principal in the last years of the war, because he'd had rheumatic fever, you see, and so wasn't physically qualified for military service. He might well have known Frankie."

"Do you know where we could find Mr. Ferguson?" James asked.

"Why at the high school, of course. Now I think of it, he'd probably know when Frankie left school. Do you think you'd be able to find the high school?"

Sammy couldn't sit there any longer on that chair. He was up, putting his glass down on the tray, and heading back down to the front door while James was still saying thank you to Mrs. Rottman. Sammy let himself out the front door. He didn't want to stay inside that iron fence, not for another second, so he waited for James in the street.

When James finally came out, all he said was, "Your manners are rotten."

"So what?" They walked on to the corner, not in step. "She's pretty stupid," Sammy pointed out to James, who hadn't seemed to notice that.

"Not stupid, just—not objective, everything started with how she felt."

"Stupid," Sammy clarified.

"But don't you ever wonder?"

Sammy didn't bother answering. James would go ahead and say what he wanted to anyway.

"I mean, we can only know what we know."

That was pretty stupid, even for James.

"I mean, if somebody is always fair to me, and considerate and all that, but is rotten to other people, can I say he's rotten? And if they tell me he is, how can I believe them, if all of my experience is that he isn't? Like Gram, when we first got here and everybody said she was crazy or something, but she wasn't crazy at us."

"People just expected her to be like what they were like. And she isn't," Sammy said.

"But if they thought she was crazy she might as well have been. If you see what I mean."

"You have to let people be what they are," Sammy protested. "She never was, no matter what anyone said."

"So how can you know what's really true?" James wondered.

Sammy couldn't see what this conversation was about or where it would get them. He stopped at a street corner and asked James to take out the map. The high school was outside of town, to the south. "Do we have time to walk that far?" James worried.

"It's maybe two miles," Sammy said, studying the map.

James stopped. "Too far."

"Okay." Sammy folded up the map and gave it back to James.

"Do you think it's too far?"

Sammy shrugged. This was James's idea, let him make the decision. It wasn't too far for Sammy, but this wasn't his idea.

James didn't move. He looked all around, as if there were an answer hiding somewhere behind the corner of one of the houses, or up in a tree. "Unless we walk pretty fast. The average walking pace is about three miles an hour, and average is pretty slow. So it might not be too far."

"Okay," Sammy said.

"We have a couple of hours, it shouldn't be too far."

As far as Sammy could see, there was only one way to find out.

"I don't think it's too far," James decided.

They walked along at a good pace, through the town, out past residential areas and then the outlying houses, farther apart, and then farmlands. "How much farther do you think it is?" James asked.

"We follow this road until it crosses a main road, and the school's right there. Want to quit?" Sammy chose that word on purpose.

"No," James said.

Sammy slowed down a little, to match his brother's flagging pace.

"I was thinking," James said, "about what Mrs. Rottman said about him. If he was as smart as she said, and she is probably right about things like that because she's a teacher, he could have become almost anything. Like she said."

"Yeah, but he didn't," Sammy pointed out.

"I wonder why."

"Dicey said the police were looking for him, in Provincetown."

"She told me, you don't have to repeat everything Dicey said. I already know it. Sometimes, you're just like her," James said.

"Good," Sammy answered.

The land emptied around them, uncultivated fields overgrown with weeds and grass and saplings. Walking fast made the warm day start to feel hot. Sammy rolled up the sleeves of his shirt. It would be a good day to play tennis, windless and clear. He wished Mina hadn't already gone back to school, because there wasn't anyone else he could play tennis with.

"I wonder where the family is now," James said, beside him.

"Does it matter?"

"Maybe not, except—just because they left Cambridge

doesn't mean they left the area. They could have started up business somewhere else around here."

"I've never heard of any candy business around here."

"But we haven't lived here all that long, and we don't travel around. For example, if I wanted to start up a confectioner's business, I'd go to Ocean City, where there's a big tourist season. Wouldn't you?"

Sammy wouldn't want to start up a candy-making business, so he had no idea what he'd do. A distant plane droned across the sky. Following the little dark shape with his eyes, he missed the first sighting of the high school.

"There it is," James said, and his pace increased, as if—now that he could actually see their destination—he had the strength to hurry to it. The school looked fairly new, long and low, surrounded by parking lots. Sammy caught a glimpse of several macadam tennis courts off behind one of the wings that spread out from the main building. Windows were open, but it was quiet outside. They headed for the doors with a flagpole in front of them; that would be the main office.

In the office, a secretary looked up at them. "We want to see Mr. Ferguson," James said.

"Down that hallway, through the glass doors, turn left, and it's the third door on your right," she told them, without really looking at them. When they found the door she'd directed them to, it had ASSISTANT PRINCIPAL painted on the glass.

"He still has the same job he had when he came," James said.

"How do you know?"

"Because it's what Mrs. Rottman said. Don't you remember?"

Sammy hadn't been paying attention. "Are you going in, or what?" he asked.

James knocked on the glass with his knuckles and a man's voice told them to come in. They entered a short narrow room with only one window, high up on the back wall. A gray-haired man sat behind a desk under the window, facing the door. He had a pouchy face, pouches of skin under his eyes and his jowls hanging down pouchy. He looked at them without saying anything, his watery blue eyes not curious, as if he already knew what they were going to say and what he was going to say. He had a thermos on his desk and some manila folders, but no phone. He poured himself a cup of coffee out of the thermos, without saying anything, then looked back at James and Sammy, disliking them.

"Well? Well?" he finally said. "Come on up here. Move it, boys."

They went up to the desk. Sammy let James stand a little ahead, because it was James's business. He watched Mr. Ferguson's pudgy fingers turn a pencil, over and over. He could feel the man's boredom with them, and his dislike for them, coming across the desk at him like heat from an open oven door. Well, he didn't care.

"Spit it out. Who sent you and what did you do." Mr. Ferguson put down the pencil and opened a drawer to take out a thick pad of detention slips. "And give me your passes."

"We don't have any passes," James said.

"Why not?" the man demanded, his voice growing larger and more threatening.

James didn't seem to be able to answer.

"Because we don't go to this school," Sammy said, stepping up beside James. He wasn't going to let this man think he could bully him. Maybe he could bully away at James, but Sammy was a different story.

"Why aren't you at your own school?"

"We're not hooking," Sammy told him. It wasn't a lie. He'd have said it, and said it exactly the same way if it had been a lie, but it wasn't. He didn't say any more than that, because he almost hoped the man would draw the wrong conclusions, and try to get them in trouble, and then they would show him.

"It's not what you think," James said, trying to smooth things over. At the expression on Mr. Ferguson's face he changed his way of saying it. "We haven't explained ourselves." Sammy wished James wouldn't interfere; he could handle this Ferguson man.

"A woman named Mrs. Rottman—"

"Her," Mr. Ferguson grumbled.

"Mrs. Rottman told us you might be able to help us. We're looking for information about a former student, here at the high school. She said you might remember him—Francis Verricker."

"Verricker?" Mr. Ferguson leaned back in his chair and smiled to himself. "Bet your boots I remember Verricker. I was the one who got him thrown out, which may be the best day's work I ever did."

"Yes, sir," James said, agreeing. "So I guess you knew him."

"I knew everything I wanted to know about him. He was a bad one. Always in fights—and he didn't fight clean, either. Bad with the girls, too."

"Is that why he got expelled? Because of the fighting?" James asked.

Mr. Ferguson folded his fingers together over his stomach. His cheeks pouched back as he smiled again. "Better than that. He got expelled for making book. Verricker was running a gambling operation—it was small-time, but he was a small-time type. He'd take bets on the games—you know? He even gave odds, he'd work them up himself, depending on what school we were playing. It didn't matter what sport, he'd be there like some weasel back in the corner—football, basketball, baseball—his pockets full of chits and his hands grubbing around the dollar bills. I caught him at it, found a couple of people who'd lost a lot to him and were happy to talk, and we gave him the boot. He was trying to act like some Chicago big-time gangster or something, like this was Chicago or something. That boy had no sense of reality. He didn't even put up a fight. He just crumbled to little bitty pieces—and went away."

"Do you know what happened to him after that?"

"No. I never asked. I've seen a lot of kids like him in my time, all thinking they can break the rules and get away with it, with no feeling for the school. He was one of the worst. None of them fooled me for long."

"Ah," James said. Mr. Ferguson leaned forward again, his pleasant memories concluded. He wanted them to leave.

"I don't know if you remember when this was?" James answered.

"Why should I remember a little creep like Verricker? Just, sometime right at the end of the war, forty-five it must have been. I remember thinking it was too bad he wasn't in time to get drafted." He opened up a manila folder, as if he was going to read it. "It would have been good to think of him being killed off." He picked up his pencil and held it over the top sheet of paper in the folder.

"Well, thank you for your time," James said. The man ignored them.

James didn't say anything, not all the way back into town. Neither did Sammy. Sammy had nothing to say. When they were finally sitting in the grass, waiting for Rev. Smiths to come out of his meeting, James opened his mouth. Sammy thought he'd want to talk about what kind of man their father had been, and he didn't feel like talking about that, but instead James said, "Weren't you even a little afraid of that Mr. Ferguson?"

"Why should I be? Were you?"

"You never are, are you," James said. He was sitting up, pulling shoots of grass and rubbing them between his fingers until his skin was stained green. Sammy watched his nervous fingers, pulling up, rubbing, dropping the squeezed grass back down onto the lawn.

"Anyway, you got busy asking questions, like always," Sammy reminded his brother.

"I guess."

"You weren't expecting good news, were you?"

"I dunno," James said. "But I always wondered, and now I can see why Momma didn't name me after him."

"She named me after her brother."

"I don't even know why my name is James," James said.

Sammy almost groaned aloud. Now James was going to go haring off to find out why he was named his own name. Well, that trip Sammy wasn't going to go along on. Besides, there was no way of figuring it out. Besides, what did it matter how you got your name, since it was your name. He got up and started just walking around the building. The stone walls went right down to the flat ground, as if they continued cutting down into the earth. The walls were flat and straight, the corners squared off even, and up above, the steeple tried to push its way right into the sky. Standing at the base of the steeple, close up to the cold stone wall, it looked as if the steeple was about to fall over on him. It wasn't true, but that was the way it looked, an optical illusion. Sammy liked that.

He thought James was probably getting het up about names to avoid thinking about what Frank Verricker was like. Sammy didn't need to avoid thinking about what their father was like: He felt like he already knew the guy, inside and out.

Rev. Smiths came out of the building among a bunch of other ministers, all wearing the exact same hats and suits. He said he hoped he hadn't kept them waiting, and James said he hadn't, and reminded him that he was doing them a favor. They got back into his car, with James in the front seat because Sammy had grabbed the back. Once they were on the highway, heading south, Rev. Smiths asked, "Did you find out what you wanted?"

"We found out some things," Sammy said, when James didn't answer.

"Seek and ye shall find," Rev. Smiths said, not asking any more questions.

"Something was opened up to us," James said then, without turning his eyes away from the road ahead. "But I guess I don't know just what it was."

"I didn't know you went to church," Rev. Smiths remarked.

"I don't," James said. "I've read the Bible."

"Really? Why?"

James looked at the driver then. He always enjoyed showing off at people with the things he'd read. Sammy sat back, away from the front seat. James explained: "In fifth grade, my teacher said the Bible was one of the underpinnings of western civilization. I liked that idea so much—the way kids get fixated on things—so I decided to read it. It took years. I didn't read much of it in fifth grade, although I started."

James was all ready for a big talk about the Bible, and things in it, like a reading comprehension quiz, Sammy thought. But Rev. Smiths didn't ask him questions to find out what he remembered. "Do you know," Rev. Smiths asked instead, "what Gandhi said when somebody asked him what he thought about western civilization?"

"No, what?" James asked.

"He said, he thought it would be a good idea."

James laughed out loud, and Rev. Smiths joined in, sort of chuckling. Sammy looked out the window, at the distant line of trees at the edges of fields. He didn't laugh, but that wasn't because he didn't get the joke.

CHAPTER 6

One thing about being a dork was that you weren't constantly interrupted by people when you had things to think about. James had some things to think about. For example, he had his father to think about. That kept him busy as he sat on the bench during the first home baseball game, and when he rode with the team, alone in his seat at the center of the bus, to the first away game. That game was up in Cambridge, of all places.

They won the home game and lost the Cambridge game, no thanks to James either way. He was busy sorting the information he had gathered into different lists. Or, rather, trying to sort the information. Because whenever he thought about it—even just to the extent of just sorting things out—his whole mind got blown over, by feelings like dark night winds blowing clouds across the whole sky. He couldn't even think whenever he thought about it. Except to recognize Francis Verricker—he figured he knew that man pretty well.

But coming home on the bus, coming home from Cambridge again, as twilight darkened into evening, sitting, looking out the dirty window while voices talked around him, James found he could look at those lists without that heavy wind rising up and knocking him over. He had finally figured out that on game days he wouldn't have to play baseball at all. Realizing that, James smiled to himself: he could get enthusiastic about games. The darkening landscape swept by the window, and he could think.

First off, there were some hard facts, that was the first list. Those facts might be clues, if he put them together the right way. He might find some kind of a lead among them. The second list was soft facts, things filtered through the eyes, or opinions, of the two people he'd talked to, who had actually known his father. The third was guesswork, intuitions, trying to put together what those people had implied and figure out the common ground between them, trying to get a sense of who the boy had been and what his life had been like then, there.

James set to work on the first list, the facts. He rode silent in the coach's car from school to his driveway, trotted silent up the driveway between dark fields, pinning down the facts. When he entered the kitchen, he heard piano music from the living room and saw that his grandmother was just sitting at the kitchen table, listening. It was Thursday. Maybeth was having a piano lesson with Mr. Lingerle. An extra place was set at the table, because Mr. Lingerle always stayed for dinner after the lessons. James didn't stop to listen, and didn't disturb his grandmother. He went right on up the stairs and into Sammy's room. Sammy was sitting on his bed, cross-legged, doing nothing.

James dropped his books by the door, with a noise that made Sammy look up. "He was years older than she was," James announced. "Our father. Because I've been thinking, Mrs. Rottman said he was in third grade in 1938, which means he was about eight, which means he was born around 1930. He could have been nine, you see," he explained at Sammy's confused look. "It's only a rough date, but Momma wasn't born until 1942, so he was more than ten years older than she was."

"So what?"

"It's not normal, it's—she'd have been awfully young for him, if you—"

"Just because something's normal doesn't mean that's the only way. Or even the best way," Sammy argued.

"But—" James tried to think of an example his brother could understand. "It would be like Mr. Lingerle marrying Maybeth."

Sammy looked at him then.

"He's old," James said. "And she's just a kid. See what I mean?"

Sammy was still thinking. Probably cooking up some stupid objection, James thought, as if this was an argument he had to win or something.

"Mr. Lingerle has got to be at least twenty-six, and she's only fourteen—" James continued.

"But that wouldn't be so bad for her," Sammy said. "Would it? Because he'd know what she was like, and she might be happy with someone who was older, who could take more responsibility. Except, he's fat."

Sammy was so obtuse, it almost had to be deliberate. James had just mentioned that as a comparison. Sammy was avoiding what they were really talking about. James got up from the bed and bent over to pick up his books. "They never got married anyway, so maybe it doesn't matter how old he was. Do you ever wonder why people get married?" he asked his brother. "And fall in love?"

"No," Sammy said, not interested.

When Mr. Lingerle was eating with them, they didn't have pie or cake, or even pudding, for dessert. Sometimes they didn't have dessert at all, or sometimes Maybeth made a bowl of cut-up fruit, oranges or grapefruit, apples, bananas. That night, as Mr. Lingerle spooned up segments of grapefruit, he told Gram that his doctor would approve.

Mr. Lingerle sat at the opposite end of the long table from

Gram. She looked down the table at him when he had told her that. "You're not ill?" she asked.

"No. It was just a checkup, but you know how doctors are."

"No, young man, I don't," Gram snapped. Because she snapped, James knew she was worried.

"I turned twenty-eight this month—" Mr. Lingerle explained. "It seemed sensible to have a checkup. I haven't seen a doctor for years." He buttoned and unbuttoned the top button of his shirt. "I know, I look older than that," he said.

He did, James realized. He looked almost middle-aged, the big expanse of blue shirt at the end of the table, with his thin hair and lack of energy.

"That's because of your weight," Gram said.

"That's what the doctor said," Mr. Lingerle agreed, without sounding upset or nervous at all, as if he didn't feel embarrassed about the way he looked. Maybe he didn't, James thought. It wasn't that he looked awful, just awfully large. He seemed to be pretty peaceful with himself, which James had trouble understanding, because he would bet that Mr. Lingerle would have been a real outcast at school. "Diet and exercise, he said."

"He's right," Gram answered. She got up to pour two cups of coffee and to bring one down to Mr. Lingerle's place. "What about it, then?" she asked, giving him his cup.

"I hate exercising," Mr. Lingerle said. "I hate every minute of it. I've tried," he apologized. "Well," he smiled at himself, "not hard and not for long, but—I have this irrational reaction, anger and frustration and every minute feels like an hour."

James could sympathize with that.

"Then why are you telling us?" Gram demanded. "Since you're determined not to do anything about it."

"Maybe I'm hoping you'll yell at me?" Mr. Lingerle suggested, laughing at himself. "You're the nearest thing to a family

I have, and that's what families do, isn't it? Both of my parents died when I was in college, so there's nobody left to yell at me. They were both heavy—fat," he corrected before Gram could say what she was about to say. "It's hereditary, I guess. I was an only child—and I have to say how happy I was, what a happy childhood I had. They were happy people, my mother and my father, and supportive of me. I had good parents. I'm lucky. My father, especially, encouraged me in my music, even though I wasn't a prodigy of any kind, and even though he wondered how I'd ever make a living at classical music. He was always interested in what I was doing, or hearing me play. He took me to concerts whenever he could, even though I don't think he enjoyed them all that much himself. We lived in Washington, so there were plenty of concerts. They sent me to Peabody, even though we all knew there was no chance of me being a concert pianist; they sent me there because it was the best around. They were so proud of me . . . I miss them, you know. I always do. My father was always asking me to play something, or explain about atonal music, or something. Just because I was interested in it, you see. They never thought there was anything strange about me, or pushed me to do something I couldn't."

"Don't you have any ambition?" Gram asked. "Do you compose?

"Ambition?" Mr. Lingerle answered her question with a question. James noticed that he didn't say anything about composing, which made James wonder why he was avoiding that subject. "You know, Abigail, when I think about it, I can't imagine anything more perfect for me than my life the way it is. Anything much more perfect than what I have," he added. "I like teaching, I am fascinated by music, and the life down here, away from so many of the ills of civilization. . . . The truth is, I consider myself an extremely ambitious person, and successful, too."

"Good," Gram said.

"I'll yell at you," Maybeth offered.

"Why?" Mr. Lingerle asked her. He waited for her to frame her answer, just patiently looking at her.

"Because it's bad for your heart."

"And my blood pressure," he agreed.

"And I think you'd look handsome." Maybeth wasn't flirting with him, or flattering him; she was just saying what she thought. Maybeth wouldn't know how to flirt or flatter, James thought. He saw that Mr. Lingerle's cheeks turned a little pink when she said that.

"Walking is exercise," Sammy suggested. "Or bike riding. We've got bikes—could you ride one of them?" He eyed the man's bulk. "Dicey left her bike here."

That wasn't a bad idea at all, James thought. "If you rode a bike, or walked places, instead of driving," he explained. That was kind of an interesting problem Mr. Lingerle had, because in both his hereditary genes and his character, he was bad for himself. James wondered how many pounds Mr. Lingerle's doctor had said he should lose, but he thought it would be tactless to ask. He wondered if Mr. Lingerle had the discipline to just eat less. James was glad that wasn't a problem he had, because he didn't think he'd be able to not eat. "I've read about people who had their stomachs stapled shut," James remembered.

"No kidding?" Sammy asked. Sammy would love anything so ghoulish.

"That sounds unnecessarily painful," Gram said.

"Or their jaws wired shut," Mr. Lingerle added. "So they can't eat," he explained to Gram.

"You're asking us to help you?" Gram asked.

"I'm not sure, but I think so. He put the fear of God in me, that doctor."

"How can we help?" Maybeth asked.

"You can yell at me."

"I'll try," she promised.

"Good," Gram said. "It's about time, anyway. When *are* we going to see you play baseball, James?"

James was halfway up, clearing the table, his dessert bowl in his hand. He didn't know how to answer. "I'm not good enough, I never get put in during a game," he said.

"You haven't answered my question."

James tried to get away, by taking his dish to the sink, by having his back to them. He wished he could disappear from the room. He didn't want them to come, but he didn't want them to know that, because then even his family would know . . . how bad things were for him at school. He wanted them to think he was smart and got along fine. He didn't know how to keep them away. The night was dark outside of the house and he was so frustrated and helpless—because he didn't want them to come to a game and he didn't know how to stop them. He never could stop the Tillermans from doing what they wanted.

"What about this week?" Gram asked. "Is there a game this week?"

"I don't know," James lied, not turning around. He'd quit first, or break his ankle, or something. He couldn't stand it, especially Sammy, and Gram, too.

"I don't think James wants us to come watch," Maybeth's voice said. "I think he really doesn't. I don't think we should."

If James had dared to turn around, he would have hugged his sister. He thought, sometimes, she was the smartest one of them all. But her remark had been greeted by a total silence, and he didn't want to look at what that silence meant. He turned on the tap water, to start the dishes. They let the subject drop.

James washed glasses, dishes, and utensils, then pots. Sammy dried and put them away. James didn't say one word, not wanting to open up any conversation, not wanting to hear what his brother might say. Sammy didn't say anything either. James concentrated hard on his next move—because he thought he'd like to go up to that Hall of Records in Annapolis, and find out whatever he could about the Verrickers. That meant he'd have to figure out how to get up there, and the only opportunity he'd have was that school trip; but he didn't have the twelve dollars it cost for the bus and to pay the guide they'd hire to take them around Colonial Annapolis; and he didn't know how he'd get any time at the Hall of Records anyway, because school kids on trips were kept together, herded from place to place. James kept his attention on that problem while his hands soaped dishes and then rinsed them off in scalding hot water. That was about all he could stand thinking about at that moment, so he thought hard. And he didn't want Sammy along, anyway. He didn't need any help from Sammy. Sammy wasn't any help anyway. He could do it on his own, since he was the only one really interested anyway, really curious to find out who their father was, maybe even to find him.

By the time he'd scoured out the sink and washed down the table and counters with a damp sponge, James felt okay. He thought the subject of games had been dropped, and he was so relieved that he hadn't had to beg them not to come that he felt like a strand of spaghetti, cooked limp, just lying there on the bottom of the pot, without the ability to do anything but lie there.

Sammy clanged the last pot back into its cupboard. "James?" he said.

Uh-oh, James thought. He heard something in Sammy's voice, and he didn't want to hear a lot of noise from his little brother, for whom things came so easily, sports and friends and all, about everything that was wrong with James.

"You should just be yourself," Sammy said, when James didn't turn around.

James didn't say anything. He was thinking how Sammy thought everything was so simple, and how just being yourself was only all right if you were good enough, and how he wished Sammy would leave him alone.

"Well, you should," Sammy insisted, ignoring the way James was ignoring him. His voice came at James from behind. "You can only be what you are, whatever that is. It won't make any difference even if you find out what our father is, because—and besides, I don't think you'll find out anything good, anything you'll like knowing. I don't think you ought to try," Sammy warned him. What was Sammy doing, warning him that he shouldn't try to know something? "I mean it, James," the voice said. "Worrying about it won't do any good and whatever you find out—" Sammy's voice almost made James turn around to look at his brother.

Things were always simple for Sammy. James heard his brother waiting for an answer, then leaving the room, but he stood by the sink, looking out the window at the darkness. He tried to figure out a way he could earn some money. Maybe he should have taken that clerking job in Cambridge, instead of pushing ahead to talk to Mrs. Rottman and Mr. Ferguson, who hadn't told him anything he wanted to hear anyway. Then at least he'd have a day's wages in his pocket.

He could have done it, too. He could file, that was just putting things into alphabetical order. He could type. He hadn't been lying when he'd said he could do those things.

He turned around to say good night to Mr. Lingerle, who left thanking Gram once again for the dinner, and the company. Maybeth was with them, and she asked James if he had time to help her with a page of math problems.

"Sure, you know I'll be glad to," James said. He sat down at the table. Maybeth went upstairs to get her books. Gram sat down facing James, looking into his face, considering him.

"All right," Gram said, nodding her head.

For a minute James couldn't figure out what she meant, and then he understood. "Thanks," he said. There wouldn't be any more talk about coming to games. Gram meant what she said, and she kept her word. She knew how not to ask questions, too, James realized, even though he knew that didn't mean she didn't care about the answers. Whatever else about his life, he was incredibly lucky to have Gram—and a feeling rose up and blew through him, taking his breath with it temporarily, as he looked at the woman across from him, with her unruly curly hair and her lively eyes.

"Do you think Isaac can lose all that weight?" she asked him.

James thought about it. "It has been done. It's not impossible. You're always seeing advertisements in magazines about people who have lost pounds and pounds."

"You maybe see them. I don't."

"You're not reading the right magazines," James teased.

"Do you believe what you read?" she asked.

"I don't know. Sometimes. There's a truth in advertising law."

"For what it's worth. Although, sometimes I think that we'd be better off without any laws, because then people wouldn't be tempted to break them. He might do it for Maybeth."

"Maybeth?"

"He thinks a lot of her."

"So do I," James said.

"That's not what I meant," Gram said.

"But he's so—old, and she's just a kid."

"Someone like Maybeth—whom I wouldn't change for the world, the world on a platter with all the stars scattered around it—someone older, a little paternal," Gram continued, as if she was just thinking out loud.

"Sammy said that, or something like that." Surprise pulled the words out of James's mouth before he thought.

"Your brother is no fool," Gram answered, getting up and leaving him alone again.

You could have fooled me, James thought, but didn't say. Then he wondered, because he didn't really disagree with Gram, why—if that was true—Sammy didn't get good grades in school. Sammy didn't think about things, either. If he was no fool, then how could he say he wanted to be a tennis player and an astronaut, both, and not go on to think about how if you wanted to do that, what you should do to get ready? As if Sammy thought just wanting things made them happen, which was pretty foolish.

In good weather, James took his lunch outside, to get away from the noise and the smells of the cafeteria. But on rainy spring days he had to eat inside. There was nobody special he ate with. Usually, he just sat himself down at the end of one of the long tables and didn't pay attention to who else was sitting there. He tried to keep clear of Toby Butz, who had been his best friend in fifth and sixth grades but had grown really weird. Toby wasn't even smart any more, except in science and math where he was A-track. All he'd talk about was extraterrestrial life-forms. He was a science-fiction nut, and you couldn't talk to him about anything else, but if you started to talk to him about that he'd buttonhole you and go on and on and on. Toby looked as weird as he acted, a short square guy, with thin blond hair that was always too long and not clean enough, with pale blue eyes gleaming crazily out from behind thick glasses. Toby still wore striped T-shirts, just like a little kid, although James knew for sure his family had the money to dress him better, because his father was a pharmacist and earned a good living. It was sad what had happened to Toby, in every respect; James remembered they used to have some interesting conversations when they were friends. Anyway, Toby was one guy James felt superior to. At least, James knew, he was skinny, and his jeans hung down around his hips in a sort of cool way, and he looked okay in the button-down shirts he wore. He didn't *look* like a wimp. Toby did: he looked like a biscuit, with arms and legs sticking out, with a round head stuck on top.

James wouldn't be shocked if Toby turned out to do something interesting with his life, like write science-fiction books as good as Frank Herbert's or Isaac Asimov's, or he might really be the one to discover the existence of extraterrestrial life-forms. That was, after all, what happened with a lot of unpopular kids—later on they got famous. He couldn't see why kids didn't figure that out, the normal ones, and try to get to know the dorky kids. But he guessed he could see why. There were a lot of movie stars, like Jane Fonda, who said they were ugly in high school, and really unpopular; but even knowing that didn't make ugly girls look any prettier to him.

James chewed his way through his sandwiches, and his banana, and then took out a thick slab of the chocolate cake Maybeth had baked last night. His sister could just go out to the kitchen and turn out a cake, or something, as if it was the easiest thing in the world. James had tried making cookies, once . . . they weren't any good; and it had taken him hours to make them, because he had trouble seeing the sense of the recipe, and then he'd had trouble getting the baking time right. But Maybeth just went out there and knew what to do, knew how to do it right. He unwrapped the double wax paper he'd put the cake into. For a minute, he just looked at it: two dark layers of chocolate, and he knew how good they'd taste, moist dark and crumbly dark; a lighter frosting, mocha, creamy without butter, which cost a fortune, creamy because Maybeth used a boiled frosting recipe, never getting anything but perfect texture. That cake was something to look forward to; it was like a present in the middle of the day. James was about to pick it up and bite into it when somebody sat down across from him and said his name. "Tillerman."

It was Andy Walker. James concealed his surprise.

"I was looking for you. You sure hide away down here."

Andy waited for James to say something, but James couldn't think of anything to say. He hoped people were seeing this, though.

"I wanted to ask. What are you going to do that French paper on anyway?" Andy asked him. "Can I take a bite of that?" He pointed to the cake.

"Sure." James watched while Andy's hands broke the cake in half. The French paper, one of the big final assignments you got in a lot of A-track classes as the year drew to a close, was supposed to get them ready for next year's course. French III was a literature course, mostly a reading and writing course. For the paper, they had to pick a work of French literature from the list Mr. Norton had given them, read it, and then write a one-page report on it. They could read the work in English, in translation, because they were only French II students, but they had to write the report in French and then read it aloud before the class. After that, the class would ask questions. James could believe Andy was pretty worried about that assignment. It was a big part of the final grade.

Andy reached over and took the other half of the piece of cake. "Okay?" he asked. He didn't wait for an answer. He just chomped away into it.

"I'm doing *The Hunchback of Notre Dame*," James told Andy.

"Yeah, well, I guess you've got the time for a long book. I

figured, you probably had some ideas you thought about but decided not to do. The way you brains always do. I mean, I'm not much on these kinds of things, reading and papers, and I've got so much to do already—the baseball season really wipes me out, and my old man's got us painting the garage, and, you know, a man has to keep up his social life."

James wished he could kid himself about what was going on. Andy was kidding himself. James didn't see why he couldn't, if Andy could. Maybe that was something else that made him a dork?

"The Little Prince," he suggested. "Did you think of that? It's good, and it's an easy read."

"Hey, did I say I was looking for something easy? I'm no dummy." Andy narrowed his eyes at James.

"I meant easy as in not taking much time," James apologized.

"Besides, Celie's doing that. I'm not going up against *her*, not with her having lived in France and all. That would be asking to look bad. Right?" Andy grinned, and crumpled up the wax paper. "Good cake. Homemade?"

James nodded.

"So, what other ideas did you have?"

"'The Myth of Sisyphus,' the Camus essay," James admitted.

"But you're not going to do it, right?"

"I said I'm doing the *Hunchback*."

"Well how about it, you must have notes, a rough draft. You're the kind of student who does all these rough drafts, right? Would you care to share that with somebody needy? Ordinarily I wouldn't ask but I'm backed up in my schoolwork and all, on account of baseball. And all."

James knew what he was being asked but he didn't dare name it to Andy. It might be that the guy really thought he could do the work in the course, or really didn't think it was cheating to copy off of somebody's homework. Or maybe he thought James had been happily going along with him all year.

Which he sort of had, James realized, admitted, almost choking on a wave of self-disgust that broke right up in his face. He had no right to accuse Andy of cheating when he'd been going along with it the way he had. He wasn't any better and maybe he was even worse. James, watching Andy's eyes watching his reactions, had a sudden cold thought: He knew, as if Andy had said it out loud, that if he called Andy on copying, Andy would say just that; because Andy knew James knew, and if James got Andy in trouble, Andy would get even.

"I'll see. Anything I have will be at home," James said.

"I sure would appreciate it," Andy said, getting up. "If you happen to have anything. No big deal, right?"

"Yeah," James said. He kept his eyes down on the table, watching his hands gather the crumpled ball of wax paper and drop it into the paper bag, before smashing the whole thing together in both of his hands.

It could be worse, he thought, almost amused. He could have other classes with Andy. They did play baseball together, but that was so different—Andy acted as if James was invisible during baseball. James wished he were, and he wished helplessly that he had the nerve to just quit the team, no matter what anyone said. He didn't have the nerve for that, either.

James entered English class after lunch the way he thought medieval criminals must have entered a church, crying out Sanctuary, Sanctuary. He felt that way. As long as he was in a classroom, sitting at his desk, he felt safe. He knew everyone didn't feel that way; he knew feeling that way marked him out as a dork. But he was glad to be there. He was even glad to be assigned a five-page paper on character in *Macbeth.* He knew what the teacher would like best—she wanted something on

Lady Macbeth or on Macbeth himself, something that would show he'd been listening to all the things she'd said about character development, and something that showed he'd picked a hard subject. An easy subject for a character study would be the witches, or Macduff. James knew he'd steer away from those. He wished, though, that he could write about Shakespeare's idea of what a king should be like. That was something he and Gram had talked about: James had said Macduff was the best man for the job, but Gram had said it had to be Malcolm because he had the right bloodlines. But the teacher said character and she meant a character from the cast; she didn't mean any other kind of character, James knew that.

Baseball practice was called because of rain, so James had time to rush into the library and take out a copy of Camus before he got the bus. When he and Maybeth got off at their driveway, Maybeth took the mail from the box and put it under her raincoat before running up the driveway. James hadn't taken a raincoat and he didn't feel like running. He hunched his body over to protect his books, and let the rain fall down gray all over his shoulders and back. He didn't even try to avoid the puddles. His hair got wet, plastered down along his face. Water ran down his nose, down his neck; it sluiced along his cheeks. It felt like he was crying, and James didn't mind that. He never did cry, because men didn't, or at least that was the idea he got. The kids at school would sometimes tell stories about their fathers yelling, or whipping them, and they'd say things about their mothers bursting into tears in the middle of a big fight, but they never said anything about a father crying away. So James figured men didn't. Certainly, not just over being pretty disgusted with yourself, and depressed about everything. The rain pushed at him, as if it were trying to get him flat down, flat with his face in the dark mud of the driveway, which was about where he thought he belonged. In the meantime, moving slow, with the rain running down his cheeks like tears, it felt almost as good as crying.

Gram didn't even bother to give him an earful when he came dripping into the kitchen. "I'll have hot chocolate ready in five minutes," she told him. James, toweled off and in dry clothes, took his mug into the living room, sitting at the big desk to drink it, while Maybeth told Gram about her day and Sammy interrupted to tell about his. James had picked up the weekly newspaper, sent out free in the mail, to look at.

He thought, turning the pages, he really wanted to get to go on that Annapolis trip. Once there, maybe they'd go to the Hall of Records, because archives were part of state history, which was what the trip was about. If he didn't get to go, then he'd never even have a chance to see what they had there on the Verrickers. He concentrated on wanting to go.

When he came to the classifieds, he looked down the Help Wanted section. He didn't see why women complained about work when there were so many jobs for them, like babysitting and housekeeping, being secretaries. For men it was mostly construction work. His eye was caught by an ad headed STUDENT WANTED. Well, he could meet that qualification. It was a job for part-time work, basic office work, some telephone answering, some typing, some filing. You had to have your own transportation, he read, which he guessed let him out. They were offering three twenty-five an hour, and he wished them luck, because most of the other jobs offered more than that, except babysitting. A person with his own transportation—in other words, a car—would be able to drive up to Salisbury to a job that would pay more. If the ad hadn't said the job required transportation he might just have written a letter to the post office box, just on the chance. He knew he didn't do well with physical labor, he couldn't work like that for hours and hours, and he'd be fired from any job that expected him to do that, but he would be able to do office work. He bet. If he only had transportation instead of just a bike.

Rather than think about anything, about finding things out about his father or doing the work on a paper for Andy, about whether or not he could be accused of cheating in French or was going to be stuck playing baseball for the next two years, about Celie and the way she looked through him, about what a creep he was and how much he needed someone or something to help him be not the way he was—rather than think about all of those things, James went upstairs and typed a letter to the post office box the ad had mentioned. He said right away he only had a bike and wasn't sixteen, so he'd never get the job, but writing the letter at least made him feel better.

Because the weather cleared overnight, the scheduled game was played. It was a home game, which James hated more than an away game. Even though he knew nobody noticed him anyway, he still didn't like being out there at the end of the bench where, if they were going to, people could see him. Not playing. And all.

He thought, at first, that the worst thing was seeing Celie Anderson and her friends sitting in the bleachers, watching the game. He thought—he wished he could pretend to be sick and just crawl out of sight, so she wouldn't see him, if she looked in his direction. But if he tried that, it would draw attention to him. James sat small, quiet. He didn't even move when the game was over, waiting for Celie to go on. But she was coming down to say hi to Andy Walker, who was waiting around among people who were telling him what a good game he'd played. Andy saw Celie, but he didn't interrupt his fans. When they were finished, she came up close to him. "Hi," she said.

"Hey," Andy answered. "Did you enjoy the game?"

"Of course," she answered.

James sneaked looks at Celie, admiring the pale orange color of the blouse she was wearing, wondering what it was about Andy that made her look at him that way.

"You don't know a thing about baseball, do you?" Andy looked over her head, and waved to someone.

"No," she admitted. "But I did like the game."

Her eyes weren't really green, but greenish, which was better than green.

"I guess then there's hope for you," Andy told her. "Listen, you know this dance coming up?"

There were two dances coming up, a sock hop on the weekend, and the Sophomore-Junior Prom in another week. James didn't know which one Andy meant.

Neither, apparently, did Celie. She hesitated before asking, "The one this weekend?"

"Naw, the prom. You got a date for that yet?"

"No," Celie said.

James wondered if this was how asking girls out went. First you found out if they already had a date, then you asked.

"Well, I need to take a date to the prom, and I thought you might want to be it."

Her, James corrected. Then, she, he corrected himself. He wished he could get up and walk away, but then they'd know he'd been eavesdropping.

Celie didn't much like that way of being asked, he thought. She wanted to say no, he hoped.

"Is that an invitation?" she asked, her eyebrows drawing together.

"So what's with the sarcasm?" Andy answered, finally smiling down at her. He knew she wanted to go with him.

"I'd love to, thank you," Celie said, as if Andy had asked her if she would please go to the prom with him.

"That's okay then. I'll let you know when," Andy said. He turned and walked away, big in his uniform. James watched Celie sort of shake her head, then turn back to her friends. When she shook her head like that, her hair brushed against her cheek, more gentle than anything else James could imagine. He watched her walk away, and then finally could get up himself.

She hadn't even noticed he was there. It was really funny, in a way, the way girls didn't want to be seen with some people, because they thought those people were dorks, even though James was willing to bet money that a dork would ask a girl out as if he really wanted her to say yes. It was really funny, but it wasn't funny a bit, and it was almost enough to make him angry.

CHAPTER 7

The answer to James's letter about the clerical job came quickly, which surprised him. A. S. Landros, the person who wrote the answer, was one of two doctors whose names were printed at the top of the stationery. The answer asked James to come in for an interview, which also surprised him. He guessed he should have known there would be an interview, however; you didn't just hire somebody from a letter. He wasn't sure he wanted to go in for an interview. He didn't know what they would ask him, he wouldn't know what to say, and people didn't take to him, so an interview would probably mean he wouldn't get the job. But he wanted the job, so he would have to go to the interview.

James wore khakis instead of jeans the day he was going to be interviewed. He rode his bike to school, because he would need it to get home on. He spoke to the baseball coach at the start of practice, to tell him he wouldn't be there.

The coach looked at him when he said that. "What's your excuse?" the man asked, as if James—who had missed just one practice, and no games, all spring long—was in the habit of making excuses to miss sports.

"I have a job interview."

"A job interview is it? Does that mean you'll be leaving the team?"

James had been thinking that with any luck it would turn out he'd have to drop baseball, but when the coach asked that, as if he really wanted to say *quitting* instead of *leaving*, he said "No, sir." It was only a few more weeks. He could stick it out for a few more weeks. All he had to do was hold on—and he'd been doing that all spring long, so a few more weeks wouldn't hurt him. He could make it through a few more weeks, he hoped.

The doctors' office was out on the north side of town, inland, a white stucco one-story building set back from the road at the end of a straight driveway. In that part of town, some of the fields had been cut up into square lots and ranch-style houses had been plopped down on them. James rode his bike up the paved driveway to the office. A sign by the door said A. S. LANDROS, GENERAL PRACTICE. LESLIE O'HARA, OBSTETRICS AND GYNECOLOGY. The letter had told James to come by any afternoon between three and five, so he opened the door and went in, not knowing what to expect, what to plan to say.

He entered a waiting room, where a couple of pregnant women sat reading magazines in chairs, and a black man of about fifty sat on a sofa, looking at his hands. An empty desk, with a phone on it, had been set at the far side of the room. The one big window looked out over the parking lot. Beside the window stood tall filing cabinets.

James didn't know what he was supposed to do. There were voices down the corridor that led off the waiting room, but he didn't feel right about just walking down there. He sat in a chair near the empty desk. After a while, a woman in a nurse's uniform came out to sit at the desk. A middle-aged black woman whose hair was streaked with silver followed and the man rose from the sofa to greet them. The man wanted to ask the woman questions, but she just shook her head at him, to keep him from speaking.

The nurse handed the woman a slip of paper. "Dr. Landros

will call you when the X-ray results come in. Your appointment's tomorrow, so we should hear by early next week."

The woman nodded her head. She opened her purse and paid her bill. The nurse gave her a receipt. The man put his arm around the woman's shoulders, but she shrugged it off.

"You're not to eat anything until the X-rays have been taken. You know that? Only water to drink." The nurse gave these instructions to both husband and wife. Both of them nodded their heads. The woman wouldn't even look at her husband. Her shoulders were high and stiff, her back perfectly straight, her elbows tight in against her ribcage. Beside her, the man looked clumsy and ashamed, with his neck bent a little and his shoulders sagging, his hands just hanging at his sides. He followed her out of the building, catching the door she pulled open for herself. The nurse was writing something on a piece of paper.

Through the window, James watched the couple as they went to their car. As soon as they were in the parking lot, the woman turned to the man and leaned against his shoulder. She was tall enough so her face fit right into his neck. He put his arms around her, and patted her shoulder, and she let him comfort her, now that they were alone together, and private.

"And what can we do for you, young man?" the nurse called James to attention. Before he could answer, she looked across the room at the pregnant women. "It'll be just five minutes before we take you in, Mrs. Grogan. Hello, Mrs. Johnson, how are you feeling today?" Before they could answer, her attention returned to James. She looked friendly enough, but in a hurry.

"I'm supposed to come in for an interview," he said. "With Dr. Landros, he wrote me a letter but I left it home."

"She," the nurse said, amused.

"I'm sorry," James said, although he could have pointed out that he had no way of knowing.

"It's a common enough mistake. Well, I can take you right in—her next appointment's going to be late, it seems. But you might get interrupted."

"That's all right," James said. "Or I could wait," he suggested, not knowing what he should say.

"Better grab the chance you have," the nurse said, leading him down the corridor and into an office with a big desk, framed diplomas on the wall, and a bookcase. She told him to wait.

James waited. He sat down and waited, and then wandered around and waited, reading the titles of the books on the shelves, reading the diplomas. Finally, a stumpy woman with short bristly dark hair and a white doctor's jacket on over her gray skirt entered the room and sat down at the desk. James returned to the chair facing her. She had a rough, square face, with no makeup. Her little eyes were brown and had pouches of flesh underneath them. Everybody in that place looked tired, he thought. He watched her blunt fingers search through papers on her desk.

"James Tillerman," she said when she had found the letter he'd written.

"Yes, ma'am," he answered, sitting up straight. He thought she was probably in her forties, from the lines around her eyes and mouth. She wasn't married.

"We had a number of inquiries about the position, but yours looked the most promising," she told him, her eyes on the letter.

"It did?"

"You can spell and write a clear sentence," she said. "You seemed to try to be honest about anything that might be against you. Your age. Your bicycle."

"Thank you," James said. She was the kind of person who made him sit up straight and pay attention.

"The letter could be a slick con job, of course," she said. "Is it?"

"No, ma'am," he told her. "I don't think so."

"Do you want the job?" she asked him. She certainly didn't waste time deciding things.

"Can I do the work?"

"James, it doesn't require one of the great minds of the Western world to file and fill out insurance forms. To answer the phone. I assume you do well in school?"

"A's," James told her, for once proud to be able to say just that.

"Unless the educational system has taken a complete dive—which, as a taxpayer, I sincerely hope is not the case—you should have no trouble with the work. It'll be only a few hours a week, I don't think more than ten to start with. We've only been down here, my partner and I, for a few months. Business isn't booming. I should warn you: We're liable to need someone full-time as things get busier, so it's not a permanent job."

"Yes, ma'am," James said.

"So you'll take it?"

"I'd like to," James told her. "But—" Her mouth moved impatiently. He hurried on. "I have to ask my grandmother's permission. We live with my grandmother. She'll give it, I'm pretty sure, but I do have to ask her first."

"I can see that."

"And for a few weeks, not long, I can only come on Saturdays. Because of sports," he explained.

"You don't look the athletic type," she remarked, looking at him.

"I'm not. But anyway the season ends in just three or four weeks, and then I can come after school. Because there won't be late practices, or games." He wondered, if she said he had to be able to come after school starting right away, if that would be reason enough to quit the team. He decided it might be, and he hoped she'd say that.

"All of that's fine by me. We have office hours Saturday

morning. Let me get my partner, so if she doesn't like the look of you she can tell us now. I should warn you, she wanted to get another nurse, not a file clerk. But I made her see reason. It's the paperwork we need help with, at this point, not the weighing-in and sampling of blood."

James didn't say anything. He wouldn't know about that. Dr. Landros picked up her phone and pushed a button. "Leslie? Can you step into my office just for a minute? That young man is here."

The other doctor was younger, but not married either. She had a stethoscope around her neck, and all she did was take a quick look at James's face, shake his hand, say "Good," and leave. James had a job.

Gram wasn't even surprised when he told her he'd been offered a job. "You're old enough," she said. She asked him what he'd be doing and he told her. "You'll do well," she said, her attention on the chunk of potato she was swooshing around in the pot roast gravy. "I've never heard of these doctors," she said.

"But—" Sammy started.

James interrupted, to answer Gram's question. "They're new here, they just opened up a few months ago."

"You make them sound like some store," Gram objected.

"But, James—" Sammy tried.

"What do you know about them?" Gram asked, in her unquestioning way. James thought to himself how he liked the way his grandmother took it for granted that he'd get a job, as if it wasn't anything so special.

"They're women," he told her.

"So," she said, looking at him, "are fifty percent of the people in this world."

James was only trying to tell her whatever was different from what would be predictable. "Actually, it's closer to fifty-two percent," he corrected.

"Present company not excepted," she continued, looking around the table.

James gave up, and laughed. "Okay, okay. One's a GP and one's an obstetrician. It's a small office and when they get busier they'll want somebody full-time."

"Yeah, but who—" Sammy tried again.

"You can wait a minute," Gram said to him. She turned her attention back to James. "Clerical work, just thinking about doing it makes my ears droop."

"Not me," James promised her. "I'll need work papers."

"I can still sign my name," Gram said. "Now, Sammy, what is it?"

"Who'll go crabbing with me?" Sammy demanded.

"I may be able to," James said. "I don't know what hours I'll be working. Or you could get one of your friends to work with you."

"But then we'd have to split the money with him," Sammy pointed out.

"I could do it," Maybeth offered.

"That's a *good* idea," James said. She looked so pleased that he admitted, "I never even thought of it." He wondered how difficult it was on her, always to be treated as slow-minded, and maybe stupid, as if you couldn't have good ideas just because you weren't good at schoolwork. James still hadn't gotten over getting the job, and so easily. He never would have thought he'd write the best application letter.

"Anyway, you won't make as much money," Sammy continued. "How much are they paying you?"

That stopped James in his tracks. "I think three twenty-five, but I didn't ask."

"I'm glad to see your self-sufficiency is flawed," Gram remarked, but James barely heard her he was so surprised at his oversight.

He was making, he learned the next Saturday, three fifty an hour, which meant he'd earned seventeen fifty by the time they closed the office at two. James had spent his time quietly at the back of the office, behind the desk, sorting and alphabetizing, finding old file folders or starting new ones, and studying the long insurance claim forms to see what information went into which boxes. When he had any questions he asked the nurse, but he didn't have many. If you thought about them, things made sense. All the five hours he was aware of the coming and going of patients in the office, of the doctors doing their work, and the nurse coming and going between the desk and the phone and the back examining rooms. He liked the work, and the office. He didn't exchange more than a few words with his bosses. "The accountant will get the check in the mail Monday, first thing," Dr. Landros said as they locked the door behind them at two.

"Thank you, ma'am," James said.

"Don't call me that. I'm a doctor."

If James hadn't known Gram, he would have been sure he'd made the doctor angry. As it as, he wasn't sure he hadn't. He made a mental note to address both the doctors as doctor, from then on.

The check arrived on Wednesday, and James signed up the next day to go on the school trip to Annapolis. How he'd get shed of the group, he didn't know; but he'd think of something, once they got there. He had a lot to think about, so baseball barely dented his consciousness, even when he was at practice and actually had to do something. He had the English paper to write. He went ahead and wrote it on kings in *Macbeth*; he didn't have time to think out another topic, and he didn't want to do another. By the time he handed the paper in, nine typed pages and one more of footnotes, he had forgotten that he hadn't done the exact assignment she'd wanted, so when she smiled at him and asked if the paper was going to be as good as usual he just answered yes. He heard a voice nearby say, "Did you hear that?" and another voice answer, "Yeah, but he doesn't have anything else to do but get the grades and butter up the teachers." James would have liked to turn around and see who had said that, but he didn't. Besides, it wasn't as if he was kidding himself about people liking him, anyway.

He didn't kid himself about the way it bothered him, either, even if there was nothing he could do about it. But after all these years, he had to admit it was starting to get through to him.

Adults liked him all right, there was that. Anyway, the doctors did, and so did their nurse. It wasn't just teachers who liked him. Kids acted as if they were the only people in the world, but they weren't. They weren't even an important part of the world, although they acted as if they were the reason the whole world had been made. It was pretty unrealistic thinking, James thought. He wished he could show everybody how stupid they were. Because they were, always trying to make someone feel bad because he wasn't just like them, or even just ignoring him because he wasn't someone like them.

Gram took James into the town dock so he could get to school by seven thirty for the Annapolis trip. It was a warm, moist morning, with clouds hanging over the flat water. Everything was gray—the clouds a smoky gray, the bay a stony gray. "Call me when you get back, if you miss the school bus," Gram said. "You have money for a phone call?" she asked.

James had five dollars in his pocket and other things on his mind. "Yes, sure," he said.

Gram didn't even cut the motor on the boat, because she was in a hurry to get back. James stood on the dock, looking down at her, waiting, in case there was anything else she wanted to say. She looked up at him, from the rocking boat. "Enjoy yourself," she said. "Whatever it is you're up to."

Before he could deny anything, she had pushed off and was heading out into the harbor. He wondered what she guessed, and why she suspected anything. But she had gone, and the red boat was hobbling along across the choppy water, so he couldn't ask her. He didn't want to know, anyway. He didn't know that he expected to find anything in particular in Annapolis, but he planned to go to the Hall of Records and see what there was there under Verricker. He might find his father's family. He walked up along the broad main street to the school. He'd be more than on time, he knew, so he took his solitary time. Stores were deserted, their fronts like sleeping faces. He might find one of those sisters, somewhere, in business somewhere, and she might know where her brother was. James didn't know whether he actually wanted to meet his father, whom he couldn't even imagine. He wondered what it would be like to see him, from a distance, or even talk to him, without James giving away who he was. He wondered what kind of a man Francis Verricker was, what kind of a father he would have made.

Toby Butz was among the group gathered at the front of the school, waiting for the bus to arrive. The U.S. history teachers were the chaperones for this trip, only three of them for the sixty kids who would fill the bus. That was good, James thought, good that Toby, someone he knew, was going, and also good that U.S. history was a junior course, so none of the teachers knew who he was. He wasn't the kind of kid they would know was there, or not there. James went to stand beside Toby.

"James," Toby said, hesitant.

"I didn't know you were going."

"Anything's better than a day here."

That surprised James. He always felt safe, in classes at least. He stared at Toby, looking at the eyes magnified by the thick glasses. He thought, Toby had always felt the same way he did about school; he wondered, what had changed Toby's mind. "You really don't like school," he said.

"I hate it. You can't think about anything."

"If we have to have partners, let's be partners," James suggested.

"If you want to," Toby said. He said it as if he weren't sure he wanted to. James wondered if Toby felt as strange about him as he did about Toby. It was hard with people you used to be good friends with, best friends, and then just weren't—especially if they turned out to be dorks.

They sat together on the bus, but there wouldn't be partners, because this was, as the teachers told them, a high school trip and they were certainly old enough to behave sensibly. If they knew what was good for them.

James looked out the window, because Toby had told him to take the window seat. He tried to figure out how much to tell Toby about his plan to ditch out on the group. Getting away shouldn't be hard; it was not being noticed that was the risky part. He was getting pretty adept, he thought, about sneaking around. He'd given Andy Walker the notes for a report on "The Myth of Sisyphus"; good notes too, so good that James was sorry not to get to make the report himself. He'd just handed them over at the start of French the previous morning, just said "I don't know if you'd be interested in this," and passed the papers over. Andy had looked at them and said, "Can I borrow them? I haven't got time now." In case anyone was listening. All Andy would have to do was work out the development of the ideas, and then translate what James had written into French. That was so close to cheating, James thought, uncomfortable and not because of the way the bus bounced under him, so close that it probably wasn't any different. Well, he thought to himself, turning away from the gray and brown landscape, he was his father's son in more than just the smartness. Besides, it only really mattered if you were caught. If you weren't caught, then it was as if you hadn't cheated. The whole thing depended on what people thought. There had even been times when cheating was admired. It was all relative, anyway, everything was relative, especially morality, and besides, there wasn't anything James could do about it now.

He turned to Toby, more to distract himself than to talk. "How are things?"

Toby shrugged.

"Do you still think extraterrestrial life-forms are a possibility?"

Toby didn't want to answer, James could see that. But he couldn't stop himself from talking about his favorite subject. And he was knowledgeable, James thought, listening, as the road rolled on and the towns rolled by, Princess Anne and Cambridge, as the miles rolled by and they crossed over the short humped drawbridge to Kent Island. Traffic got thicker around them, and the voices in the bus grew louder. They rumbled up the long bridge that headed west over the bay. James looked down at the trail of a tanker in the gray wrinkled water, then up to where the low mass of the western shore came toward them.

James was going to have to trust Toby. There wasn't anything else for it. If he didn't tell the kid, then he'd . . . have to stay with the group all day, pretending to himself that he'd tried to get to the Hall of Records but circumstances had overwhelmed him, while all the time he'd know he'd been too chicken to take a shot at really doing it. But if he did tell Toby, then he'd have to try.

He kind of hated to interrupt Toby, in the middle of an explanation of the possibilities of life on Venus. "Not humanoid, of course," Toby was saying, earnest and engrossed. "The chemical composition, the environmental differences, it wouldn't be anything like human, but—"

"Listen," James interrupted. "I have a favor to ask. A big one. I want to finish talking about this on the way back, but—"

"I guess I've been doing all the talking," Toby said. He smiled, then hid it behind his hand. "I always talk too much, if anyone listens." He smiled again, as if smiling was a nervous habit. His smile looked like an apology.

"You are a bit obsessive," James told him. "But listen—I have to get away from this group."

"Why?"

James shook his head. He wasn't going to answer.

"For how long?" Toby asked.

"As long as I can. It's nothing dangerous or anything."

"Nothing dangerous? Annapolis is a city, James, you could get—anything could happen. Do you expect to just wander around in it? And not know where you're going or anything? Aren't you afraid?"

"No." Not of anything Toby had mentioned, James wasn't. "Will you cover for me, if you need to? Or tell them where I am if they find out?"

"But I don't know where you'll be."

"Just tell them I'll be back to get on the bus at two. That's if they miss me, which I strongly doubt they will."

"Do you know how much trouble you could get into?"

James didn't want to worry about that. He just . . . hoped they'd never notice him, like they'd never noticed him so far. "That's okay," he said.

Toby envied him, James could see that, and admired him.

Toby's reaction made James feel like a pirate, like an adventurer, like someone the rules couldn't hold in. Like his father. Toby was all wrong about him, James knew, but it still felt good.

At the front of the statehouse, where the legislature met, they all clambered off the bus. A guide, dressed up like a colonial woman in long skirts and a little white cloth cap, was waiting for them there. First everybody had to listen, looking up at the brick building on top of a green hill, while she told them how to behave and what the legislature was going to be discussing. Then she led the group up the shallow steps, to begin the first part of the tour.

It was easy to hang back, to hold the big doors open for other people and then just not step inside. It was hard not to just grin and wink at Toby, looking back over his shoulder at James from inside the building.

When the last student had gone through, James let the door close and stepped back, against the brick building. His heart was thudding. He didn't know if it was fear or excitement. He waited for whatever it was to die down so he could think. He half expected one of the teachers to come back out through the doors, to yell at him to come along quickly, right now.

That didn't happen.

James went back down the steps, feeling as good as if the sun was shining right down all over him. It was a sort of adventure, his own adventure.

The statehouse had been built at the top of a low rounded hill. Green lawns spread down all around it, forming a circle around which cars drove slowly, a big necklace of cars around the legislature's green hill. James walked all the way around the circle once, then went into a store to ask directions. The store he picked had men's suits in the windows, and naval uniforms. It had a round clock hung out from over its door. Ten ten, the clock read. James entered the store and moved through a room crowded with shirts piled up in glass cases and ties hung on racks, with trousers and shorts stacked up on tables. He asked one of the men behind the counter, "Can you tell me how to find the Hall of Records?"

The man was wearing a suit and a knitted tie. His shirt was crisply white and his face looked freshly shaved. He looked like he should be buying these clothes instead of selling them. He pulled a small folded map from under the counter, to show James where he was, and where the Hall of Records was. It was just around the corner, James saw, trying to memorize the map.

"You'd better keep this," the man said.

"Thank you, I can use it," James said. "Thanks a lot," he repeated, because things were going so smoothly he wanted to share some of that feeling with the stranger who had been so helpful.

He left the store and turned down the narrow street, in the direction he had been told. The street was lined with little shops on both sides, bookstores, a window where tin soldiers lined up in regiments facing off against one another, antique stores, a window filled with wicker baskets of more shapes and sizes than James would have guessed possible. At the stoplight, he turned left and the stores disappeared, leaving tall square houses, with an occasional shorter one, many built of brick, many shingled, only one with any kind of front lawn to it. At the end of the street lay the broad green lawn of the college. The Hall of Records was at one corner of the front campus, the salesman had told him that.

James walked slowly along, enjoying the heavy moist air and the way the low gray clouds made colors look deeper. He liked the uneven bricks under his feet, liked the way the roots of trees had broken up through them. He liked the neatly painted doorways. He liked occasional glimpses into small gardens hidden behind houses. He liked being there, on his own. He liked being away from his usual life, his usual self.

He crossed the street and entered the campus of the college. Two tall rows of trees marched up the main sidewalk, one on each side, leading to a perfectly symmetrical brick building, situated on top of a rise of land. At the center of its slanting roof was a cupola, in which a bell hung. As James entered the campus, the bell started to ring, swinging back and forth, its notes swinging back and forth out over the campus. He knew it wasn't ringing because he had come there, but he felt—looking up between the two lines of trees at the gold cupola glowing under smoky clouds, at the dark bell swinging right, swinging left—he felt he was going to find out something. He knew that today was his day, somehow.

Because he knew he was going to discover what he wanted to, that his luck was running, James wanted to move into it slowly. Instead of turning across the grass to the little corner building he knew was the Hall of Records, he went on up toward the bell, looking around him. He didn't know what they were, dormitories, classroom buildings, whatever. He walked up the broad brick sidewalks, approaching. A number of students, young women and young men, ran down into and up from the cellar of the building he approached. Most of them looked a little ragged, but some of them didn't. Older men and women, in jackets and ties, in dresses and suits, were probably the teachers. Professors, they'd be. James walked up the sidewalk and then turned down another brick path that led toward the Hall of Records. He listened to snatches of conversation, the voices flowing on away as he went down the hill. He entered the Hall of Records through painted wooden doors. To find—almost as if these were magical doors—what he was looking for.

He was back out in five minutes. The receptionist had been nice, but they couldn't help him, they didn't have records of that sort; he didn't have the library skills to make use of the records they did have. She was awfully sorry, but much as she'd like to, she couldn't help him. No, she said, she didn't see any need to ask anyone else. No, he couldn't stay and just look around; these were irreplaceable historical records, they were strict about letting people wander around. No, she said, no.

James sat on the stone steps, his feelings as gray as the sky, and as heavy. He should have known. He should have guessed. He would have, if he'd stopped to think, and he knew that was why he hadn't stopped to think. He hadn't wanted to know. It was about ten thirty and he had to kill hours before he could get back on the bus. It was a waste of time, just another one of his bright ideas. It was a waste of money. He'd been so sure, too, not ten minutes ago. Well, maybe that was the way to tell how things would go: If you were sure they'd go well then they'd go badly. But if you were sure they'd go badly, then they went badly too. They just went wrong, things. One thing after another.

James wondered if he wasn't even good at what he was supposed to be good at. Like, having ideas and being able to find things out. Then, he thought, sitting there with his shoulders heavy, he got depressed when things didn't go his way. That was the kind of person he was. The kind of person who would run out on somebody, looking for the easy way, rather than sticking around to help with responsibilities that were of his making. Like four children.

Maybe, James wondered, he didn't want to find his father after all. Who needed more bad news? In any case—he stood up—he was going to have to think of something to do with all this time. He pulled the map out of his pocket.

Looking at the map, James was struck with memory, struck

down by a memory so clear he wasn't sure for a minute it wasn't happening all over again. Of course—they'd been here before, right here walking in front of this college campus, six summers ago, the three of them following Dicey. He guessed, things had sure been worse for him then. He felt like he was occupying two time zones at the same time. There was the present, where he was standing with the sidewalk under his feet, facing down the line of trees that edged the front of the campus. At the same time, he was in the past, walking along toward himself, on the sidewalk by the street, beside the hedge of tall boxwood that marked the end of the campus, following Dicey, not knowing where they were going. Hunger he remembered, feeling hungry. He was hungry now.

James explored the campus, partly to be doing something, and partly to see if he could find something to eat. He went back up the hill to a kind of patio area behind that main building. The patio looked down over broad flat fields, with a squat modern cement building on the left and a heavy brick building on the right. James turned back and went down the steps into the cellar where he had seen students going. There, he found a coffee shop. Inside it students, sometimes alone, sometimes with other students, sometimes with professors, sat around talking or reading. James got himself a couple of tuna sandwiches at the counter and sat alone at a thick wooden table while he ate. The ceiling of the room hung low and the voices were kept pretty low, too. Nobody stared at him. They didn't think it was odd for him to be there; they didn't think he looked odd.

When James went back outside, he drifted down the front lawn to a flat-faced three-story building opposite the Hall of Records, at the opposite end of the campus lawn. Broad steps led up to glass doors. It seemed to be a place you could go into.

It was a library, the college library. James pushed open the heavy door; he always liked libraries. In the foyer, a croquet set stood against the wall, mallets, wickets, and balls all held in a special rack. That was pretty strange for a library. Well, James didn't mind strangeness. He entered the building proper and was stopped by a girl sitting at a little table. "Are you just looking around?" she asked him, marking her place in the book she was reading with her finger. The page was filled with diagrams of conic sections; she had been making notes on it with her pencil.

"Just looking around," James echoed, glad she had asked him and given him his answer.

"Are you visiting the college?" she asked.

"Yes," he agreed. He knew that what she meant wasn't what he meant, but she didn't need to know. "I like libraries."

"The reading room's over there." She pointed toward a room filled with sofas and chairs, where magazines and newspapers hung on racks, all visible through glass doors. "The card catalog is right behind me. The stacks are all in the lower levels. What would you like to see?"

"The stacks," James decided. That would kill the most time.

She told him how to get there. "You can enter at any level, they all look alike. If you're not out by four, I'll come rescue you." Her smile told him she was joking.

James went through more doors and down stairways. He didn't want her to think he'd been lying, so he had to. He hadn't been lying, anyway. He entered the stacks at the first level below the ground floor.

The stacks were rows and rows and more rows of books, narrow hallways of books, books from floor to ceiling of the room. Along the outside wall were desks, each one separated off by a shallow wood partition, each with its own lamp and straight chair. Some of them were occupied by students, reading or writing. Halfway along the length of that wall the pattern was broken by a low round table surrounded by four comfortable chairs, a place where you could sit and talk, or slouch, and read with your feet propped up.

When he had walked down the length of the room, James stepped into the stacks. Books in tiers stretched out before him, towered up above him, went down to within an inch of the floor. He had known there were so many books, but he'd never actually seen them gathered together. They were all hardbound. He ran his hand along some of them, touching their stiff spines. A heavy quietude filled the air, more than quiet but not silence.

James didn't know most of the authors' names. He didn't see many familiar titles in the books he was moving slowly past. He came to the end of one row and turned back along the next, just killing time. All of those books . . . it was like all the stars in the sky: The books seemed to pour their thinking out into the air of the library, like stars poured out their light. Every one of the books had been written by somebody, and every title was different, and every somebody was different.

The books seemed to be bound only in dark colors, and they seemed old. Row after silent row, they waited to be noticed. Some of them, he guessed, would never be taken down and read. He walked on, back and forth along the rows, not skipping any. Sometimes he ran his hand along the spines as he walked by. The books lined the narrow passageways like walls holding up the whole building.

You'd think, James thought, with all those books, there would be an answer. You'd think, with all those words and all that thinking, somebody would have figured things out and written down the clear truth. It didn't have to be in English; it could be in any language. But nobody had, in any language. Even James's simple question they couldn't answer, about who his father was. Not the man's name, but the man he was. But the real question was why—why was that a question James wanted to know the answer to? Because then he'd have some idea of how to be a man, what you did when you were a man—not a dork. He'd know how to change himself, or at least do a better job of hiding himself so people wouldn't know what he was like.

But James didn't have a father and the father he'd had wasn't much of a man, unless running off on responsibilities and looking for the quick easy way was what men did. Which James doubted. So he was better off without a father maybe. He looked around at the tiers of books. They couldn't tell him even that. They all argued with and contradicted each other and didn't agree on anything. There should be only one book, and that one true for sure: that was what James thought.

He went slowly back up the stairs from the stacks. It was all pretty depressing. He said thank you to the girl behind the table. Everything sort of hung down off of him: the waste of hope, the waste of money, all the time left to waste before he got back home; shame hung like a cloak from his shoulders, hung heavy: shame for who he had been and the things he'd done, or shame for who he would be and the things he'd do, and it wasn't even as if he had done or was going to do anything much.

Once outside, James stood at the foot of the library steps. He couldn't breathe in. He felt like his heart was being pushed in and he couldn't breathe. He wondered if he was having a heart attack, and he didn't think that would be too bad. At least, he wouldn't have to live his life then. He just sat down on the bottom step and waited.

Two young men, college students, wearing no shirts, their chests and backs and faces and arms tanned, were throwing a Frisbee back and forth. Throwing and catching, catching and throwing. The round disk soared through the air in long arcs.

They ran to catch it, leaping up, stretching low. They didn't notice James. Their bare feet moved over the grass.

There were hundreds of thousands of blades of grass, maybe millions. There were thousands and thousands of books boxed into the building behind him. James let his mind go back to wander along the stacks. He guessed the books didn't mind not being brightly colored, or being ignored. He guessed he wouldn't mind being a book. Books just did what they were made to do, like stars just shining out in case anyone cared to look. In a way, James felt sorry for those books, individually.

He sat there for a minute, feeling sorry for the books, and all the thousands of people who had written them, and the stars, and the grass—and himself. What had Sammy said to him, Just be yourself? Sammy didn't know what he was saying.

Unless Sammy was miles smarter than James and knew something. Because even if your self was James Tillerman, and that was pretty depressing, you couldn't be anything else. It was pretty lucky, in a cruel way, that it didn't matter much who you were.

James felt the cruelty of that on him; he forced air into his lungs to prove he could still breathe. With his lungs filled, he felt the luck of it. Because if it didn't make any difference, then it really didn't matter. Really didn't. And if it didn't matter—

If it didn't matter, then it wasn't a big thing to be a dork. It wasn't anything at all, because he was so small and unimportant—like any individual star, or any individual book or blade of grass, he was just any individual human being. It was like "The Myth of Sisyphus," James thought and he wished—he wished he hadn't turned those notes over to Andy. He would have liked, he thought—standing up, wishing he was alone to spread out his arms and stretch, stretch out until his fingertips touched the sky—he felt like they could—he would have liked to think Camus's ideas out for himself, think them out completely. He would have liked to try to explain them to the class, even in French; to himself, too. Camus understood what the voiceless books knew: All that James had to do for himself, all he could possibly do, was just be himself.

Whether the young men playing Frisbee saw him, and thought he was weird, or not, James did stretch out his arms and touch at the sky with his fingertips. But maybe they knew it too, that because you weren't important it wasn't important who you weren't. They weren't keeping score in their game. The only reason the game took place was for the catching and throwing, the running. Nobody was out to beat anybody else or worried about being beaten. Because both of those young men, and James, too, and everybody, could only live for the short time a life took. That was a terrible thing, that brevity—terrible but not frightening.

At least, it didn't frighten James. It couldn't frighten him because he felt, like night lifting off of the sky, the shame and depression lifting off of his shoulders at the thought that he really didn't matter, whoever he was.

Without looking back—he didn't need to look back—James left the campus. He took the map out of his pocket and just wandered, keeping an eye on any clock he passed, keeping his eye on where he was in relation to where he had to be at two. Sometimes he recognized a street, or a store—he'd been here before. He wondered how Dicey had done it, had gotten them down to Gram's and kept them safe. She was something, his sister. He couldn't have done it, even if he'd been the oldest. He wondered if he had ever thanked her, and he didn't think so, and he thought he wanted to. If all you had was the one brief life, then someone who, like Dicey, had pushed and pulled you along through a bad and dangerous part of it, had done something for you you could never pay back.

The last time they were in Annapolis, he thought, as he waited for the school group on the steps of the statehouse, they were looking for their grandmother, even though they didn't know at the time that was what they were looking for. This time, he'd come to find his father. He hadn't found him, but they didn't have a father, and they couldn't, and maybe it didn't matter. Maybe it wasn't anything important after all. Maybe it would have been good, maybe not—probably not, if what they knew about the man was half true. But it didn't matter because it wasn't what had happened.

Sammy, he thought, maybe already knew that, which was why he'd just been going along with James. Sammy saw things more clearly than James did. Sammy, he realized—seeing the three familiar teachers come around the curved sidewalk followed by the long mass of kids, slipping in beside Toby, who pretended not to notice—Sammy was pretty smart. But if he was so smart, why weren't his grades better? There *was* something not right about that.

James and Toby sat down in their same seat. Toby got the window for the return trip. James wondered about his brother. It wasn't as if good grades meant anything, necessarily; it was just that, someone smart got good grades, almost without trying, in elementary school. Which meant that, if he didn't, there should be some reason.

"Well?" Toby asked him.

"Thanks," James said. "It was okay."

"I can't believe you got away with it."

"It wasn't anything much to get away with," James pointed out. "So tell me, what are your conclusions about Venus? Remember?" he said to Toby's puzzled expression. "You were telling me when I interrupted you."

Toby gladly started in again. James listened, carefully, thinking of Toby as just one brief life, but thinking how Toby was all wrapped up in something much larger than himself, something that really interested him. Toby was doing all right by his life.

"Do you know?" James interrupted. "I wouldn't be at all surprised if you turned out to be really famous. One of the pioneers of astrophysics. One of the really big men, the men who really contribute something." He said it because he meant it.

Toby's eyes got watery for a minute, but James didn't mind. Even if Toby had burst into tears, what did tears weigh in all the time that had passed? If Toby felt like crying, and cried, that was what was important.

CHAPTER 8

Sammy cut James off in the middle of asking "Do you ever wonder—?" with "You know I don't."

He'd about had it with James standing around as if he didn't have two hands like everybody else, standing around while somebody else did the work. It wasn't that Sammy didn't like hard work, or this work. In fact, kneeling there in his grandmother's vegetable garden, pulling out weeds, loosening the soil around the plants, his hands covered with dirt and the sun hot on his bare back, on the soles of his bare feet, too. There wasn't much he liked better.

Then why was he getting angry at James? If James helped, it would just be more work for Sammy. Sammy knew how James worked at things he didn't like—carelessly, that was how. If James were to help out, Sammy would have to watch him, to be sure his brother was thorough enough, getting the tiny new weeds as well as the bigger more full-grown ones. He'd have to check that James picked them all up, because if you left any behind they'd just root where they lay. That was the way weeds were. Weeds would just root down wherever they found themselves. Like the Tillermans, Sammy thought. That idea made him smile.

"We're like weeds," he said, over his shoulder to James's legs. James had just returned from the long Saturday hours at his job, where they paid him for sitting down.

"No, we're not," James said.

"Maybe *you're* not," Sammy said. And maybe James wasn't, maybe James wasn't strong enough and needed more careful tending. For sure, James didn't want to be a weed. He wanted to be a lawyer and wear three-piece suits and rake in the money.

Not Sammy. Sammy just wanted to be left alone, like a weed to grow on his own. Into whatever he was going to grow into. Something that had sunlight and sweat, he thought. Like a tennis player. His fingers dug down around the wide-spreading root system of some grassy weed, loosening its roots. Sammy pulled the thing out of the soil and tossed it into the heap he was making. He looked back up the row of eggplant bushes. Their long leaves were opened now to the sun, like pairs of hands cupped out to catch the heat and light.

Or an astronaut. In his own way, even though he lived in an enclosed environment, an astronaut worked with sweat and sun. Or a farmer, too, he thought, moving on his knees to the next plant. He picked up the clawed cultivator and dug into the tight soil around the plant's slender stalk. James wouldn't even offer to gather up the piles of weeds. James just stood there, thinking. Not doing anything. Just standing there, probably thinking about this father business again. He'd never told Sammy what he found in Annapolis. Sammy hadn't asked, either. He wasn't going to ask—this was James's fixation, James was the one interested. But he wondered what had been so bad that James had found out, so bad that he wouldn't even tell Sammy. Who didn't even care.

James sat down on the long grass at the edge of the garden, at the end of the row Sammy was weeding. The grass needed mowing, too, but James would never think of doing that until you told him he had to. James picked at the soles of his sneakers. Sammy pulled at weeds. The sun poured down. Inside the house, Maybeth and Gram were working on the upstairs—opening windows, emptying closets and drawers to wash everything out. If James wasn't going to work out here, he should go help them. From the garden, Sammy could sometimes hear their voices, sometimes a distant car, or gulls a way off, fighting over something. The buzzing drone of insects was the only steady noise on this windless day. Sammy straightened back and wiped the sweat that was rolling down his forehead. He could feel the way his hands left another smear of dirt along his face.

He liked dirt, liked being painted up with it. He liked sinking down into a tub full of warm water to get clean again. Even if he'd rather be playing tennis right now, if there was only somebody he could play with, there wasn't anything he'd rather be doing right now than what he was doing. It was contradictory, he knew, but it was true, both of it.

"In Annapolis," James began. Sammy looked over at his brother. With his narrow face and thick dark hair, something about the way the button-down shirt looked on the slender body, James looked like he came from an entirely different family from Sammy. Sammy waited.

"When I was there," James said. He was watching his own clean hands pull grass out of the ground.

If he was going to pull things up anyway, Sammy thought, why not weeds. He waited. Finally, he asked, "You never told me about Annapolis."

"It wasn't a big success. The Hall of Records didn't have anything, or, if they did, I couldn't get in to find it. So I just hung around most of the day. We've been there before, do you remember?"

"Yeah." Sammy remembered. Except for the worry about Momma, he'd enjoyed that wild summer, or a lot of it.

"It was weird, being back there, with everything so different. But there was a library full of books—"

Sammy didn't want to hear about books.

"And it made me wonder about—all the different lives people have lived, all the different things there are to be. It's really amazing, how many different things there are to be in your life."

Sammy returned to the work at hand.

"Because he was smart, they said, they both said."

"Who?"

"Him. Our father. And he had a regular family even if they weren't having an easy time of it—besides, I don't think much of anyone who had an easy time during the Depression. But out of all the things to be, he turned out a sailor. He wasn't even an officer. And before that he was some kind of crook."

"A gambler," Sammy corrected. "Not even a real professional gambler."

"Yeah, but he was crooked. The thing is—" Out of the comer of his eye, Sammy saw James lean forward, the way he did when he was having ideas and trying to tell you about them. "It makes me wonder if there was something in him, some character flaw. Something wrong about him."

"He just sounded to me like someone who always tries to find the easy way out," Sammy said, thinking that there was a lot of that in James.

"But don't you see? If he was so smart, he couldn't kid himself about that. Because it takes just as much work to figure out and then take the easy way. Anybody knows, there isn't any easy way."

The way James handled ideas, following them down like fingering loose the root systems of weeds, that wasn't any easy way. So Sammy guessed maybe he didn't have to worry about James.

"Maybe he just liked trouble," Sammy suggested.

"Yeah. That's what I wonder. But you know you told me to be myself?" Sammy didn't remember, but it sounded like something he'd say. "You were right—don't look so surprised, you're not stupid. You were right about that, because it doesn't matter—if you imagine all those lives over the thousands of years, any one little life doesn't matter a bit."

Why, Sammy wondered, did James find that such good news? What was so great about not being important at all? Sammy was pretty important to himself.

The sun was getting hot, which made him think of summer, which made him remember the end of school coming up and the question of how to get someone to take James's place crabbing, which made him remember the projects that teachers seemed to like to have due right at the end of school. "James? You had an English project, didn't you? When you were in seventh grade?"

"Yes, why? Do you?"

"A'course, and in science, too. What did you do?"

"When?"

"For your English project." Teachers tended to repeat assignments from year to year. The English was anything you wanted to do, but you had to write a five-page report, with a list of the books you'd read, and you also had to stand up and talk about it in front of the class for about five minutes. Sammy wasn't worried about the talking. He knew he could fool around for five minutes easy. He wasn't worried about the writing, once he sat himself down to it. But he couldn't think of anything to report on.

"I did a report on Ursula LeGuin, the science-fiction writer."

"I remember." Sammy got back to work. His hands were clearing the soil of any weeds which might choke the growth of the vegetable plants. "That was the year you and Toby read all that science-fiction stuff."

"And fantasy." James wasn't paying attention.

"What happened to Toby? I haven't seen him for—ages."

"Nothing. He's still around."

"I kind of liked him. He was weird. You must have had other ideas, though, didn't you? What were some of the ones you didn't do?"

When James didn't answer him, Sammy turned his head to see why. James had leaned to crouch forward on the grass, he looked like some dog at the water's edge the way he was crouched there next to the garden. James looked—bad. He looked—not exactly sick, and not exactly frightened, not exactly furious, but—bad.

"What's the matter?" Sammy had his hands full of weeds.

"Don't you do that," James said. Sammy didn't know what James was talking about. "Don't you dare ask me to do that report for you."

Sammy didn't even *want* him to and he'd never said that. He opened his mouth to inform his brother of just that, but James stood up.

"You tell me, and you act like all you do is just be yourself, but you aren't being as much of yourself as you can. So don't ask me."

Sammy dropped the weeds and stood up to face his brother, because he didn't know what James was talking about, but James was spitting words at Sammy like Sammy had done something awful. If it was a fight James wanted, he'd get one.

"Listen—" Sammy warned.

"No, *you* listen. You act like you're so stupid—"

"I do not." He did not.

"Like you're not smart, then, and you are, but you never get around to using it. Your brain. You just let it sit there in your head, lazy. And ask me to do the work for you. That's cheating, Sammy. Don't go lazy-brained kidding yourself about that."

"I don't cheat," Sammy said.

James didn't listen, as if he were talking to himself, not Sammy, or talking to somebody who stood where Sammy stood but wasn't Sammy. "Like our father," James said.

"I don't cheat," Sammy repeated stubbornly. "And you know it. Take it back, James." Nobody could say something like that to him and not have a fight coming. Sammy watched James figure that out, and back off, the way he knew James would.

"It sounded like cheating to me."

"That's because you weren't listening. I don't want you to do the report, just suggest some ideas. I don't have any idea what to write about. I'm not the one with ideas, you are. Remember? So don't go throwing all this cheating stuff at me—and where you got it from I don't know, but it's from you, not me—when all I was asking you for was what you thought might be good topics."

James stood, and stared, and said nothing.

Sammy was ready to fight, but he was just as ready to get worried. Here he'd been thinking that James was cruising along, a little conceited about his job, maybe, but feeling okay. Then it was as if Sammy had opened a little door just a tiny crack and all this dark poisonous stuff came pouring out—and it stank, too, whatever it was. James should know better than to accuse Sammy of being a cheater, like their father. James should know better and probably did. Then what was all this stuff about?

"Just possible topics?" James finally said.

"Yeah. But never mind." Sammy hunkered back down to work. He almost didn't want to talk to James anymore, again. He didn't even care if James took it back or not. It was scary, all that stuff pouring out of him.

"I'm sorry, Sammy. I really got it wrong, didn't I?"

"Yeah. You did." Sammy looked at James. Their glances connected, and Sammy was glad of that because James was worried too. "You don't often get things so wrong."

"Tell that to some people I know. Or, people I don't know, that's more true."

"Whaddayou mean, you mean girls?" That would make sense—maybe; James and girls, or a girl.

"Oh, girls, who ever knows what they think." James sat down again. "I'm really sorry, Sammy. I didn't mean it."

"Okay," Sammy said. "It's okay."

"Except about selling yourself short," James corrected himself. "That part, I think I do mean."

Sammy didn't let his face show that he'd heard, but he had. He just didn't want to talk about it.

"I thought about doing a history of Crisfield," James said, then. "For my report."

What a snore, Sammy thought. That was a snore and a half.

"Or Tolkien, because we'd been reading him, too. And I really wanted to do Plato, but that was just to show off because nobody, not even Toby, knew about Plato."

"Probably the teacher didn't either." The only reason Sammy knew the name was because James had talked on and on about the guy for a while.

"Yeah. So, anyway, I didn't. Or mythology, I considered mythology, too. Toby thought about doing the tarot cards, you know?" Sammy didn't. "Fortune-telling cards, they're really old. I think they're Egyptian in origin, and there are some strange stories about them."

"Maybe I'll do mythology," Sammy said.

"We've got a lot of books on that here," James told him. "I guess our grandfather got interested in it. It would make a good topic."

"Maybe I'll look for them after dinner. Thanks for the help, James. The only thing I could think of was that old Francis Scott Key report I gave in fourth grade."

"A report you gave in fourth grade? You'd give it again?"

"I'd have added stuff. I'd have changed some stuff." Even so, Sammy grinned to himself, it would have sounded like a fourth grade report, which would have been pretty funny. As long as you did something, teachers would pass you. He could picture how it would be, he could hear himself giving this fourth grade report and the way the class would catch on. Miss Karin would probably catch on first and he bet she'd enjoy it, too; she did a lot of laughing. She seemed to think seventh graders, and especially Sammy, were pretty funny. It was tempting, and maybe he *would* just rewrite that one; he didn't mind looking stupid.

Sammy pulled out a clump of weeds and tossed it over, then moved down the row. What did James mean, anyway, calling him lazy?

With less than four weeks until summer, it was as if all the teachers suddenly woke up. Tests and projects, all the wrap-up things, everybody was assigning more homework, making the classes toe the line because there was so much to be done before they graduated from seventh grade, before they moved on to the high school, where, if they thought things were tough here . . . Even in PE they had wrapping up to do.

At the end of every year, all the students were weighed and measured during one of the PE classes. The weights and heights were entered onto their records. The school nurse was in charge, but the PE teachers did the actual measuring, writing down, and keeping the gym quiet. While this record keeping was going on, the kids milled around in groups that moved slowly along toward the scales.

When it was time for the seventh graders to line up, Sammy made sure he was next to Custer. Custer would be a good person to work with. "So what are you doing this summer?" he asked.

Custer kept his voice low to answer, although his eyes looked eager, excited. "I'm going out West. To a ranch. It's a camp, actually, but—I'll learn to ride western style, not this eastern stuff for shows, but like cowboys. There'll be some white-water canoeing, too. And I'm going to learn how to shoot. A gun."

"A real gun?"

"No, a water pistol." Custer punched Sammy on the arm. "I'll learn how to use one of those Darth Vader death rays, too, there's a two-week course on death rays."

Sammy laughed. "How to shoot like a storm trooper?"

"They never hit anyone," Custer pointed out.

Sammy explained it to him: "It used to be black hats. Now it's bad shots. That's how you can tell the bad guys—they miss. How come you're doing that?"

"My father grew up out West. Not California, that's not the real West, he lived in the Rockies. In the mountains. He didn't live on a ranch, but he had some friends who did and they used to go off, on horses, with bedrolls just like in the movies. They'd camp out. They had to take their guns, because it was dangerous—and he wasn't any older than I am. He shot rattlers and jackrabbits. My grandfather used to shoot moose and deer for their winter meat. You know that moose head we have?" Sammy remembered it, a huge gentle-faced hairy head under wide antlers. "My grandfather shot that." Sammy used to feel sorry for that moose. He didn't tell Custer that. "My father would wear just an Indian loincloth, they all would, and they'd fish for their meals and cook the fish over the fire. He says the West is an experience he doesn't want any son of his to miss, so I'm going to this camp. We're all going to drive across the country, my sisters and everyone, and I'll fly back at the end of the summer."

"That sounds great," Sammy said. It did. He wouldn't have

minded it for himself except he didn't have any father to want him to do it.

"I'll probably go back for lots of summers. Dad says, the mountains are a good place to grow up. He says it teaches you things about being a man."

Sammy guessed he just couldn't understand that.

"They used to pan for gold, too. Like the old miners, they'd be up there beside some stream, panning for gold."

"Did he find any?"

"Not enough to spit on, he says. At camp we're going to do a lot of trail riding. Hiking, and climbing, too. There are marksmanship contests."

Custer was really looking forward to the summer, talking fast. Their line moved slowly forward.

"My dad says he thinks I'll make a marksman, because I've got a steady hand and a true eye." Then, as if he could see that Sammy was getting tired of hearing all this, Custer asked, "What're you doing this summer?"

"The usual." Custer knew what that was. "I was going to see if you wanted to be in the crabbing business with me, but I guess you can't."

"I guess not." Custer didn't sound like that bothered him.

Sammy shuffled forward with the rest of the kids. He could see why Custer would rather go to camp out West, and learn how to shoot a gun, and all. It wouldn't make sense for Custer to wish he could stay in Crisfield and go crabbing with Sammy—Sammy wouldn't wish that, if he were Custer and his father wanted to take him West.

"I thought your brother—" Custer started to say, but then he fell into the silence that was spreading backward from the head of the line as Ernie stepped onto the scales. Everybody always wanted to know how much Ernie weighed. It was a standing joke. Sammy stuck his elbow into Custer's ribs and Custer punched him lightly on the shoulder. They stood side by side to watch. One PE teacher settled the height bar on top of Ernie's head, while the other adjusted the metal weights on the scale. Ernie slouched there, chewing gum; he didn't care. His gut hung down over his belt, all around his body. Ernie already looked like he had a beer belly.

"One forty-seven," the teacher said, neither raising nor lowering her voice. The third teacher entered the figure on a piece of paper, then called the school nurse over. "Just stay right there, young man," she instructed Ernie, who had started to slouch down off the scales.

Ernie looked back at the kids. He lifted his arm and scratched at his armpit, letting everyone see how bored he was. He grinned, making his face hang loose, like a retard's face. Then, slowly, he started to pick his nose.

"Ugh," Custer said, turning his back. But Sammy watched. He hadn't had much to do with Ernie for years, not since second grade when he was new and thought he had to prove he wasn't a sissy, and Ernie had been the biggest and meanest kid in the class. Mostly, now, he didn't even notice Ernie was in the world. Nobody had anything much to do with Ernie; nobody was even frightened of him any more. Everybody just—didn't like the kind of trouble Ernie got into. Ernie got in trouble for cussing at teachers, which was pretty stupid, and for saying the kinds of things you were never supposed to say to girls. He'd slam little kids around in the hallways, sometimes. And here he was, standing there, picking away at his nose, trying to gross everyone out. And succeeding.

Maybe that made him happy, Sammy thought, although he kind of doubted it. What made Ernie happy was being able to bully people, only now he couldn't any more.

The nurse came up and Ernie gave her a bored look. At least, Sammy thought, with Ernie around, things got knocked off their rails. The nurse started talking at Ernie about diets and health. Ernie slouched there, his head lowered so she couldn't see his face, his face bored and inattentive. "I'm going to have to talk with your parents," she finally said.

"Go ahead," Ernie answered. He didn't care.

"Don't they worry about you?"

"Nah," Ernie said. "My father says he went through a heavy phase, too. He says I'll outgrow it." In Ernie's voice was absolute confidence that his father knew better than the nurse, better than anyone.

"Lucky for you that he knows all the answers," the nurse said, sarcastic.

"Yeah. He says besides I can always be a wrestler on TV. Can I get down now?"

The nurse wanted to keep him there and talk at him until he changed, but she knew it wouldn't do any good, so she let him go. Ernie slouched on away. Sammy watched him slouch along. He'd be willing to bet Ernie was ashamed of himself, but he wasn't sure he'd win that bet. Ernie sounded pretty sure of what his father said. Sammy didn't know—he sure didn't want anyone telling him that what wasn't true was true. And asking him to believe it.

You certainly wouldn't want to work on a fourteen-foot boat with Ernie. Sammy looked around, trying to think of someone else to ask, someone he wouldn't mind spending hours in the boat with. But he didn't know how to tell who'd be able to work and who'd give up easy. He knew how these people behaved in school, and who played sports how, but that didn't necessarily mean that would be a person who could haul crabs, day after day. What you really needed was patience, Sammy thought, but how could you tell if someone had enough of that? He thought, some people did know how to tell, because people hired men to do jobs, so they must be able to tell something.

For reasons he didn't quite understand, it was the new kid, Robin Kelly, that Sammy asked next. He asked Robin while the boy was waiting in the bus line after school. He tried to explain how hard the work was, but he could see by the excited way Robin kept interrupting that the kid was more interested in being asked than in anything else. He wasn't listening. There wasn't anything Sammy could do about that. Besides, he thought, while he was trying to say how early you had to go out, and how uncomfortable it often was, he'd really picked Robin because Robin looked like James—dark and skinny—and like Jeff Greene, too. Sammy had worked with both of them, so Robin literally looked like someone he could work with. That wasn't much of a reason, but Sammy knew it was as good a reason as any.

"I'd have to have my mother's permission," Robin was saying, practically bouncing up and down. "Boy. Boy, does that sound great."

"I'm trying to tell you—" Sammy tried to tell him.

"She'll have to meet you. Because . . . anyway, she won't say yes until she meets you. So you should come home from school with me tomorrow, and you could stay and have dinner with us. My mother's a good cook. Ask your parents, okay? I'll ask mine. Then we can all talk about it. They like to all talk things over. Once they meet you, they'll see."

See what? Sammy wanted to ask, but didn't. "I have a bike."

"That's okay, I'll get a note so I can walk. It's not that far. Don't forget to ask?"

"I won't," Sammy said.

"This is great," Robin said, again. "Boy, would I like to be able to."

Sammy just went to get his bike and ride home.

The Tillermans talked things over too; that was what families did when there was something one of them wanted to do. Sammy pedaled energetically, listening to the wind in his ears, feeling how strong his legs were. Just because you didn't have parents, that didn't mean you weren't a family. He pushed down, standing up to get more power into his thrust—left, right, left. His speed built up. A car overtook him, and passed him, with a rumbling motor sound that drowned out the wind.

In that temporary windless second after the car had rushed on, where he heard only echoing silence, a voice in Sammy's head called his name.

"Sammy."

He heard it, clear. He looked around, as if he weren't sure the voice was really in his head, although he knew it was. This had happened before, not too many times, but enough. He'd heard his name being called, like some kind of optical illusion in his ear. When he was little, he'd almost thought it was Momma calling, and he'd try to rehear the voice, trying to hold on to it. He'd finally figured out that it wasn't, and it couldn't be. It was something like a dream that happened in your ear while you were awake. Sammy didn't know if other people had the same experience, because he'd never told anyone about it.

But something was different this time, he thought, sitting down on the bike seat, slowing down. The voice had seemed closer, realer. He didn't know the voice, but he thought it was a man. He knew he didn't believe in ESP and things like that, but there was something strange here.

He wanted there to be something strange. He hoped there was some ESP going on. But that wasn't like him. What was like him was to see how things really were.

He could almost still hear it, if he concentrated on remembering, the way the voice had called the two syllables of his name. "Sammy."

Sammy shook his head, but the voice stayed hooked there in his mind. He reminded himself to ask Gram about having supper at Robin's tomorrow, and that he had to finish the rough draft of his English report that night. That would give him the weekend to recopy it. He had done it on the Greek myths about the sun god, and he'd had a pretty interesting time doing it.

Now that he'd distracted himself, Sammy listened inside his head for the voice, to hear if it was still there. He couldn't find it, but he thought it was still there. He could almost re-create it from his memory—but that was a pretty strange thing to want to do. In fact—he turned onto the driveway and rode fast over the ruts, bouncing himself in the seat and laughing aloud as the bike jolted and twisted under him, like a bucking bronco—he was having some pretty strange ideas recently, now he thought of it. Sammy decided not to think of it.

CHAPTER 9

Robin lived a couple of miles inland, in one of a half dozen ranch-style houses lined up on the road's edge, backed by fields of corn and soybeans. Sammy walked his bike, because Robin didn't have one. "I wish I did. I'm old enough to ride to school," Robin said. "You ride to school most of the time."

Sammy just nodded his head.

"My dad says it's because we used to live in the city, because we lived in Kentucky before they got married. He says my mother keeps thinking Crisfield is the same as Louisville, with city streets. But it's not at all like a city."

"I guess not," Sammy said.

"He's not my real father," Robin said.

"Who isn't?"

"My dad. They only got married last Christmas. He's a French teacher but my real father is a jet pilot, in the air force. He flew in the war, in Vietnam. He's got lots of medals. He's a colonel."

The kid was really proud of his father. Sammy guessed he could see why.

"I've got his picture, I'll show you," Robin said.

They turned off at one of the houses, different from its neighbors only in being light brown instead of white or red. There was a car parked beside it, with Kentucky plates, a beat-up blue sedan. "Is that your car?"

"My mom's. She's a teacher too, but she teaches art, in the elementary school. But she can't get a position until next fall, so she just substitutes. She promised she'd never substitute for my class. Her name's Norton, not Kelly."

"Okay," Sammy said.

Each of the other houses had a car parked beside it. Each house sat on its little flat square of lawn in exactly the same position, like houses on a Monopoly board. A couple of the backyards had swing sets in them, but most just had grass that stopped abruptly at the edge of the field that lay behind, where soybeans grew low and bushy. Robin waited by the back door at one end of the long rectangular house while Sammy kicked down the stand to park his bike. The front door of the house was smack in its middle, facing the street, just like all the rest of the houses. It was all so neat and tidy, and all so much the same, it made Sammy nervous.

"Are you coming?" Robin asked.

"Okay," Sammy said.

Sammy expected the inside of Robin's house to be boxes, like the outside. But the inside didn't match the outside at all. The inside felt bigger than it could possibly be. They entered into a kitchen, where plants in brown clay pots hung down in front of the windows, and the walls were crowded with posters in bright crayon colors. A little table in front of the windows had two glasses and a plate of cookies set out. "I'm home," Robin called. A woman's voice answered him, but she didn't appear.

"Hungry?" he asked Sammy.

"Sure," Sammy said. He sat down at the table, in one of the three chairs, and looked around the room. He liked those pictures, with their shapes that almost looked like something, almost like a person or almost like a flower, almost like stars. He liked the way the counters and refrigerator and stove sparkled. This kitchen was entirely different from his grandmother's kitchen, which was old wood colors and yellowy light. This one was bright and new looking. Sammy knew he liked the old, worn-down-with-living look of his grandmother's kitchen; but he liked this one, too. Every place he looked he saw something to like: the potholders, their colors as bright as the pictures, hanging over the stove; a wooden bowl filled with apples and oranges and bananas on the counter by a shiny metal toaster; the leaves of the plants hanging down ferny green in the sunlight that came through the window. Robin poured two glasses of milk and sat opposite Sammy. "We just moved in, practically," he said. He picked up a cookie and ate it. Sammy did the same. These were peanut-butter cookies, made from scratch, with marks where the fork had flattened them and a perfect, almost crumbly, texture. He took a couple more.

"Your mom's a good cook."

Robin, his mouth full, agreed. "It's because she isn't working. She has lots of time for cooking and things when she doesn't go to work. Want to see my room? We have to wait for Dad to get home, anyway, before we can discuss things."

Sammy finished his milk and put the glass in the sink. He grabbed some more cookies and followed Robin out of the room. They went through a long combination living and dining room, a wooden table at one end with a bowl of flowers on it, Indian rugs on the floor, and bright nubbly cushions on the sofa and chairs, then down a narrow hallway. Robin opened the second door.

Robin's room should have been just a little box with two windows, but it had been turned into something wonderful. "Hey, wow," Sammy said, looking around.

He saw a ladder, leading up to a kind of loft, and underneath that, in what looked almost like a cave, was a desk, with bookcases beside it. A bureau and some open shelves filled with games were on the opposite wall. The floor had a bright red and blue rug on it. "Neat," Sammy said.

"Dad built the bed, go ahead up," Robin said. Sammy scrambled up the ladder and saw that the whole loft was a bed, with a wall light above the pillows, and a shelf to put books on. The ceiling above the bed wasn't painted white, but covered with an intricately designed fabric that hung over the bed like the underside of a fancy cloud. There wasn't room to stand up, but there was plenty of headroom if you were sitting up. Sammy sat there for a minute, trying to forget the boy below. In this bed, you'd almost be in a tree house; it felt a lot like a tree house, the bed. It would be like sleeping in a tree.

He leaned over. "Your father built it?"

"No, Dad did. And Mom found the fabric for the ceiling. She made the rug, too. She weaves."

"I thought you said she was a teacher."

"She does crafts and all kinds of things. Weaving, sewing, too."

"Did she do those paintings in the kitchen?"

Robin started to laugh. "You mean the Matisse cutouts? Wait'll I tell her you thought she'd done the Matisse cutouts."

Sammy didn't know why Robin was laughing at him. "So what," he said. "So what's so funny?"

"Because Matisse is—I'm sorry, Sammy, I know you wouldn't know anything about Matisse. I'm not laughing at you."

"Yes, you are." Sammy climbed back down the ladder.

Robin started to object, then stopped. "Yes, I guess. But I am sorry, I know it's not your fault if you don't know something. I mean, I only know because my mom's been taking me to museums from about the minute I was born. That's one of the things my father didn't like. Look, here he is."

The photograph had been put into a silver frame. It was an officer, with his cap on exactly straight, and his expression serious. He had dark hair, like Robin, but his face was more square, the jawbone square, the mouth a thin straight line. He didn't look alive, Sammy thought; he looked like a wax figure, not a person.

"That was five years ago," Robin said. "He gave it to me. I guess he'll look older now, probably. You can't see his medals."

"What do you mean five years ago? Haven't you seen him?"

Robin shook his head. He looked at the picture, not meeting Sammy's eyes.

Understanding, Sammy had a little jumping feeling inside him; not a nice feeling at all, he knew, like a little black imp jumping up and down; because he guessed things weren't so exactly perfect for Robin after all. But why should that make Sammy glad? Unless he was jealous? But Sammy didn't get jealous of people, and why should he envy Robin, anyway. Why should he envy anyone? He didn't, that was the truth. Except for just that little short jumping feeling—gone now.

"Let's go outside. Do you have a soccer ball, or another lacrosse stick?"

"We've got a baseball and two gloves," Robin said. "Let's."

Mrs. Norton was in the kitchen as they went through, and Robin introduced her but Sammy barely paid attention other than to say hello. "The cookies were good," he said, turning at the door to tell her.

For some reason that made her laugh. He didn't mind.

They had to play out in the narrow backyard, because Robin said he wasn't allowed to play in the street. "It's because we lived in a city," he said. He had an okay arm, and the ball went back and forth between them with satisfying speed. "Dad says all Mom's reflex reactions are a city person's. So we have to be patient with her, until she gets used to how different things are here."

"Dad?" Sammy was having trouble keeping these fathers straight.

"He's my stepfather but he wants to adopt me. So I call him Dad."

"Why do you need to be adopted?"

"So we'll all have the same name and be a family. Because he likes me, mostly, that's what I think."

"Do you like him?"

"Sure. He's not my real father, though."

"Yeah, but it doesn't sound like your real father is anywhere around."

He shouldn't have said that, he could tell, but it was too late. Robin held on to the ball, kind of rubbing it into his glove, twisting it there, studying it. "It's a lot of work being a colonel," Robin said. "He flies F-110s. I've got a model of one of those. I'm going to be a jet pilot too, if I'm good enough."

"By that time," Sammy said, trying to ease things up a little, "jets will probably be obsolete. You'll have to fly—I dunno, some kind of spaceship, like—"

"In *Star Wars*?" Robin's face lit up. He tossed the ball to Sammy. "Do you think things will move that fast?"

"How would I know?" Sammy joked, glad Robin was so easy to distract. "I left my crystal ball at home."

"I can never tell," Robin said, "whether I should be scared, about the bombs and all, or excited about space exploration."

"I know what you mean."

"My dad says he can't tell either. I thought I wanted him to say something different, you know? But it turns out I feel better knowing that he doesn't know. Isn't that weird?"

What was weird, Sammy thought, was the way Robin had this terrific stepfather but kept insisting on his real father. If Sammy had had a stepfather, he wouldn't have minded: and now he wondered why his mother never did have another boyfriend to marry. Maybe it was because she had all those kids. Or maybe she didn't want any boyfriend except his father, maybe she loved him and didn't know how bad he was. Maybe if you loved someone, it didn't matter how bad he was.

They tossed the ball, talking a little every now and then, until a white sedan pulled up behind the blue one. A man got out of it. He waved to Robin, then went into the house. "My dad," Robin explained. Sammy had figured that. "He stays at school to get his work done there, so he can concentrate on us when he gets home. Mostly that works, but sometimes he has to bring work home anyway. He likes us. Well, Mom especially. They met at a teacher's convention and he wanted to marry her right away. As soon as he clapped eyes on her, he says. I dunno, Sammy, can you imagine that?"

"Getting married? No."

"Anyway, she wouldn't, not for a couple of years. Dad came and took a summer job in Louisville, so he could see us a lot. See her, especially. He told me my father sounds like the kind of man it would be hard on a woman to be married to. Dad says they were just all wrong for each other. He says some people shouldn't ever get married, but he's the marrying kind."

Sammy thought of his own father, who was the non-marrying kind. But he couldn't imagine that it could have been worse for Momma to be married, and almost missed the catch.

"What about you?" Robin asked.

Sammy didn't want to talk about himself. "What about me?" He fired the ball so hard it burned out of the kid's glove. Robin wasn't stupid; he ran to pick up the ball and when he turned to toss it back he didn't ask any more questions.

Robin's mother called them in to wash their hands, and then they sat down at the dining-room table. Mr. Norton sat at one end and Mrs. Norton sat at the other. All the plates and serving dishes were in front of Mr. Norton, who was a round-faced man, with thin light brown hair that needed cutting. He smiled a lot and asked questions as he served them their plates. "How do you feel about succotash? Do you want your ham sliced thin or thick? Robin, will you pass your mother the mustard?"

Sammy got the second plate, after Mrs. Norton. He started to pick up his fork to eat, but then he noticed that Robin's mother hadn't started, so he put it down again. He guessed maybe every meal in this house was as fancy as Thanksgiving.

Once they started eating, they got down to the business at hand. The grown-ups ran the discussion, like school. "Robin tells us that you want him to go crabbing with you this summer," Mrs. Norton said.

She was looking at Sammy as if she wanted to look right inside him to see what he was like. Her hair was soft curls, held up on top of her head by a big wooden barrette, but wisping like strings of coiled cornsilk around her face. She had big, round brown eyes, gentle.

"Yes," Sammy said. He just looked into those eyes. "We've been doing it for about four years. Before, my brother worked with me, he's fifteen, but he's got a job in an office now, so he can't."

"Is your brother named James?" Mr. Norton asked.

Sammy didn't want to have to look away from the brown eyes, but he did.

"I have him in class," Mr. Norton said. "I teach French in the high school."

"Oh," Sammy said. He didn't know what he should say next, so he took a big forkful of his baked potato. "This is a good dinner," he said to Mrs. Norton. She laughed, and agreed with him.

"We don't know what working with you would entail for Robin," Mr. Norton said.

Sammy explained about how you had to get out to the boat at about dawn, and then set the line and run it, for a couple of hours or sometimes longer, depending on how the crabs were biting. He told them about taking the haul to the town docks, to be picked up by the restaurants. He ate and explained. He estimated how much money Robin might earn, after they'd paid for bait and gas. "It's hard work," he said, looking at Robin's excited face. "And sometimes it's cold, and wet—the eel smells, and when the jellyfish come in they can sting you."

Robin just sat there looking excited.

"So you and James have been running this business?"

"Mostly me and James," Sammy told Mr. Norton. "Sometimes someone else—a friend of my sister's, he has a car so we drive around to the docks, but he's in college now but—sometimes he'd give James time off. Sometimes we'd take his boat instead. James doesn't like it as much as I do."

Mr. Norton nodded, listening. He painted mustard on the top of his second slice of ham, and cut a bite.

"But if you've been doing this for four years, you must have been awfully young when you started." Mrs. Norton turned her brown eyes on Sammy again. He agreed. She was impressed and he liked that. He liked the way her eyes rested on his face. He liked having her look at him. He liked looking back, too. She was awfully pretty. "Didn't your parents worry about you?"

Sammy shook his head: No, they didn't. It was the truth, anyway; neither of them did, not his mother or his father, for one reason or another. He answered the question she really meant to ask. "There are life preservers—my grandmother makes us wear them. We never go out in rough weather, because the crabs just don't bite on windy days. We take good care of the motor, and there are oars, too."

"I can't get used to that much independence," Mrs. Norton

said, smiling at herself and looking down the table to Mr. Norton.

"We know you can't. Don't we, Robin?"

Mrs. Norton didn't mind their teasing. "But how would we get Robin there so early?" she asked.

"In summers—you've never been through a summer here—I get up at dawn or before and then take a siesta in the early afternoon when the heat is at its worst. The heat can get pretty bad. I've warned you about summers, love. But since I'm up anyway, I could drive him over. Wait till you see the summer dawns, Robin—everything sort of silver before the sun rises . . ."

"You think this is a good idea, don't you?" Mrs. Norton asked Mr. Norton.

Robin was practically holding his breath with excitement.

"I think it'll be fine. It'll be hard work, but Robin's up to some hard work," Mr. Norton answered. "I think you ought to let him, yes."

"Then it's okay with me," Mrs. Norton said.

"All *right*," Robin said, smiling at Sammy as if he'd just heard that the world was perfect after all.

"And if it doesn't work out—" Mrs. Norton continued.

"It'll work out," Robin interrupted her. "It'll be great."

"If it doesn't work out," she insisted, "then you'll tell us. One or both of you will tell us. Promise?" Mrs. Norton asked Sammy.

"That sounds pretty fair to me, Robin," Mr. Norton added.

"Okay," Robin agreed. "Is that okay with you, Sammy?"

"Sure," he said.

"That's that, then," Mr. Norton said. "Summer might also be the right time to get Robin that bike. That's yours by the door, isn't it, Sammy? Do you ride to school?"

"Sure," Sammy said.

"You don't ride by yourself, do you?" Mrs. Norton asked him.

Sammy could tell by then what Mr. Norton had meant about her having city reflexes. "I've been riding a bike for years, because—well, we don't have a car. At first, my sister always rode with me, to make sure I knew how, and to be safe, but ever since then. I mean, when I had a paper route, I had to ride my bike because the houses were so far apart."

"How old were you?"

"About third and fourth grade."

"And your parents didn't worry?"

"No," Sammy said. Which was the truth.

She looked at him, then at Robin, then at Mr. Norton. "Go ahead, say it, Ben, I know you're thinking it. You too, Robin, I can see you two ganging up on me. I'm too protective, that's what you're thinking, isn't it?" She smiled at Sammy. "I guess, I'm beginning to think they might be right. Just beginning," she told the two of them. "So don't get too many ideas. And now it's time for dessert. Does anyone want lemon meringue pie?"

Everybody did. They all helped clear the table. Mrs. Norton brought out the pie, its meringue topping looking like white waves, toasted white waves; Mr. Norton brought out two mugs of coffee, and the cream for it in a little pitcher. When they had settled down around dessert, Mrs. Norton asked Sammy, "What does your father do?"

She didn't ask it like it was an important question, more as if just for something to say. But Sammy still didn't know what to answer. He took a bite of the pie and put it into his mouth, and he didn't taste it. While he chewed, he looked at Robin, who was eating away at his own piece, and then at Mr. Norton, who was watching Sammy. As soon as Sammy met his eyes, Mr. Norton looked down the table at Mrs. Norton.

As soon as Sammy swallowed, she had her eyes on him again.

He looked right back at her, and he didn't want to tell her any lies. Or the truth, either.

"I've said something wrong, haven't I? I'm sorry," she said. She meant it. She didn't like hurting people.

"It's all right," Sammy told her. "Really. I just—don't have a father. I mean, I do, but I've never seen him."

"Oh. Then it really was the wrong thing to ask," she insisted. "I really am sorry, Sammy."

Sammy didn't mind.

"Your poor mother. How does she manage?"

Sammy took a deep breath. "We live with my grandmother, my mother's mother, where my mother grew up. All of us do, I'm the youngest. There are four. Gram adopted us, five years ago. She has a farm and a big house and it's pretty nice. We used to live up in Massachusetts, on the Cape, when I was little. Then we came down here. My mother died, and—Gram takes care of us, and my sister Dicey, she's at college right now, and we take care of ourselves."

He never stopped looking at her while he told her this. She didn't stop looking at him. "I guess, it's no wonder you're pretty independent," was all she said about it, when he'd finished.

Sammy grinned. "Yeah." He tried to explain to her: "My grandmother is—I really like my grandmother. Some of the things she gets up to—" He couldn't explain, so he stopped talking.

"But if you don't have a car, how does she get around?" Robin asked. "Does she have a bike too?"

"No, she uses the boat to get downtown in. Or Jeff—he's Dicey's friend, the one who sometimes comes crabbing—he's got a car. Or Mr. Lingerle, Maybeth's piano teacher, he's our friend."

"Isaac Lingerle? The music teacher?" Mr. Norton asked.

Sammy nodded. He didn't know why Mr. Norton asked in that wondering way, but "He's our friend," he repeated, to let Mr. Norton know.

"I can't imagine living that way," Mrs. Norton said to all of them. "I can't imagine not having a car. It isn't anything I can even begin to imagine."

"Positively un-American?" Mr. Norton asked.

"Bikes and boats. No horses?" Mrs. Norton asked. She was teasing now, too.

Sammy was enjoying himself. "No horses, no animals. I tried to have chickens, for a long time. But Gram says the only good chicken is a fried chicken."

Then they all laughed, sitting around the table where the plates sat on bright woven mats and the pie had the same golden color as the light outside the windows.

After they cleared the table, and Sammy was told that Robin and his dad always did the dishes so he should get on along home before the sun went down, Mrs. Norton said she hoped he'd come again, soon. Sammy said he'd like that, which was true. He told her, if she let Robin have a bike, he'd ride with him for a while, to check him out and be sure he was safe. She said thank you, not teasing at all. Sammy said thank you, for the dinner. Robin walked down to the end of the driveway with him, just bubbling away with excitement. "I knew if they met you it would be okay."

"It's hard work," Sammy warned him.

"That's fine."

"I had a good time," Sammy said, looking back at the house.

"Good. I wanted you to. She used to be nervous about guests, and worry about not being able to have things nice enough, but Dad doesn't care so now she doesn't either."

Sammy waited.

"I don't mind if my dad is only a schoolteacher. I probably shouldn't say that."

Sammy didn't know about that. "He acts like a real father, doesn't he?"

"Yeah. He likes me."

"Yeah," Sammy agreed. "Look, I'll see you tomorrow, at school. Okay?"

Riding alone back to town, through town and out the long road home, Sammy's mind was whirling. The trouble was, he kept remembering the way Mrs. Norton's eyes had looked at him, and it made him feel sort of squishy inside, it made him feel good. And that made him nervous, because—he'd never had that feeling before. Then he looked around him, as the road swept under the wheels of his bike, and he couldn't stop smiling. It was a perfect evening. The sky was filled with dark gray clouds moving across from the east. The lowering sun shot out long bars of golden light under the approaching clouds. The whole landscape around him, fields and trees, was washed over with that light.

Sammy was looking forward to having James check over his English report for spelling and grammar errors. James wouldn't find any, he almost never did, but that wasn't what Sammy was thinking of. He was thinking that he'd done a good job, and he thought James might be impressed. James ought to be impressed—it was about the best thing Sammy had ever done for school. But he wasn't sure if it was as good as he thought. He wanted James to read it. Sammy didn't like that feeling of wanting James to be impressed, and he thought maybe he wouldn't let James read it. Anyway, it wasn't anything written by a lazy-brained person, that was for sure.

CHAPTER 10

James licked the final envelope, and sealed it. He put it on top of the three-inch pile of envelopes, to go out in the mail Monday morning. Leaning his elbows on the desk, he rubbed at his eyes. He had the office to himself on this Saturday afternoon. He'd come in at eight and been working steadily for almost six hours. During morning office hours, he'd been interrupted by the phone ringing and patients arriving or leaving; but since noon, when he'd wolfed down the sandwiches Gram had packed for him, not even noticing what kind they were, it had been relatively quiet. Dr. Landros had told him, as she left, that once she'd had lunch and done her grocery shopping she'd be at home. Dr. O'Hara had gone up to Salisbury when a patient went into labor about four weeks early. "I don't like it," she had said to Dr. Landros. "Neither do I," Dr. Landros had agreed. "I'll be on call this afternoon, so you go see what can be done. It might be false labor. You were just boasting about the premie unit up there, anyway."

"Or it might be something wrong, and I'll have a lawsuit on my hands. I saw her Tuesday, she looked fine, but—"

"Leslie," Dr. Landros had said, as if she was speaking to someone pretty stupid, "this isn't the big city, there aren't lawyers on every corner offering percentage deals on malpractice suits. You'll cross that bridge when you come to it."

"I better run. I'll talk to you later," Dr. O'Hara had said, running out of the office.

They were cousins of some kind, James had learned. Dr. Landros had practiced for years, but she said everybody wanted specialists or psychiatrists, and she was sick of locking her car and double-locking her apartment and being robbed anyway. Sick of accident cases where people swore at her because she insisted on the strict truth about their injuries. Sick of . . . about everything. "I figured, what the hell, if I'm going to hit change of life, I might as well change my life," she told James. She liked being near the water. She liked fishing. She liked the quiet. She liked being a GP, too. "I'm a doctor," she said, "not some specialist."

James looked at the stack of duplicate forms, now ready to be filed in the tall cabinets behind him. He was tired, bored, ready to go home. But if he filed them now they'd be out of the way. He started sorting them into alphabetical order, separating Dr. Landros's cases from Dr. O'Hara's. Most of them were Dr. O'Hara's, the final entries after the six-week postpartum checkup. Dr. O'Hara said that statistically more babies were born in March and April than any other months. "It's all those June weddings, the people who aren't getting married still get feeling romantic, sentimental—it's something about June."

Dr. O'Hara had been married, but she didn't have any children. James thought that had something to do with her going into obstetrics. She'd been divorced for about six years now, but she didn't have anything good to say about men. He'd gathered, from bits and pieces of conversation, things he'd overheard and things he'd been told, that Dr. O'Hara's husband had treated her pretty badly. Not hitting her, or abandoning her, or anything like that, just ordinary bad treatment between two people. She had paid the cost of sending him to law school, working as a waitress at night and a checkout girl in a supermarket during the day.

Waitressing was better money for the hours, she'd said, but the supermarket job was a steady income, and had the benefits, too, the medical insurance. Her husband—James didn't even know what his name was because she never named him, and had gone back to her maiden name after the divorce—went to school. During the summers he couldn't work, at first because he had to write his paper for law review, because if you were on law review then you got a better job, and then because he was offered a position clerking for a judge that didn't pay anything but had a lot of prestige. Then, once he'd graduated, he was working six, seven days a week, to beat out the other new lawyers in the company he'd joined. He said he didn't want children yet, he wanted a house instead, and a Mercedes, he wanted to enjoy himself after all that work; then he said he wanted to marry someone else.

Dr. O'Hara had gotten her own lawyer when he did that, and she said she'd really put the screws to him. Let him pay for her to go to school now, that was her attitude. She wasn't too proud to use him the way he'd used her. She sounded like she didn't like him a bit. If she'd talked to him like that, James could see why he wanted to be married to someone else.

Except for when she talked about her ex-husband, Dr. O'Hara was a pretty nice person, sort of anxious but with a good sense of humor, and she really cared about her patients. James figured, the guy must have been pretty much of a snake. He'd thought, a couple of times, of saying to Dr. O'Hara, "Look, you didn't get the only bad one. My mother got one too." But he didn't, even though knowing that made him feel better. It might not make her feel better.

James was filing and thinking—the filing made easy because all he had to do was go through the big drawers from front to back, finding the right folder—when the phone rang. Until he left the office—at which time he would notify the answering service to pick up the calls—James was responsible for answering the phone.

He leaned over the desk, pushed down the flashing button, and picked up the receiver. "Doctors' office. May I help you."

"Hello, doctor. I don't know if I got a problem, but I thought, I maybe might call." It was a man's voice, rumbly and deep, spewing off its words so fast James didn't have time to interrupt and say he wasn't the doctor. "It's probably nothing, but I haven't been able to urinate for almost two days now. Is that serious?"

James wasn't any doctor, but that didn't sound good. The man didn't sound good either; he sounded under too much control, he sounded frightened.

"What's your name anyway?" the man asked.

"James, but—"

"Listen, Dr. James, I know I'm not one of your regular patients, but I wondered. If you could tell me. If I might should come in. Or go to a hospital. Or what. I don't have a doctor—I haven't been to a doctor for—since I can't remember when. But I think I'm running a temperature, see, only I can't find where my wife put the thermometer. She's off at Ocean City for a few days. So, what should I do?"

"Dr. Landros is on call. Let me get in touch—"

"I don't feel good," the voice rumbled. Some people, James had learned, always didn't feel good; but this voice didn't sound like that kind of person. This sounded like the kind of person who when he said he didn't feel good meant he felt terrible.

"I'm not a doctor," James finally got in. "I'm just—"

"See, my wife took the car so I'm out here alone. Please, can't you think of something?"

Yes, James could: He needed to get the man's name, address, and phone number, then track down Dr. Landros. But he could hear panic in the voice.

"I read a book once—" he began.

"I don't need any book. Unless it's a medical book."

"Travels with Charley," James just continued, trying to get his calm voice through the man's panic. "And the writer's dog couldn't go to the bathroom."

"Okay. You think I should call a vet?" The voice sounded as if this was a reasonable suggestion. The man must be even more panicky than James had thought.

"So he gave him tranquilizers, and a drink—to relax him."

"I don't have tranquilizers. We don't have things like that."

"Look," James said. "I've got to get off the phone and find the doctor for you. If you have a drink and, I don't know, sit in a hot tub and—the writer rubbed the dog—"

"That hurts," the voice said, small and ashamed.

"Let me have your name, and your telephone number, and where you are," James asked.

"Herbert Wilkinson," the voice obeyed, and rattled off information that James wrote down. "Did that work for the dog?"

"Yes, but—"

"We've got whiskey. I already took aspirin."

"That's good," James said. "I'll find Dr. Landros, it won't take long. She'll be in touch with you as soon as she can, either on the phone or she'll come out."

"She? It's a woman?"

"She's a doctor."

"I guess. Yeah, okay. How long will it take?"

"I don't know," James said.

"What about you, will you be there? Where you are now? In case . . ."

"I'm not a doctor," James repeated. Then he thought he understood. "But I'll be here. Can you hang on for a little while longer?"

"I guess." The voice sounded more confident. "The dog was okay?"

"The dog was okay," James said. "It was nonfiction."

"It's just that—I mean, what if I explode or something."

James couldn't pretend to know about that danger. "I'll find the doctor."

"Okay, Dr. James. I'll be here. I'm not going anywhere," he made a rough joke, "unless it's to my eternal reward."

"You don't sound *that* bad," James answered before he thought, just saying exactly what he was thinking.

"I don't? I guess I don't. Okay. Thanks, Dr. James."

"I'm not—" James started to say, but the man hung up.

James called Dr. Landros's home first, but nobody answered. She wouldn't be out on her boat, because she was on call, so he didn't worry. He called the restaurant where she would have gone for a crab-cake sandwich, what she called her Saturday celebration. She had been there, but had left twenty minutes earlier. So James called Tydings grocery store, where Dr. Landros did her shopping. "Millie? It's James Tillerman. Is Dr. Landros there?"

"Just leaving," Millie said. "How are you all?"

James didn't have time for Millie's usual slow conversation. "Can you catch her? It's an emergency."

"An emergency? You want her for an emergency," Millie repeated the information. "Hold on, James. I'll try."

Impatient, James listened. The receiver clanked down on the countertop. Then he heard not much of anything, until a distant door banged and Dr. Landros's voice came on. She didn't waste any time. "What emergency?"

James told her what the man had told him, and what he had told the man. He gave her the number. She didn't even say thank you. "Got it, James," she said, and hung up.

It wasn't until James had called the answering service to tell them the man's number where Dr. Landros could be reached that he sat down at the desk and buried his face in his hands.

What had he been thinking of? That was just like him, wasn't it. Somebody says I'm sick and he talked about something he read in a book. Just because John Steinbeck's dog . . . It could hurt a human being to drink whiskey and sit around in a hot bath, maybe, if there was something wrong with his bladder, or something.

All alone in the office, thinking of what he'd done, James groaned. He didn't blame Dr. Landros for being angry at him.

He read so many books, anyway, who knew what was true and what false? As if life were a book, real life. What if the man died? What if James—acting like himself and talking about books he'd read, when there was somebody really sick—had told him the wrong thing, the exact wrong thing, and he died?

James didn't know anything, and especially nothing about the human body. There was so much to know and he only knew what they'd taught in school biology and health courses. He knew something, he guessed, but not much. He knew just about nothing compared to how much more there was to know.

James did the only thing he could think of. He was just waiting for Dr. Landros to call in, or to be able to call her and find out if the man was all right. In the meantime, all he could think of to do was walk into the doctor's office and look over the shelves of medical books there. At least he could find out if he'd given dangerous advice. It took him a while to find the right book, but once he did he took it back to the desk in the waiting room. There, he opened it and read, waiting.

He had no idea how much time passed before a scratching at the lock interrupted his appalled recognition of how many things could go wrong with the human excretory system. It was the scratching, and a clicking noise, that distracted him. Without thinking, James fell from the chair to the floor. Fear seized him, at the first faint sound, and it held him as the sounds continued. His whole body was cold, sweaty cold. If it was someone breaking in, because they thought doctors had drugs . . . if it was someone crazy on drugs, you didn't know what they'd do, they'd cut you to pieces for no reason at all. James had read about it. He crawled under the desk, curling himself up in the kneehole. His heart was thumping away and he had no idea in his head except being afraid. He closed his eyes, listening. "Oh no, oh no. Please, no," his mind said, over and over. The noises stopped.

He heard the door open. Footsteps, hesitating. Whoever it was didn't even close the door. A fresh current of air found James out easily where he was hunched there in the blindness of closed eyes, trying to be invisible. Whoever it was, moving slowly into the room, wasn't even thinking enough to close the door. James's jaw hurt and his stomach was holding so tight against breathing that those muscles hurt. He felt like he was shaking. "Oh please no." He opened his eyes.

He kept his eyes fixed on the flat panel of wood that was the front of the kneehole—trying not to see anything, hoping whoever it was would just steal something and go away—he didn't want to see anything because if he couldn't see anything then nothing could see him—but he couldn't help noticing something moving, feet coming toward the desk. Shoes.

The doctor's shoes, her legs.

The air emptied his lungs in a rush and his head banged up against the underside of the desk. How could he be such a jackass? Jerk, dork, wimp—James started to crawl backward out of the kneehole. Weenie. Ashamed, he was so ashamed. Not overly heroic, he said to himself sarcastically. Not too brave. But that, he thought, backing out, was just what he was like, wasn't it? All confident and acting big when it was only thinking and books, but anything physical—like baseball even—anything physical and he was no good at all. He stood up.

"Ah, Dr. James," Dr. Landros greeted him. "I saw your bike. I wondered where you'd gotten to."

"I didn't hear your car," James mumbled. "I told him I wasn't a doctor."

"You thought I was somebody breaking in?"

James waited for her to start laughing at him.

"Well, it's a hazard. One of the hazards of the medical profession. I don't blame you for hiding out. It makes good sense."

That made James feel better, except that he knew it wasn't common sense that made him hide. It was fear. "What about Mr. Wilkinson?" he asked.

Dr. Landros didn't answer. "I see you've been doing some research on your own."

"I'll put it back," James said. He took the book and followed her into her office. He replaced it on its shelf. Dr. Landros had pulled out a new file folder and a blank patient information sheet. She sat down at her desk.

"Did I tell him something dangerous?" James asked. "I guess I shouldn't have said anything. I didn't mean to." He stood in front of the desk, ready for a scolding. He just wanted to know the truth.

"He's all right. I got out there and he was jaybird naked, lying in the bathtub, drinking whiskey. You shouldn't have told him anything, James."

"I'm sorry. I won't ever again. I'm glad I didn't hurt him."

"Although what you told him was right enough, if that's worrying you. Didn't do any harm, and gave him the feeling he was doing something about it. You were lucky. You read the right book."

"I promise, I never will again." James waited. "He's okay now?"

"Temporarily. It could be one of several things—well, you were reading up on symptoms, you must know that. I'm sending him up for testing Monday. His wife came home, in the middle of this—they'd had some kind of a fight and she'd gone off to her sister's, so the whole thing could even be psychosomatic. But whatever, it's given him a scare. I don't know, James, men act as if—all of their manhood is in their penis. Everything that makes a man a man. I can't believe men are so foolish."

What was she doing talking to him like this? James thought. It was . . . you didn't . . . and what did he know about manhood anyway, what did she think he knew about it. Not much, he felt like telling her; but more than she did, because he was one. "Yeah, well, if they do, they do," he answered grumpily, because he didn't see why anyone should be looked down on just because he was male.

Dr. Landros stared at him, then she started laughing. "That's right, put me in my place."

"I didn't mean—"

"I know you didn't. Besides, I think you're right to object, if that's anything to you: I've got to be careful not to be sexist. So I'll try. Isn't it time for you to go home? You're a glutton for work—I don't know where you get your endurance from. Go on home," she said, adding—just as he reached the doorway—"Dr. James."

James just burst out laughing.

Riding his bike along the quiet roads, the air mellow around him as he rode through it, clouds chasing one another slowly across the sky and their shadows chasing themselves slowly over the flat land, James wondered along. His thoughts, wondering, followed one another, drifting like the clouds, almost aimless, maybe aimless, but maybe following the direction given by some invisible wind.

James rode into a breeze he made himself by riding along. He was feeling pretty good, so good he didn't even mind the work of pushing the pedals, pushing the bicycle along. He'd helped somebody. He'd just said what he was thinking, just acted natural, and it had been a right thing to do. He knew he shouldn't have given any advice, and he wouldn't again, but he really liked the way helping someone made him feel. He wondered: Doctors made good money—they made good money and they helped people too. James felt pretty good about saying the right things to Herbert Wilkinson; he could almost imagine how it would feel to be a doctor and know what to do to really make a difference, the way Dr. Landros must feel.

James had never thought of himself as the kind of person who could do things and make other people better. What, he wondered, had he been thinking of not to realize that if you were as smart as he was you could really choose what to do? What had he thought all this smartness was good for?

He guessed maybe he didn't mind being James Tillerman, didn't mind being himself. No matter what other people, kids, thought of him. He'd grow up, and being grown up would be easier; one thing about adults—he thought of the adults he knew—they seemed easier just being themselves. He'd be okay, if he didn't get lost from himself along the way. Francis Verricker, he thought, had gotten lost. How, or why, James didn't know, and he never would know, he guessed. But that didn't matter for James. It was up to James to see that he didn't get lost. James pedaled along, just feeling good.

Until he remembered that he was virtually cheating on that French report—more than virtually cheating, he told himself. Actually cheating. Even if Andy Walker had instigated it, and would do the actual act of cheating, James had gone along. Had helped out. Had done it. He tried to push the thought away and forget about it. But this time it wouldn't go away. James slowed down, no longer eager to get home, or get anywhere. Because if he did that, that was the kind of person he was.

All right, he said to himself. That's done. What's done is done. But never again, he promised himself. I can't do anything about that now, but I won't ever again let myself do anything like that, not in any way.

The promise helped . . . some.

CHAPTER 11

Sammy leaned back in his seat and stretched his legs out. Ernie was up there babbling away about baseball. Sammy kept his face turned toward Ernie, so it would look like he was paying attention. He had the evaluation sheet in front of him.

Ernie's was the second report of the day, following Shirley's report on how the Chesapeake Bay was getting polluted. What Shirley said made Sammy uneasy, uncomfortable: How could people be so dumb? The dumbest thing of all was to keep on doing it, even after they could see the bad effects it had, cutting down the trees, and using fertilizers that ran off into the bay. He was glad when Shirley finished and sat down, even though he gave her high marks on every category of the evaluation sheet. You'd think, Sammy thought, that somebody, the governor or the president or someone, would just stop the destruction. You'd think that somebody who had the power, and was in charge, would do something.

It was almost a relief to have Ernie standing up there, looking like a potato, a couple of notecards in his hand. Ernie wasn't nervous at all. It sounded to Sammy as if Ernie had spent maybe ten minutes, tops, looking up baseball in a little kid's encyclopedia. It was a terrible report. Ernie would tell some fact, then look up and say something—usually something stupid—about that fact. After people stopped laughing he'd read off his next fact.

"Baseball was invented in 1839," Ernie said. He looked at the class. "Which was a pretty long time ago." People giggled, because if there was anything stupider than Ernie acting like Ernie, nobody knew what it was. It was a joke, Ernie giving a report. Ernie was a joke. "In 1939 the Baseball Hall of Fame was opened, in Cooperstown, New York. That's New York State, not New York City, in case any of you are wondering. Nineteen thirty-nine is a hundred years after 1839," he added.

Sammy was giving Ernie pretty high marks for engaging interest, because most people were enjoying themselves; the low marks came on content and organization, preparation and delivery.

When Miss Karin stood up from her desk and said, "Thank you, Ernie. Are there any questions?" Custer muttered into Sammy's ear, "Yeah, I'd like to know how he got into seventh grade." Sammy snickered, as did others who'd heard.

There were thirty-six kids in the class, and about half of the reports had been given. Reports made an easy week of English, because all you had to do was come to class and listen, checking off the evaluation sheet. After class, people told one another what their evaluations had been. An awful lot of the evaluations had to do with how popular someone was. Robin had given a pretty good report on jet fighters. Sammy had liked it and Miss Karin had said it was good. Even Custer, who'd been asking Sammy why he was friends with a wimp like Robin, thought it was interesting. But most of Robin's evaluations had been bad ones, just because Robin wasn't well liked; everybody agreed with Custer about Robin, so they gave him low marks. Sammy didn't see why Custer was so down on Robin. "I bet he cries, too," Custer had said. So what? Sammy wanted to say, but he didn't. Instead he got sarcastic: "Real men don't cry?" "C'mon, Sammy, you know what I mean," was all Custer answered. Sammy guessed he did know, but "No, I don't. Tell me," was what he'd said. "Why are we fighting about that baby face?" Custer had asked.

Sammy didn't know. He didn't like someone telling him who to be friends with, for one thing, even if that someone was a friend of his. He didn't exactly know how he felt about Robin either, because the thing he liked best about Robin was his mother. Maybe. "I'm not fighting," he'd said to Custer.

Miss Karin called Sammy's attention back to class. "You're on, Sammy," she said, smiling at him.

Sammy got up from his desk. He was never nervous. People liked him, and they liked listening to him. Mostly, he got off some good jokes, and he kept things short; he tried to give the kind of report he liked listening to. He didn't have any notecards, because he never had any trouble remembering what he planned to say. He stood at the front of the class and looked around at everyone. Making eye contact was what they called it on the evaluation sheet.

They sat in straight rows, in their desks, all of them looking at him. The girls were looking at him and the boys were looking at him. They each had a fresh evaluation sheet, waiting. They each had a pencil, ready to write things down. They were mostly his friends—Chris and Jason, Billy and Pete and Tom Childress, and everyone except the ones he didn't like. He looked at them.

Sammy couldn't remember a word of what he was going to say. He couldn't even remember his topic, practically. If he opened his mouth, he knew no words would come out. He just stood there, staring stupidly back.

He had no idea what was going on with him. If this was nervousness, he could sympathize with people who got nervous. But why should he be nervous?

Sammy jammed his hands into his back pockets and kind of spread his legs apart. He did this because he could feel his whole left leg just shaking, vibrating away, and with his legs apart he could lock his kneecaps. It felt like his stomach was jiggling and he didn't know how to get himself going. He opened his mouth. "Um," he said. But nothing came into his mind. Nothing else came out of his mouth.

He looked out the windows: The sky was smoky gray with low clouds and a misty rain filled the air, not falling, but sort of floating down.

"Um," Sammy said again. Mythology, that was it. Greek mythology. James's idea.

But what was wrong with him that he was suddenly nervous?

"My report is on Greek mythology," he said. A lot of people didn't like to hear that; he could see it on their faces. He looked at Miss Karin and she smiled at him, to encourage him. She smiled at him with her red mouth. She always kept her lipstick fresh and bright. Something about her red smile drove any other thoughts out of his head.

"Um," Sammy said. "My report is on Greek mythology," he said.

"I guess we know that by now," Ernie said. Some people laughed so he asked, "Is the report over?"

Shut up your fat face, Sammy wanted to say. Ernie made him mad, trying to submarine his report. "But what I'm going to talk about," he said, remembering now, "is just one story. Because I thought it was interesting. But first, I want to say a couple of general things about Greek mythology." He was saying it all wrong. He should have said "What we call Greek mythology was their religion." That was the important thing and he'd omitted it.

Robin was watching Sammy, looking interested. Custer had a little smile on his face, probably waiting for the jokes. Sammy was okay now, he hoped.

"The important thing is, that this was a religion. We treat it the same way we treat fairy tales, but it was a religion. People believed in it. The kind of religion it was, is a nature religion." He heard how he was repeating that word, religion, and how wrong that sounded, repeating it like that. "The Greeks believed that different parts of nature had gods who controlled them." What a little kid sentence; it didn't even say what it meant. Shut *up*, Sammy said to himself. He took a breath and tried again. "Like, there was a god who controlled the ocean, and a goddess of war, and every river or field had its own little god or goddess. So that everything had a reason for it. If lightning struck, for example, that was Zeus—or Jupiter, to the Romans—he was the king of the gods, he would send lightning bolts to destroy something. Or, if you fell in love, that was Eros—or Cupid—who had shot you with a golden arrow and you couldn't help it. So that, in a way, the people were helpless, and everything that happened was the gods' idea. So you can see it's different from what we think." Now he was really off the track. But he'd never thought of that before, the way believing that the gods had all the power kept you helpless.

Not too interested, most of the faces. A few were, Sammy saw: Custer was, and Shirley he thought, although she was doing that trick of pulling her hair down over her face and chewing on it. Robin, too. But most of them weren't too interested at all. He hurried along. In a way, he just wanted it over, because it didn't look like his report was as good as he'd thought.

"My report was actually about the god of the sun, Apollo. The Greeks thought that the sun and moon were chariots, driven across the day sky and night sky by twins, Apollo and his sister Artemis, or Diana. Do you know what a chariot is?" Sammy asked. He hadn't planned to ask that, but it struck him that some people might not know, and for the story they needed to know. So he explained what a chariot was, and how it was pulled by horses. He got back on the subject. "Apollo was mostly the sun god, but he was also god of prophecies. When you wanted to find out what was going to happen you'd go to his temple at Delphi and the priestess would go into a trance and tell you his answer. He was also the god of music. He was always pictured as a very handsome young man." There were a couple of giggles at that. Sammy ignored them.

"Anyway, I thought I'd tell you one of the myths about Apollo," he said. That sounded so bad—he almost wished he did have notecards, and had written down how to say things right. "The Greek gods," he began the story, "often fell in love with mortal women, and they'd have children. I guess these children were half-god, half-mortal. Apollo once fell in love, and the woman had a son named Phaëton. Apollo didn't live with his family, because he was a god and he had to drive his chariot across the sky every day. Besides, the gods would fall in love and then just forget about the woman and never see her again. So this Phaëton lived with his mother, down on earth. She told him who his father was, but it was supposed to be a secret. Well, Phaëton was just a kid, and the other kids started teasing him, telling him he didn't have a father, and all. He got angry one day, and told them who his father was." Sammy wondered if they needed a reminder. "That his father was Apollo, the sun god." No, he'd been wrong, they hadn't needed a reminder.

"The kids didn't believe him, of course. I mean, would you?" Nobody would, they agreed; at least they were listening now, interested. They liked being told a story.

"So Phaëton got really upset, and he went to his mother. I don't know what she said to him, the story doesn't say, but he made up his mind to prove to the other kids that he really was Apollo's son. So what he did was, he went up to Mount Olympus, where the gods all lived, and he went up to Apollo. Apollo knew who he was. Phaëton asked his father if he could have one wish granted. Apollo wasn't thinking, I guess—he just said yes. Phaëton made him promise first, he made Apollo swear by the river Styx—which is one of the rivers that surround the underworld in Greek mythology. That was the most sacred vow a god could make, to swear by the Styx. When a god swore by the Styx that he'd do something, he had to do it. Then, once Apollo had promised, Phaëton told him what he wanted."

Sammy waited there, just for a minute, letting their curiosity build. He had them, he could see. Waiting was the way to tell the story—that at least was right and he was sure of it. He waited just the right time and then told them.

"He wanted Apollo to let him drive the chariot of the sun."

"I wouldn't have asked for that. I'd have asked for money," Jason said.

"I'd have asked for immortality," Custer said.

"What happened?" Tom Childress asked.

"Apollo tried to talk him out of it, but the more his father tried to convince him the more Phaëton wanted to do it. Apollo had to give in, because he'd sworn the sacred vow. So, the next morning, Phaëton—who was just a kid, like us—climbed up into the chariot of the sun. I guess, Apollo was probably still trying to get him to ask for something else, even when he was handing over the reins. But Phaëton only wanted the one thing, because that would show the other kids he'd been telling the truth."

"Anyway, what was so bad about that, driving the chariot?" Shirley wondered.

"Because it was dangerous," Sammy said. "Because the horses—nobody knows how many there were, maybe two of them, maybe four—they were huge. Strong and fast. I mean, they pulled the *sun.* They were pretty wild and strong. And Phaëton wasn't a god or anything, he was just a kid. Would you be able to do that? Be the one who controls horses strong and fearless enough to pull the whole burning sun across the sky? Anyway, when Apollo unbolted the stable doors, the horses knew they were supposed to go out and follow dawn across the sky. So they went tearing out of there, like every day. I guess, Phaëton probably felt pretty good right then. There he was, about to drive the chariot of the sun across the whole sky where everyone would see him.

"But it didn't take the horses long to feel that there was somebody different holding the reins. They could feel how weak he was and how inexperienced. And they started to run wild. The more they ran wild, the more they ran wilder, if you know what I mean. Phaëton couldn't stop them, no matter how hard he pulled on the reins. The horses just went where they wanted to. They went up high and then they just—rushed down, really close to the earth, and where they came close they scorched the land, burning up forests and drying up rivers—destroying towns and people, too. They went sideways, zigzagging across the earth, and nobody knew what was going on because the sun had gone crazy. They went way up, and then down. Phaëton couldn't do anything about it, he couldn't even begin to control them. Things were pretty bad. So Zeus—remember, he's the king of the gods?—heard the commotion. He saw what was happening. I guess he was probably pretty angry at Apollo, and Apollo had to go along with what Zeus said because Zeus was the king. Zeus had to stop the destruction, because he was king. So he fired off a thunderbolt, and killed Phaëton, right there in the chariot. He just blew Phaëton away. Then Apollo got in and got the horses back under control, and things got back to normal. But Phaëton was dead."

That was the end. It took people a few seconds to realize that. Then, Miss Karin said, "Thank you, Sammy. Are there any questions?"

Sammy waited. He didn't know if he wanted any questions or not. He was thinking: He'd rather have gone back and tried to do a better job of telling the end of the story. He could see it happening, but the way he'd told it wasn't anything like what he could see. He could see the terrified boy, and the blinding gold ball, and the spittle flying back from the horses' mouths. And Zeus, cool and sad, with the thunderbolt in his hand and Apollo, wise and sad, beside him. And Phaëton's mother, watching up from below. He could see it but he hadn't said it. He was also thinking: if he were like Phaëton with wanting to be an astronaut, which was kind of like driving a chariot across the sky, except your ship would go across space skies. Sammy realized that he didn't know why the idea of being an astronaut was so appealing to him.

Ernie's hand went up. "I guess that Phaëton guy was a bastard, hunh?"

A few snickers greeted his boldness, and people waited to hear Miss Karin say something, which she chose not to. Sammy didn't say anything either—it wasn't a question, it was a way to get to say something you weren't supposed to say. Sammy just looked at Ernie. And what was so wrong with being a bastard, anyway. Not every mother got married, as he had reason to know. Did Ernie know that, and was he trying to get at Sammy? Because, Sammy stared on, if that was the case, it was time Ernie learned better. Maybe Momma should have gotten married, and he didn't know why she didn't except he figured it was his father's fault if she didn't want to, but he wasn't going to let anybody say things about her. Maybe there was something wrong with her that she didn't get married, but he didn't think so.

Ernie's eyes dropped as the silence built louder.

"Are there any other questions?" Miss Karin asked.

"I want to know how they could believe the sun was a chariot that got driven across the sky," Custer asked. "It doesn't even look like a chariot. And besides, it isn't the sun that moves around the earth, the earth rotates around the sun."

"People used to think the earth was flat," Miss Karin reminded them. "Remember, the way everyone thought Columbus would sail off the edge of the world? It wasn't until Galileo invented the telescope that people understood that the earth does in fact revolve around the sun."

"Besides," Sammy added, "if you imagine it, doesn't it make sense? If you just look at the sky, the way it looks like a bowl upside down over the earth, and the sun goes up one side and then down the other."

"I guess," Custer said.

"Does the girl's name Diana come from the goddess of the moon?" a girl named Diana asked.

"I think," Sammy said.

"So I'm named after a goddess. Neat," Diana said.

"I thought," Chris asked, "that the god of war was a man. You said it was a goddess of war."

"There were two kinds of war," Sammy explained. "There still are, I guess. The male god, Ares or Mars, was the god of offensive war, when you go out to conquer territory or something. The goddess was Athena, or Minerva, and she was goddess of defensive war, when somebody was attacking your home. That's different."

"Did anyone ever think," Shirley asked, "if maybe what really happened was that a comet came close to the earth? A comet's tail could really burn the earth, all those particles and things, and heat. Did anyone say that's what might have actually happened? And it got turned into a story."

"Not that I read," Sammy said. Shirley was the smartest girl in the class and that was an interesting question. "But I guess it could have. You mean if myths might have some basis in reality? Except the story gets changed around. Like George Washington chopping down the cherry tree and saying he couldn't tell a lie. That probably didn't happen, but probably something like it did?" Shirley nodded, and chewed on her hair. But why should she look embarrassed?

"I don't understand, Miss Karin," Pete asked. "Is it a report if you just tell a story?"

A number of voices seconded the objection. Sammy didn't know what to say: Was Pete trying to get him in trouble? Even if Sammy had thought that a report someone made didn't meet requirements, he wouldn't have said so to the teacher. But why should Pete want to make Sammy look bad? Pete had been one of the first to give his report, and it wasn't very good but that was because he hadn't worked very hard on it. Sammy didn't understand, and he didn't understand Pete, and he didn't understand why people were agreeing with Pete. He looked at Miss Karin, where she sat at her big wooden desk.

"That depends," she answered, "on what story you tell, and why you tell it."

"Because you didn't tell us we could do that," Pete continued stubbornly.

There were more, and louder, murmurs of agreement. Sammy thought, he didn't know anything about these supposed friends of his. He'd done something wrong, he could feel that they were thinking that; they were thinking he was getting away with something. And they didn't want him to get away with it. He stood up there, in front of everyone, feeling that.

"Where did you learn all that stuff, about the gods and all?" Tom asked Sammy.

"We've got books at home. My grandfather had a lot of books, I guess he used to read about it," Sammy said. He didn't know anything about his grandfather, either, he thought. That was funny, the way Gram almost never talked about him; even when she did, then she didn't say anything good. His father, his grandfather, that Uncle John—the only one she ever talked about was Bullet, and then not much. What was wrong with the Tillerman men? But he couldn't stand up there, thinking private thoughts in front of everybody.

"Sammy?" Shirley had another question. "Why did Apollo let his son drive the chariot? I don't understand that. He knew—he must have known what would happen. I mean, he was a god, and you said of prophecy, so he knew the future. He must have known Phaëton couldn't control the horses. Didn't he? So he shouldn't have let him do it. He should have stopped him."

"Or gone with him," Robin suggested.

"He promised," Sammy explained. "He'd sworn by the Styx."

"Yeah, well, my father makes a lot of promises. That doesn't mean he keeps them," Jason said.

"But he was a god," Sammy argued. "The gods can't just break their word."

"My father thinks he's God, if you ask me," Ernie cracked. "Doesn't everybody's? Doesn't yours?" he asked Sammy, grinning at him.

Sammy couldn't answer. He had no idea.

Robin's hand went up. "What do you think is the moral of the story? I think it's that he should have listened to his father. Is that what you think?"

"I don't know," Sammy said. "Because—once he'd made up his mind, Phaëton couldn't change it. He was just thinking about proving to the kids that he was really Apollo's son."

"I think the moral is that he should have listened."

"Maybe," Sammy said. He didn't think it was as simple as that, but he didn't know why.

There were no more questions, but there was one more thing he wanted to say. “I don’t know if anyone noticed, but it sort of struck me that in this story, the father is also the son, because Apollo is the sun.”

A few groans were the only response he heard.

The bell rang then, so Sammy didn’t have to say anything else. They all dropped their evaluation sheets on Miss Karin’s desk, and hurried out the door to lunch. The teacher held Sammy back for a minute. She was gathering up the sheets, and Sammy saw that almost no one had given him top marks. And he’d thought it was such a good report.

“I just want to thank you,” Miss Karin said to him.

Sammy didn’t know why she said that.

“I’ve suspected—not that you gave me much reason to hope—but I suspected all year you could do excellent work, and this report was excellent. You really knew your stuff, didn’t you?”

“Yes,” Sammy said, his eyes on the sheets. He almost wished he hadn’t done such a good job.

“Sammy, you know as well as I do that these evaluation sheets are never—or rarely—much more than popularity contests. Believe me, it was excellent.”

“Thanks.” Sammy didn’t know why he was feeling sorry for himself anyway, and he’d never thought he was the kind of person who did that. But he did do that about playing tennis, didn’t he?—acting as if he wasn’t going to be able to play with a tennis class next year, acting as if he couldn’t wait until then, as if it wasn’t fair that he had to wait.

“If the written report is nearly as good—”

“It’s different, it’s a straight report,” Sammy warned her.

“Good. Because I’d dearly love to give you an A on the project. How’d you like that?”

Sammy shrugged. He didn’t know. “I never thought about it.”

That made her smile with her bright-mouth smile, and her eyes smiled too. "All right, Sammy Tillerman, have it your way. I'm just saying thank you for proving to me that I was right all along. There is one thing, though. . . ."

"Yeah?"

"I don't know Greek, but I don't think in the original language you'd get that sun-son homonym," Miss Karin told him.

Sammy hadn't even thought of that. "So what?" he said.

"As you say. Okay, you're finished, you can go eat your lunch now."

Sammy did as he was told, but not because she told him.

In the cafeteria, he went to sit with Custer, although he saw that Robin had saved him a place. He didn't want anything to change, he thought, taking his sandwiches out of the brown bag. He wanted things to stay the way they had been. He had a terrible feeling that they weren't going to, but he sat down next to Custer the way he had for years and years, as if things hadn't changed a bit. The trouble was, he thought, nodding his head while Custer said he liked Sammy's report, the way friends were supposed to whether it had been a good one or not—the trouble was that he would really rather have sat with Robin. But was that because he wanted to be invited back to Robin's house? Or because he felt sort of sorry for the kid? Or because he wanted to talk about the real moral of the story? Sammy didn't know, and he wanted to know. Not knowing made him feel helpless, and angry. But he didn't even know whom he was angry at. And he wasn't helpless, was he?

Ernie leaned over from behind him, his potato face grinning. "Hey, Tillerman, you never said whether your father thinks he's God."

He was doing it on purpose. Sammy knew that now. Knew it for sure. Knowing it for sure made him feel good; it made things clear.

"Why it's Ernie, Mr. Baseball Expert," Sammy started. He waited for the laughs to die down. He knew how to handle this. "I get the feeling that you're trying to pick a fight with me." He grinned back up at Ernie's stupid face. He looked—he knew it—all friendly and joky, which was a lie.

Ernie hadn't expected such a direct attack. "Now that you're going to go getting smart on us," he muttered.

"Do you remember the last time Ernie and I had a fight?" Sammy asked Custer, keeping his voice loud so everyone could hear. "I kind of enjoyed that, didn't you?"

Custer was laughing.

"He looked so cute with all that mud all over his face. Sort of like a pile of mashed potatoes with lots of gravy. Remember that fight, Ernie?" Sammy asked, still smiling away.

"I didn't say anything about a fight," Ernie's eyes looked around.

"Gee, you could have fooled me," Sammy answered. Poor Ernie, Sammy was twisting the words so he had to either fight or look stupid; he could almost feel sorry for Ernie.

"But if you want one," Ernie's voice tried to sound threatening.

"Hey, sure. It would be fun," Sammy said. Then he started laughing and his words came struggling out because when he thought of it, it just made him laugh. "As long—" he gulped in air, trying to finish—"as long—as long as you don't—fall on me."

The laughter—Sammy's and everybody else's—drove Ernie away from their table to the far side of the big room. Sammy almost fell over, he was laughing so hard.

CHAPTER 12

James didn't know *what* had gotten into Sammy. Sammy was suddenly coming at him, and coming back at him, about their father. "Did he steal that money from Mrs. Rottman's purse? I bet he did," he'd say, and "What about that gambling, do you think that was crooked? How would you go about fixing a high school game? Would you make a lot of money that way? Would he have been poor, do you think, would a candymaker have made much money?"

James didn't know any of the answers, but Sammy just kept asking anyway. "If you never graduated from high school, could you get a job as a sailor?"

"Merchant seaman," James corrected, his mind elsewhere.

"Whatever. Do you think that requires a high school diploma? There's more ways of being smart than in school you know."

"I know," James said, trying to keep his ideas for the French report clear, while Sammy talked.

"But he was smart in school, too, wasn't he? He must have loved Momma, don't you think? Because he kept coming back. I mean, I never saw him so I don't remember, but there are the four of us. That proves something, doesn't it?"

James guessed it did, but he had decided to forget about it, to forget about wondering about it. It wouldn't do any good to wonder, or worry, and besides, he didn't know that he cared anymore about his father. Whoever he was. It wouldn't make any difference, it wouldn't bring back those years when he hadn't been there. James was busy, anyway, between school and work. "Let it lie until summer," he finally asked.

"What's the matter with you?" Sammy demanded. "You were all hot to find out not so long ago."

James shrugged. He didn't know what was the matter with him. If anything was. He was feeling mostly content these days—he was always busy, and he was doing things the way he wanted to do them, even when it meant he didn't get the grades he was used to. Like in English, where she gave him a B- because he didn't do the assigned topic. He thought he had done it, and he knew why he thought so; but she didn't ask him what he thought, she told him it was wrong. James knew he'd be singing with the chorus next year, instead of trying to play baseball and prove he wasn't a dork, if playing baseball had anything to do with that. It wasn't as if you had all the time in the world, it wasn't as if you were going to live a hundred years, it wasn't as if anybody guaranteed you any amount of time at all. James figured he'd spend his time the way he wanted to. Figuring that—it was as if a dark shadow that had been riding around on his back all of his life had floated away. There was a dark clinging thing and he had unwrapped its fingers from his throat and tossed it back into the darkness it had come from. That wasn't exactly true, he knew, but it was the way he felt.

"I bet if we could find out something about the boats he sailed on, I bet we could find someone who knew him. Or maybe him. Do you think?" Sammy asked.

James nodded, his mind on the fairy-tale aspects of *The Hunchback of Notre Dame,* which was like *Beauty and the Beast,* only without any magic spells or happy-ever-after ending.

"Do you think you have to join a union? To be a merchant seaman. Where would you have to go to do that?"

"I don't know, Sammy. Look, I've got work to do. Why don't you ask Gram?"

"I can't," Sammy said. "She'd think I wasn't happy to be living here. She wouldn't understand."

"She might. Don't underestimate her."

Sammy shook his head, his face serious, his hair, bleached to white-gold from the hours outside, falling into his eyes. "Maybe, if I can find him, then I'll tell her. But it would be different if I ask. She wouldn't know what I need to know, anyway. Did I tell you that Robin Kelly can work this summer, with me?"

James tried not to get impatient, or look too obviously at the door of his room. He really wanted to get back to work. He really wanted this year to be over—so he could begin forgetting it. He wanted to give a report that was as good as he could make it, as good as he could make it, working as hard as he could—to make up for Andy Walker's Camus report. Nobody but James would know, but James would, and he'd feel a little better about himself if he'd done his own work as well as he possibly could.

"Anyway, I thought Maybeth—"

Sammy shook his head. "She was just being nice. She works around the house, and Gram needs her."

"How do you know she didn't mean it?" James wasn't so sure, but Sammy was usually right about Maybeth.

"It makes sense," Sammy said, as if that was an explanation.

James didn't want to worry about it. "Go away, Sammy. I've got mountains of work to do."

"So you can get A's and be a lawyer?"

"I'm not so sure about that any more," James admitted.

"I don't believe you," Sammy said, but he did go away, leaving James alone. James had been almost hoping Sammy would ask why he wasn't sure, so he could talk with his brother about maybe being a doctor. But Sammy wasn't interested, apparently.

Sammy believed what he'd always believed about James, as if he didn't know people could change.

Within a few days, Sammy had found out that the merchant seamen had a union, that you had to belong to it to be anything higher than a sailor, and that the union headquarters were in Baltimore. "So we have to go to Baltimore. But I can't figure out how to get there. Will they be open on a weekend? Are there buses? How long would it take us to hitchhike up there do you think?"

"Hitchhiking is pretty stupid," James told his brother.

"Oh yeah?" Sammy asked. He was weeding the garden again, and he'd called James over when James arrived home from work. "So what?"

"People sometimes—especially with kids, they think kids are helpless so if they mean harm they'll go for kids. You know that. Why do you think Dicey never tried hitchhiking, when we came down here?" Sammy thought a lot of Dicey. He thought everything Dicey did was about perfect.

"Jeff's father goes up to Baltimore to teach," was Sammy's answer. James didn't let his face show the smile he was feeling, at the way Sammy wouldn't admit that James had convinced him. He didn't know what had gotten into Sammy, but he knew that if Sammy thought James thought he'd won, then Sammy would make sure to correct that impression. Even if he had to do something stupid to prove it. Sammy went on, thinking out loud.

"He goes on school days and Gram wouldn't get us out of another school day. Besides, he stays up two or three days, anyway. I could ask the Professor, he likes me."

"Everybody likes you," James reminded his brother, who was hunched there among the spreading zucchini plants, his hands working away, working without even thinking about it.

"Yeah, sure," Sammy said. He was pleased James thought, even if he was trying to sound sarcastic. "I'm Mr. Popularity."

James turned away. Sammy just didn't know and couldn't imagine how things could be for other people.

When Mr. Lingerle left after dinner that Thursday, Sammy followed him out the door. It was only a few minutes later that he came running up the stairs, his feet pounding as he took them two at a time, and burst into James's room. "He'll take us, this Saturday, he'll take us to Easton and we can get a bus, and he can spend the night with his friend who has an antique store and so can we. He'll drive us home Sunday."

James didn't know what to say. He had to go to work Saturday. He had the final draft of his report to write, because it was due to be given next week. He didn't want his life interrupted.

Sammy stood in the doorway, his eyes eager and his jeans filthy. His feet were bare, because once the weather got warm, Sammy stopped wearing shoes except to school. James looked at his brother's feet, and his ankles. Those bones fitted together like a beautifully made machine, to enable walking, running, turning corners—all kinds of positions worked in the ankles. They were pretty incredible, if you thought about them. "You need a bath," James said.

Sammy just laughed. When Sammy laughed, it made you smile; there was something about Sammy. "How did you get him to agree?" James asked. "What did you tell him?"

"The truth," Sammy said, as if there were no other possible answer. "So, will you? I'll go by myself, but I'd rather have you with me. With the twenty dollars I've got, and the money you've been making, we can stay in a cheap hotel or something if it takes too long and we miss the bus back. I called the bus company."

That was what convinced James, that and seeing how young his brother looked, for all his stocky strong body—he still looked like a kid. If Sammy was going to go up there, regardless, James thought he'd better go with him.

"We can just ask Gram if we can go to Easton with Mr. Lingerle," Sammy said. "We won't have to tell her anything. She'll say yes. I'll ask her."

"Okay," James said. He could call Dr. Landros, that would be all right. He could do his report on Friday evening. "I guess you've got this all planned out."

"You don't think you got all the brains in this family, do you?"

James didn't know what the answer to that question was.

Things certainly went smoothly for Sammy. Mr. Lingerle got them to a noon bus in Easton, and then gave them a slip of paper with the name and phone number of where he could be reached. "Call me about meeting you," he said, his round face looking a little worried. James suspected that the man hadn't thought very hard before he answered yes when Sammy asked; now Mr. Lingerle was thinking of all the bad things that might happen, and he was worried. "Call me, collect, if you need anything."

"Sure," Sammy said, putting the paper into his pocket.

"We'll be all right," James told the piano teacher. "We've got enough money for a hotel and all if we miss the last bus." There were three buses on Saturday, at morning, noon, and evening, from Easton to Baltimore, and three back.

"I know you're all much more independent and self-reliant than I was," Mr. Lingerle said, almost as if he were talking to himself, convincing himself. "Probably more than I am even now," he added. "Take care, then. And good luck." He reached out to shake their hands, which was a little weird, James thought. Then he went back to his car, hitching his trousers up, his gait rolling and slow, relaxed.

"Is he losing weight?" James asked Sammy. They hadn't talked about diets at all since that one night, but now James wondered.

Sammy was staring at the piece of paper, which he'd taken out of his pocket to read. "It's a woman. Her name's Mary Millay."

"Women own businesses," James reminded Sammy. "Especially antique stores. Or clothing."

"But his friend is a woman," Sammy said. He looked at James, and he looked a little angry.

"Is there a law that says men and women can't be friends?" James asked.

"But what about Maybeth?" Sammy asked.

James didn't even bother answering that. Sammy really was just a kid.

The bus cost them thirty-six dollars for two round-trip tickets. Sammy hadn't expected them to be so expensive. When he called to find out about if the buses ran, he hadn't asked how much the tickets were. He wanted to just get one-way tickets, but James wouldn't do that. James wanted his return ticket safe in his pocket. If the bus hadn't been about to arrive, Sammy would have quarreled; but he had to either give in or miss the bus. He gave in.

James let Sammy have the window seat. This was his brother's trip. He reviewed the financial position, as the bus moved out of Easton and onto the highway, crossed the Bay Bridge and went into Annapolis to let off and pick up passengers. Sammy's twenty dollars was all they had left, so if they missed the evening bus back down to Easton they'd need to spend the night in Baltimore. There were places, like the Y, where you could sleep overnight for only a couple of dollars. Those places were safe enough. You could eat pretty cheaply if you had to, doughnuts and milk, or hot cereal; breakfast wasn't an expensive meal. Sandwiches or hamburgers—you could probably feed two fine for not more than five or seven dollars. It would be close, but they had things covered. Besides, they could go without eating a day; nobody starved to death in a day; so the worst possibility was safe enough. Anyway, they'd just eaten a couple of huge sandwiches apiece, which Sammy had packed for them, and cookies and oranges; so that would hold them for a while. It was lucky, too, because James had just plunked down all but a couple of dollars of two weeks' wages for those round-trip tickets. Sammy was carrying the rest of the money, but it was enough. Unless something like being mugged and robbed happened, they'd be okay. And they could always call Mr. Lingerle, if they needed help. James thought, he'd thought of everything you could think of in advance. He leaned back in his seat, smelling the conditioned air of the bus. He didn't much like its flavor, but it wasn't as bad as the diesel fumes the bus trailed behind it.

The route the bus took followed the main highway, but cut off it to the left and right to stop in the little towns along the way. The highway was lined with new shopping centers that had big chain stores and four movie theaters together, and with old roadside businesses—bars, food stands, garages surrounded by cars that had been in accidents. It was a couple of hours before they approached Baltimore itself. They traveled then without stopping, through a belt of industrial parks with boxy windowless buildings in thick rows, past little houses packed close in together, and then along the rebuilt area around the harbor, where the fancy aquarium poked right out into the harbor. At the bus terminal Sammy stood up before the engines had even stopped. He and James were the first ones off. "We've got a ways to walk," Sammy told James. "It's a couple of miles. Let's get going."

Sammy turned to walk off. James just followed. At least, when they went to Cambridge, James had explained where they were going.

"It's down by Fort McHenry," Sammy said.

"That's where the 'Star-Spangled Banner' was written," James said. He didn't ask what *it* was. "You want to take a look at it? The War of 1812," he explained. "The British came up the Chesapeake Bay. I guess, Baltimore was a more important city then." Sammy just moved along the crowded sidewalk, moving between and around the other people. James stayed beside him. "The prime military targets have changed entirely, now. Nobody'd bother bombing Baltimore now."

"I can see why," Sammy said.

James looked around him. Crowded streets—crowded with lanes of traffic, cars and trucks and buses; crowded with the sounds of motors working and horns hooting, and with the heat-swollen odors of gas engines—the crowded street ran between sidewalks crowded with people either walking along or waiting in lines at a bus stop. The people in cars, except for a few that had their windows down and radios blaring out, rode sealed in, windows rolled up tight, air-conditioned; but the people on the sidewalks, or clustered at crossings, talked to one another or studied the displays that crowded store windows. You never saw the same face twice. Each building, even though they were all similar in their mass and general design, had its individuality, in molded ledges under upper story windows or in the way blocks of glass and steel had been put together in the more modern buildings. The sidewalk was filmed with black, grimy dirt, and so were the store windows. Papers and empty food containers, cigar ends and cigarette butts, puddles of melted ice cream, all kinds of litter, edged the sidewalk and gathered in the gutters. He wished the city was cleaner, because it was so filled with life and variety and possibility, all swirling around, filled with energy and with going places. All ages, colors, sizes, shapes of people moved past them or along with them. James could have spent the whole afternoon just walking up and down that street, his brain trying to take in and remember everything he was seeing and hearing, his brain working away on what he was seeing and hearing, wondering.

But Sammy turned them off to the right, onto a street than ran beside a highway. They walked parallel to the harbor, through open areas, open lots, and occasional clusters of newly built row houses with straggly grass struggling up through packed dirt, with narrow windows on their brick façades, like old-fashioned border fortifications where the windows were just wide enough to let a bowman shoot through. James was interested by the ways in which the architects and city planners had contrived to make this development look both attractive and safe to potential home-buyers. Nobody was outside, although a couple of lawns were being sprinkled.

"I hate this place," Sammy said. James didn't answer, because he was busy looking and thinking, but he didn't agree. The downtown needed cleaning up, and this area needed time for the grass and scrawny trees to do some growing, but that was all. And there was so much life packed into such a small area.

They moved on, to older, unimproved blocks, where older row houses crowded up close to the sidewalks and leaned up against one another. Here, people sat on stoops and watched the two boys walking along. Here James began to get nervous, to listen for footsteps following them. It was something to do with the doorways that had two-by-fours nailed in a cross to keep them closed, to keep people from breaking in. Something to do with windows that had been broken and not mended, their curtains hanging out into the heavy air. Little kids quarreled and ran around on the cracked sidewalks. No lawns, no trees, and plenty of expressionless faces, expressionless eyes looking at the two of them. What did they see, James wondered: just two kids, one young but broad-backed, strong-looking; one taller and bonier; both in jeans and sneakers with sweaters hung around their waists in case the day grew cold.

James felt vaguely threatened. He didn't know how Sammy felt. He looked at his brother, and saw that Sammy's round head was cocked back a little, and his shoulders were squared. Sammy's eyes kind of danced and he looked around him, to the side, ahead, with a little smile of excitement at the ends of his mouth. Sammy looked sure of himself, which James wasn't sure was any too smart around this place. Around here, it was smarter to look invisible, that was his guess. Sammy was walking along like if anyone wanted to fight he was ready, and happy, to oblige.

Sammy turned off the street to go on beside a park area, with the harbor visible sometimes along to their left. Sailing boats were moored here, sleek white yachts, their sails furled along the booms and covered with weather-resistant fitted covers. Trees spread out along grassy parkland.

"How far is it?" James asked.

Sammy didn't hesitate. "We're past halfway."

"What did you do, memorize the map?"

"I couldn't afford to buy it, could I? I've got a good memory. Don't worry."

They walked on. Their route skirted the edge of the harbor, running behind big warehouses, and docks where cranes drew up high into the air. An occasional dock was busy with people unloading a freighter. Sammy didn't stop to look at any of this. They were the only ones on the sidewalk.

Sammy led James inland, onto something called Fort Street. They crossed over railroad tracks, empty and rusted, and into a more densely inhabited area. It was densely inhabited, but not prosperous. When Sammy had found the building he wanted, another square brick one with carved cement over its doorway, he walked up the steps and into it, as if he knew exactly what he was doing. "This is the place where people come to get hired to work on boats," he said. James just nodded. Inside, it was a big room, like an auditorium without any chairs. The raised stage at the end had no curtain, just blackboards, like a schoolroom except that the blackboards were the old-fashioned black kind, not green. The big room was empty except for a guard sitting at a table, reading a newspaper and eating potato chips from a bag. “What do you boys want?” he asked.

James looked at the man’s mouth. Crumbled and moist chips covered the tongue. He looked away. Let Sammy do the talking.

“Where is everybody?” Sammy asked.

“It’s Saturday.”

“Ships come in and go out on Saturday,” Sammy pointed out.

James stepped back from the conversation. He might get to see Fort McHenry after all, which would be interesting.

“Not this Saturday,” the guard said. He picked up a can of Coke and swilled the drink around in his mouth. “You’re not allowed in here.”

“If we wanted to find someone, a sailor, where would we look?” Sammy asked.

“Kid,” the guard said, half amused, running his hand over his white crewcut, “there are thousands of sailors all over the world. Up to God knows what. I don’t know where you’d look. Is it your brother or something?”

“Yeah,” Sammy said. He stood there, waiting.

“Does he have a name?” the man asked, sarcastic. He put his hand into the bag of chips, and took out a handful, which he crammed into his mouth. “I’ve been sitting here for four years, ever since they put my pacemaker in. I know almost everyone.”

Sammy threw the name down defiantly, “Verricker.”

The man leaned back to laugh, his mouth open. Then he pointed out, “He’s never your brother.”

“You said *or something*.”

This was like some kind of contest, James thought. Like some kind of game they were playing. The man knew their father, knew his name at least, but he didn’t say that directly. Sammy was playing the game as if he knew how. James felt uncomfortable, not knowing the rules, and frightened a little at the hostility behind the game. He wondered how Sammy managed to miss the hostility.

"If he owes you money, I'd say you didn't have a chance. There are a lot bigger men in line for Frankie Verricker, all of them ahead of you. You better go home, kid."

"Is he around?" Sammy asked. He stood there, straight and not moving, his hair the only bright thing in the hollow room. James watched his brother, and waited.

"Frankie's never around when you want him. That's his way. I haven't seen him in here for—it must be almost three years now. Or heard of him being around. And believe me, if he'd been here word would have spread. There are always some people waiting to catch up with Frankie Verricker." The guard took another drink, another swallow.

Sammy stood there.

"Unless he's been here and they caught up with him and he'll never show up anywhere again," the guard said.

Sammy stood. James was ready to leave.

"Tell you what, kid," the guard finally said. "If you want some news more up-to-date, you should go down to a place called Al's. It's about three blocks from here. Head toward the water and ask if the chief is in there."

"The chief? What is he, an Indian?"

The guard laughed again. "I wouldn't let him hear you say that, if I were you. The chief's a pure-blood white American and he wants to keep things that way. He's a chief mate, first mate."

"But there must be lots of those. How will I know which is him?" Sammy insisted.

"You'll know," the guard assured him. "If anyone knows anything about Frankie's whereabouts, it'll be the chief. He's had a keen interest in old Frankie for a long time. Now get out of here, both of you."

That was the end of that, James knew. They couldn't go into a bar. Besides, nobody knew where their father was. They'd walk back to the bus station, call Mr. Lingerle to meet the evening bus, and have dinner. He was ready to be out of this part of town.

Back on the street, Sammy turned without a word and went in the opposite direction from James. "Not that way," James said.

"I want to see if this chief is around," Sammy said.

"We can't go into a bar," James argued. "We're underage. It's against the law."

"We can try," Sammy said. His face was locked into its stubborn look, jaw set, eyes not focusing on anything in particular. "All they can do is throw us out. You can go back if you want to."

Sammy knew James couldn't do that. Not alone. "We'll miss the bus," James said.

"So what."

"What's got into you, Sammy?" James demanded.

Sammy shrugged and didn't say anything. Then he said, still not looking at anything, "We're close. We're really close. It's no time to turn tail."

"I'm not turning tail," James told his brother, because if Sammy thought James couldn't think, couldn't feel this hostility, couldn't look ahead and see a door about to be slammed in his face, then Sammy was underestimating him. "You don't think you'll actually find him, do you? And if you did find him, what would you say, anyway?"

Sammy grinned. He looked right at James, grinning. "Nothing. I don't have anything to say. I'd just like to punch him out." James thought it sounded like he meant what he said; and he probably did mean it, knowing Sammy. James couldn't stop him, and he didn't see anything funny. But he couldn't let Sammy go alone. He didn't want to wait alone either. Not around here.

"Come on, James," Sammy said.

James followed along beside his brother.

CHAPTER 13

Al's Bar and Grill was on a block where tall narrow houses, advertising rooms to rent by the week or month, were jammed in between small restaurants that looked too dirty to want to eat in—Mexican, Chinese, a pizza-and-sub shop, a couple of other bars. There were no trees, just the pale concrete sidewalk and narrow black street where battered cars had been parked. The early evening air seemed chilly, even though the temperature was in the seventies. James guessed, not thinking about the other things he was noticing—a man asleep against trash cans, the high shrieking woman's voice that came from the top room of one of the houses—that the street must be a place where transients lived, people who were always staying just until they went on somewhere else. Nothing—not houses or cars or businesses—looked taken care of. Pieces of newspaper blew around at their feet, and the wire baskets the city had put out for trash at street corners stood empty. He didn't let his eyes look down the occasional narrow alley that lay dark between two buildings.

There was nothing to be afraid of, James told himself, not believing it. He reminded himself that he was pretty much of a coward, a real chicken. Cowards fueled their own fears, he reminded himself. He noticed that there were no kids on this street, in this part of the city; he saw neither little kids nor older kids. He'd have felt better with some kids around. He'd have felt better if the few people out at this hour on a Saturday didn't look at the two boys as if they didn't like them, as if they personally didn't like them.

James couldn't believe that Sammy didn't know what kind of an area they were in. He didn't say anything, but he looked over at his brother. Sammy was just walking on along, looking like he didn't care about anything, didn't notice anything, heading for the neon sign that hung out over the street, spelling out AL'S BAR & GRILL in pink neon letters. Looking strong, able to take care of himself.

James couldn't look like that if his life depended on it. He hoped his life didn't depend on it. "Cool it," he muttered to himself.

The door to Al's stood open onto the sidewalk. James followed Sammy through a screen door where the bodies of flies had been mashed into the netting. Inside, the bar was dim, a smoky narrow room with a long bar down one side, a few battered tables down the middle, and booths along the opposite wall. It smelled of beer and latrines. A television screen added what it could to the shadowy lights. Some men sat on tall stools at the bar, watching a baseball game. Except for a solitary man hunched over his glass at a far booth, the tables and booths were empty. The bartender, who was probably Al, leaned back on his elbows against the bar and watched the game. He turned around to see who had come in.

He was a skinny little man, with lips so thin James thought for a minute he didn't have any mouth at all. A skinny little mustache grew over his upper lip, making him look like a rat. "Bug off, you two," he greeted them.

James would have obeyed, but Sammy just moved on toward the bar.

"You deaf?" the bartender asked. A couple of the men sitting there looked over, looked bored, looked back to the TV.

Sammy leaned on the bar, like someone in a cowboy movie. James hung back, from whatever trouble his brother was about to get into. "We were told we might find a man called Chief around here," Sammy said.

"What do you want with the chief?"

James studied the row of bottles lined up under the long mirror behind the bar. He studied the names and logos of the different brands of beer.

"Just some information," Sammy said. His voice was still high, like a kid's, but his calmness wasn't like a kid. James, jittery with nervousness and feeling out of place, wanted to pull on Sammy's sleeve and tell him to be more polite, to ask him if they couldn't please leave. Sammy acted like James wasn't there.

"Yeah? What kind of information?" the bartender asked. He had little black eyes that shifted from Sammy to James and back again.

"Whether the chief is here or not, to start with," Sammy said.

The man gave that some thought. He watched the TV set while he thought. James watched it too; it was an Orioles game, of course.

"And if he is, then what?" the bartender asked, his nose sharp as a rat's.

"About a man named Francis Verricker," Sammy told him.

The bartender's smile was like a rat that had just found a baby to chew on, James thought. "No kidding?"

Sammy didn't say anything.

"Sammy," James said, but Sammy ignored him.

"Well, he's here."

Francis Verricker was there? Right then? James looked again at the men at the bar, who looked like they never went anywhere, just sat there drinking and chewing on pretzels. He looked at their backs, and the backs of their necks, and the backs of their heads.

"Yeah?" Sammy asked.

"Chief's in the back room," the bartender said, nodding his head toward a dark corridor that led off the back of the barroom, without taking his eyes off Sammy. Sammy started to move off toward the corridor, but the bartender stopped him. "Off limits. That room's not for kids."

Sammy stopped, and turned around. He looked briefly at James, who thought, appalled: He's enjoying himself; he likes this.

"Neither's this one, either," the bartender said.

"We're not asking for a drink or anything," Sammy told him.

"Bet your butt you aren't," the man said. "I could tell the chief there's someone out here to see him. I could *tell* him."

"Would you?" Sammy asked.

"Since it's about Francis Verricker. Chief's always interested in Frank. You think Chief would be interested in Frankie?" he asked down the length of the bar.

Heads nodded, but faces stayed turned away.

"You two sit down. No, you don't. Not in a booth. Take that table by the door. I'm not going to serve you anything, no Cokes, no water, nothing. Got me? The cops would like to have my license, so no kid drinks anything in my place. Anything. Got that?"

James nodded his head and swallowed back the bubble of air that was rising up his throat. He went right over to a table and sat down on the scarred wooden chair. Sammy came more slowly behind him. That left two empty chairs at their square table. James looked across at his brother. He wanted to warn Sammy to be more careful, but his brother looked almost like someone he didn't know. He looked like he might do all right in this part of the city, in this kind of place. James felt better when he saw that, even though it meant he was depending on his little brother to take care of him in case of trouble. He wondered how much of their father there was in his brother.

"I almost thought he was here," James said. "Our father."

"Don't say that," Sammy warned him. "Not around here. Not unless you know it's okay."

James agreed: He should have thought.

The bartender came back and stood beside their table. "He says, he might like to talk to you, but not right now." While he stood there, his little black eyes flicked around the room, watching everything.

"When then?" Sammy asked.

"Wait and see," the bartender said, and turned his back on them.

James let his brother digest that thought before he suggested, "We could leave, anyway," ashamed of himself for suggesting it, but unable to stop the idea from coming out of his mouth.

"We can wait," Sammy said. "It's probably something going on in a back room, poker or something."

"With gambling," James guessed. That would explain why they kept it secret. "I have to go to the bathroom."

When James asked him where the bathroom was, the bartender pointed down the hallway. James went to it, leaving Sammy alone at the table. When he got back, Sammy went, leaving him alone at the table. James looked around him, then back at his own hands. It was better not to seem to stare. He felt out of place, and he thought his strangeness showed. This was his father's world, the kind of place where his father hung out. James felt uneasy, nervous; he knew that anything at all would tip him back over into feeling afraid.

A young man, maybe twenty, maybe a little older, came in, and went to the bar. The men there seemed to know him, although nobody spoke to him. James did stare at the young man: He looked too young and clean for this place. His jeans were worn soft, his workshirt hung from broad shoulders and needed an ironing just like everybody else's, but he looked different. He had shining clean brown hair, brushed back from his face and longer than most of the crew cuts in there, and a flush of pink on his milky skin where the high cheekbones turned flat. His eyes, when he looked around the room, were blue, the blue of a spring sky before the heat of summer has bleached it out. Although his body looked full grown, his cheeks looked like he didn't need to shave yet, and his expression, looking around and seeing James, was frankly curious. Not hostile, not nosy, just curious. His face had a friendly expression on it, about the exact opposite of the rat-faced bartender.

Sammy sat down, smiling. "Some graffiti, hunh?"

"You're too young," James reminded him. That wasn't true though. Every minute in here Sammy seemed to get older and James younger. And there were a lot of minutes they were spending, waiting. They didn't talk much, just sat, as time wore on and the booths and tables filled with groups, the bar with men alone. The bartender scurried up and down, across the room, his fingers greedy around bills and coins, jamming them into his apron pocket as if trying to conceal them. The baseball game ended and some show with car chases came on, car chases, shooting, and long-haired, long-legged women. Deep men's voices carried on indistinguishable conversations, occasionally bursting into laughter or brief quarrels, sometimes yelling across the room for another drink.

The minutes became an hour and then two hours. Sammy, for a wonder, waited patiently. James had no idea what Sammy was thinking about, as the time ticked by. James thought about his French report and his English grade, Toby, Andy Walker. Then he began to think about Celie, just remembering pictures he carried in his memory, from the very first time he'd seen her. From the first, she had snared his eyes, the way she looked, the way she moved, and he didn't even really know why, why this one particular girl. James was settled down to memories, trying to ignore everything around him, when Sammy leaned toward him to say, "Some fun, hunh?"

"No," James answered, cross at being interrupted.

"He just wants to make us wait."

"I don't much care if he never comes out."

"It sounds like he's sort of King of the Mountain around here. That's what kings do, show how important they are by making people wait to see them."

"Not real kings," James said.

"What do you know about real kings?" Sammy demanded. "You talk like this is some fairy tale, or something stupid like that."

James leaned his elbows on the table. He'd done some reading for his French report, with the help of the English teacher, whom he'd asked about books about fairy tales. He'd read an essay from *The Uses of Enchantment*, by somebody named Bettelheim; she'd lent him that from her own library. He leaned forward to explain to Sammy how fairy tales weren't all pretty-pretty. Take Hansel and Gretel for example, with a stepmother who wanted to lose them in the woods for the wild animals to eat and their father went along with it; take that idea just for starters, that idea wasn't any too stupid. He leaned forward and took a breath to begin.

"James," Sammy cut him off, his voice low so only James could hear it.

James looked up and around. Nobody was coming to their table.

"It doesn't look good for us to be talking," Sammy explained. "People are looking."

James just stared at his brother's face. Sammy looked calm, maybe a little amused, certainly relaxed: but his eyes had darker, almost dangerous undertones, James saw, and his face was a mask over whatever his real feelings were.

"Why do you think they're so interested?" James asked.

Sammy shrugged, leaned back in his straight chair, jammed his hands into his pockets, and let his glance go lazily around the dim room.

James wanted to move over to one of the chairs next to Sammy, to have their backs to the same wall. He scolded himself: They were just two kids, they didn't have any money or anything, these men wouldn't think they were worth paying attention to, they'd be all right.

"My guess is, these people don't like Francis Verricker much," Sammy said. Smiling away as if he were making a joke.

"Then shouldn't we leave?"

"No. I want to know what's really true. Just the truth, I don't care what it is. As long as it's true."

So they waited some more.

At last, a line of men emerged from the narrow hallway. Sammy had his back to them so he couldn't see them. James could see them.

There were half a dozen, the first five like attendants. It was the last man they were waiting for; he was the one everyone was waiting for. James knew that as soon as he saw him, a big, broad man—not so tall really, but heavy-muscled in his arms and legs, barrel-chested, his shirt unbuttoned down a ways, his square head planted on a thick neck. The man was tanned, like leather. James watched his approach.

The bartender, too, watched, his little eyes eager, his long nose pointing, like some rat looking out from its hole, ready to run out and grab the chunk of food that might fall, if things went well. James thought he knew, with a cold fear that reached up to finger his heart, who the chunk of food was.

The man pulled out a chair and sat down between the two boys. His hair was grizzled, the crew cut, the stubble on his face, the hairs visible on his chest with the colors of a tattoo showing through.

"I'm Chief," he said. And waited. "You were asking for me."

James looked at Sammy, who wasn't saying anything.

"What about Frank Verricker?" the man asked. He didn't lean forward, didn't sit back. "The son of a bitch owes me twelve hundred dollars. What about him?"

"He owes us, too," Sammy said.

"Yeah? Well I'll tell you, kid, you are behind me in line to collect. Got that? The next time he shows his face around here, I'm collecting—in cash or in blood. Maybe you can have some of what's left."

"How long has it been since you saw him?" Sammy asked, still slouching back. James was sitting up straight.

"Too long."

The man waited. Sammy waited. James clutched his hands together in his lap.

"That IOU is long overdue."

"He lost the bet," Sammy guessed.

"He lost the whole game," the chief said. "It's usual to buy a man a drink if you're going to ask him questions. You buying?"

"Sure," Sammy said.

The chief raised his pale eyes and the bartender hustled over. "Brandy, Al, the best. Double brandy. The kid's buying."

It cost Sammy five dollars, which he paid without a murmur of protest, without looking at James. James wouldn't have protested either. He'd be satisfied just to get out of this with his skin safe and his nose unbroken. There were an awful lot of broken noses in the room. And broken hands, too, he thought, watching the chief's big hand wrap around the glass of brandy.

"But I don't much expect to see Frank, or my twelve hundred, not this side of hell. Frank has a way of running out on his debts. So what's your name, kid?"

"Tillerman," James said quickly, just in case the anger he saw flare up on Sammy's face took over.

Then the chief looked at him, measuring. The chief smiled at whatever he saw, just opening his mouth. "What are you, brothers?" James nodded. The man's two upper front teeth were dead, a black color the outer layer of enamel muffled to gray; if James had teeth like that he wouldn't smile much either.

"Well, you can tell your old lady that if she thinks she'll see him again, and see her money again, she better think again. I've known him for years, and I never knew Frank to do more than take a woman for all she'd give him, and then leave her. He was something—I'll admit it—there's nobody like Frankie for women. They can't say no to him. But he never went back to any of them. Kids like you wouldn't have money worth gambling for or borrowing. Am I right?"

"Yeah," Sammy said. "I guess you don't happen to know where he is now."

"With some dame, somewhere. Not here, he wouldn't dare come back here again. Not with empty pockets, the way he always does. Taking people for money—not paying up, that's Frankie. Tell you why—the bastard thinks he's the whole reason the whole world exists; he thinks he's the center of the world. He's always watching out for number one. Only thing he's good at is double-crossing. But he double-crossed the wrong man this time." The chief lifted his glass and emptied it. "I could use another one of those."

"Sure," Sammy said. He paid out another five dollars.

"You're okay, kid," the chief said to Sammy. "You're an okay kid. You wanna see something?"

Sammy shrugged. It was almost as if Sammy didn't care if the man wanted to impress him. He unbuttoned the rest of the buttons on his shirt, and pulled it out of his trousers. He leaned back to show them both a thick scar, circling his waist like a bullwhip.

James didn't know what he was supposed to say. *Wow* somehow seemed like the wrong thing.

"That's some scar," Sammy said.

"Boiler blowout," the chief told him, buttoning his shirt again, tucking it in. He drank from his glass. "That kind of thing happens. Tell you what though—" He turned heavily around in his chair and yelled out to a booth behind him. "Nairne, hey, Nairne—over here."

The man he'd summoned brought his beer to their table and sat down with them. He was tall and thin, and his features all drooped down, eyebrows and mouth, mustache, giving him a look like a bloodhound, sad and tired.

"These kids are asking about Frank Verricker. You sailed with him a couple of years ago, didn't you?"

"Yeah, he was on my ship. So what?"

"So what about him?" The chief asked the question, then sat back.

"What about him? Frankie? What I think about him, is that what you're asking? He should have been at least third mate by this time, long ago, probably a first mate. But he'd never take the tests. He always spent his time figuring out how to get around the regulations. He could have been making good money and really using his abilities."

"Nairne went to college," the chief leaned over and spoke to James, in a voice that was supposed to carry. "That's why he doesn't know how to answer a straight question straight." Then he leaned back away. The thickened vowels and the blast of alcohol on the chief's breath worried James. The other man,

Nairne, didn't like what the chief had said, but he didn't say anything, or look up from his glass of beer.

"Nairne's a baker—you know?" James didn't. "The baker's one of the galley crew, a cook's assistant. Nothing like a college education, is there, Nairne? If his parents could see him now . . ."

"Okay, Chief, but Verricker *is* smart, even you have to give him that. And he's good in a fight, too. A good man to have on your side in a fight."

"So long as you don't turn your back on him. Long as you're not losing. Long as you don't lend him money," Chief listed off.

"He jumped ship on us," Nairne said. "I'm not sticking up for Frank Verricker, Chief."

"I heard you talking." The young clean man stood beside James, asking the chief for permission, "You're talking about Frankie. Can I sit down?"

"Alex, come sit down, we're just having a talk about Frankie," the chief answered.

For a second, a puzzled expression was on the young man's face. Then it cleared. He brought a chair over, and squeezed it in between James and Nairne.

"You remember Frank, don't you?" Chief asked him.

"Yes," Alex said. "You know that."

"Frank Verricker?" the chief insisted.

"Yes," Alex repeated, his expression not changed at all by the repeated question.

"He owes me twelve hundred dollars," the chief said, as if it was Alex's fault, somehow.

"I know that. I'm really sorry, Chief," the young man said, and he sounded like he meant what he said.

The only good face in the whole place, and he didn't even know when he was being made fun of, James thought. What had Sammy gotten them into?

"Whaddaya say, anybody want to have a round? The kids are buying," the chief announced.

"Un-unhh," Sammy said. The man's eyes fixed on Sammy's face. If eyeballs could grow hairs, James thought, he'd have little grizzled stubbly hairs growing out of his eyeballs. "You're the man we came to see," Sammy told him.

The chief didn't like being crossed. "Then *I'll* have another," he said, watching Sammy's reaction. James thought the man probably shouldn't have any more to drink. He still had some brandy left, and he sounded a little drunk, and he looked like a mean drunk anyway. But Sammy went ahead and paid for it. Which left them about six dollars, which wasn't much at all. James didn't know how much longer he could just sit there, silent at the table, being anxious, being afraid, being worried. He felt like he'd been in this room all his life practically, and it would be easier to die and get it over with than to sit much longer.

"Where did Frank Verricker leave the ship?" Sammy asked Naime.

"Fiji, where else? We were loading on copra which really stinks—"

"He said Fiji is like heaven," Alex interrupted to tell Sammy. "He said of all the oceans, the Pacific is the best, and in all the Pacific, Fiji is the best. Like heaven is the best."

As soon as Alex stopped, Nairne started again, as if Alex hadn't even spoken. "He just disappeared one night. He just wasn't there in the morning."

"Somebody maybe might have slit his throat for him and tossed him overboard," the chief suggested.

Nairne didn't disagree, but Alex did. "I don't think so. Frankie always said he'd like to settle down there. Because of the beaches, and how happy life is," he explained to the chief. "And the girls, too."

"And the girls, too, I'll bet," the chief answered, angry for some reason, growing more angry. "Tell these kids how old you are, Alex."

"Why?"

"They want to know. Don't you, kids?"

He asked them both but he was looking at Sammy. Sammy didn't move a muscle.

"I'm thirty-one. My birthday's in August, and I'll be thirty-two then." Alex was pleased with himself. "Frankie talked to me a lot, and he liked to talk about the islands. He'd take me ashore with him, too, if I wanted to go. And help me—change money and pick out a present my mother would like—because he wanted me to be his friend." He raised his voice to speak over the others' mocking responses, but he wasn't upset by them. "He didn't have friends but he wanted them."

The chief made laughing noises, but he wasn't laughing. "And how much money did he take off you?" he asked Alex.

"I gave it to him," Alex said. "That's different." But he didn't entirely believe himself, and James was sorry for that. He didn't think the chief should have raised that doubt. You made allowances for someone like Alex, you handled him differently. But these men didn't. Maybe men didn't? But Francis Verricker had.

They had run out of things to say at their table. James noticed then that the rest of the room was pretty quiet too—like an audience sitting ringside, they'd been watching the conversation. He looked around at all the watching faces, and at the unwatched flat face of the TV screen. The bartender was back safe behind his bar again, leaning on it with his elbows.

There was something wrong about to happen. James knew it in his stomach. He tried to tell Sammy, without words, that it was time for them to get out. Sammy wouldn't meet his eyes. James didn't dare do anything more than look at his brother, hard, and will him to realize what was about to get started—whatever that was. James didn't have the nerve to get up himself and leave; he just felt the blood racing around his body, warning him, scaring him, the blood itself panicky like a mouse cornered by the cat. The proverbial mouse. Or the proverbial rabbit, he thought, his body frozen where it was, not responding to his will, the rabbit mesmerized by the snake. *Sammy,* he yelled out inside his head, and his brother didn't answer. He couldn't tell from the voice whether it was a warning or a cry for help.

"Now," the chief leaned forward, practically pushing his face into Sammy's, "you tell me something. You tell me what your interest is in Frank Verricker. What's a piece of slime like that got to do with you?"

Words caught in James's throat, because fear had cramped up the muscles around his voice box. *Say money,* he silently urged Sammy. That lie had been given to them. Telling it would put them on the side of these men. *Say he owes us money. Pick any number, anything reasonable, two hundred dollars would be good.* His heart was being squeezed and the words being pushed up—like toothpaste—but his throat was capped by fear and he couldn't speak.

"He's my father," Sammy said, quiet and angry.

The chief smiled, showing his two dead teeth. "Well, well. Imagine that. Frankie Verricker's your daddy."

James couldn't even think. He could only wait to see what happened next, and hope it would be over soon. "Your daddy too?" the chief asked him.

James wanted to say no. He wanted to stay clear. He looked at Sammy—Sammy didn't mind whatever James said, because Sammy was speaking only for himself. James nodded his head, yes. He couldn't do any more than nod.

"Really?" Alex asked him. James nodded again. "No kidding?" Alex's smile was entirely happy. His blue eyes shone. "I didn't know Frankie had any kids. He never said. Wow." He reached out to shake James's hand. Dazed, not thinking, James shook hands with the young man. "I'm really glad," Alex said, turning to Sammy, shaking Sammy's hand. Sammy smiled back at him, looking like he meant it. "That's so great," Alex said to the rest of the table. "Isn't it?"

"I guess," the chief said, "old Frankie really did take your old lady—"

Frozen in his seat, riveted down by fear, choked by it, James tried to warn his brother's face—*don't.*

But Sammy went ahead and interrupted the man. "I'd rather have him for a father than you. Any day."

The man lifted his arm and hit Sammy, backhanded him across the face. It happened so fast, James didn't really see it. Then it was over, and Sammy's head was back where it had been. Maybe, James hoped, it hadn't happened. Maybe that would show Sammy they were in over their heads. Maybe the chief wouldn't remember that he, James, was there and then he, James, would get off without being hurt.

"Any day," Sammy repeated. "And twice over."

Shut up, Sammy, James thought. *Please.*

But Sammy hadn't, and the big hand returned, and when Sammy's face was back in place again, there was some blood coming from his lip.

"Hey," James protested, squeezing his voice out. Alex laid a hand on his shoulder, to quiet him.

"I said," the chief told Sammy, "I'd take my twelve hundred in cash, or in blood." He was threatening Sammy, menacing him, challenging him. The whole room waited, as if this was what they'd been waiting for.

Sammy didn't hurry and he didn't hesitate. He got up out of his chair and stood clear of the table.

"Kid," Nairne protested. "Don't be a fool. Sit down."

Sammy ignored him.

The chief got up, satisfied. James looked around the room, to see who would help. Grown men didn't fight a kid; it wasn't even a fight. Somebody had to stop the chief. The bartender had moved back against the mirror, as far into safety as he could, and his little black eyes watched eagerly. You could almost see his nose twitching over the thin mustache.

"You're as dumb as your father," the chief said to Sammy. The chief was huge, thick chested, thick muscled.

"He's just a kid," James squeezed out the words. "You can't—"

The chief looked at him then, and his heart shriveled up inside him, and his voice faded away, slinking back down his throat. "It's like the good book says," the chief said, to a round of laughter, "the sins of the fathers shall be visited upon the sons. Until the seventh generation." He was pleased with himself, at the Bible quote, at the joke.

James got up then—he didn't know what he was doing. He moved around toward the space between Sammy and the man, and he talked at the same time. "That's ridiculous." He didn't want to move closer, but he couldn't stop himself now, any more than he could make himself move just a minute before. "It's entirely irrelevant." He could barely hear his own voice, his heart was beating so loudly in his ears. "That has nothing to do with—"

James thought, in the rush of movement that followed—which he was somehow at the center of although he had no time to figure out what was happening—he thought he heard Sammy's voice. But he wasn't sure. He wasn't sure what was happening. Until he felt his chest slammed into the wooden front of the bar, he didn't know he couldn't breathe. Until he could breathe, he didn't realize that his head was being held down, his ear in some wet smelly unwiped spill, held by hands that were more like rat claws, clawlike fingers digging up his nose and wishing they could dig into his eyeballs. His feet barely touched the floor and he was held there. He'd been tossed across the room, like—like a duffel bag or something.

Thumping noises behind him. Men's voices saying things he couldn't distinguish and didn't want to. James didn't fight—he didn't know how to fight. He didn't want to—but he couldn't see. And he couldn't see his brother.

He wrenched his body free, which was a mistake. Fear had gone to his legs and he collapsed onto the floor. He wasn't angry, he was frightened—every cell in his body wanted to curl up and be invisible. He was frightened that he'd be hurt and frightened of fighting and frightened of standing up because he couldn't and frightened he'd wet his pants and—

James forced himself up. He saw Sammy sort of catapulted toward a booth, his arms loose and flailing. Sammy crashed into the side of the booth and his arms crashed down. The men nearby backed away.

Sammy didn't even hesitate, he just turned right back—with his head lowered and his nose bleeding too, now, along with his mouth—moving toward the man in the center of the room.

James pushed his body off from the bar, like pushing a boat away from the dock. An arm went across his chest, pinning him back. He didn't look to see whose it was. His eyes were on Sammy, on his brother's yellow head which the big man held now under his arm, choking Sammy's neck. A voice spoke low in his ear. "Chief's always mean when he's lost at cards. He lost a month's wages in there tonight. It'll be over soon."

It wasn't being over soon, it was lasting forever.

Sammy twisted in the huge arms. His legs kicked backward, not often connecting and those blows weak, anyway, because he wore sneakers. Deep voices commented on the fight, saying *what* James didn't know, didn't care. Watching, James saw what the chief couldn't see—Sammy's mouth opening to bite down hard on the hairy arm that held him, even while the huge hand twisted at his head.

Don't do that, James thought and at the same time *Smart move.* He didn't know what he thought.

The teeth—in a time zone that stretched out into slower than slow motion—closed on the flesh of the arm.

"You little bastard," the chief roared. He was hurt, James saw, glad. But he spun Sammy around and slammed a fist against the boy's ear. Sammy careened backward, and fell down.

That was it then, James thought, relieved. KO, knockout.

But Sammy got up again. His legs started to buckle but he pulled himself up with the help of a chair. He headed back to the man. Sammy just wasn't going to quit.

The chief held his arms out, his fingers motioning Sammy forward, encouraging him—like a father teaching his kid how to walk, James thought. It was all wrong and somebody had to stop Sammy.

"Come on, kid," the chief coaxed Sammy.

And Sammy came on.

James—trying to slip out from under the barring arm because—it was his brother, it was Sammy—trying to breathe—heard the low voice in his ear reassuring him that Frank used to get the chief going and then he'd slip out of the trouble somehow. He heard the voice urging him to relax, promising it would be over soon—and now James was afraid he'd just burst into tears. He was so useless, so helpless—and he was supposed to be so smart. If he was so smart, what had he been doing letting

Sammy get them into this mess? And what was he going to do? There wasn't anything he could do, for all his useless brains. For all his brainy philosophy about how because life was brief things didn't matter. Sammy mattered.

He couldn't get Sammy out of this. He looked at his brother's battered face. The chief was taking his time now. Everybody was quiet. They were just two kids, and helpless—

"I think you'd better stop this now," a voice spoke.

James almost looked around to see who it was, speaking, except he didn't want to take his eyes off Sammy. As long as he had his eyes touching Sammy, maybe things might—and besides, it was his own voice anyway—sounding normal almost. Sounding cool and sure, like he was giving the right answer in class.

His voice went on and he knew what it was going to say. "Unless you want to really beat up on him. But I can't imagine any jury being sympathetic about men beating up on a couple of kids."

He said *men* on purpose, not *man.* He said *men* because he wanted everybody in the room responsible. Because, he knew, as if he'd had time to think it out, if each man thought he'd be held responsible, and arrested, then each man would have something personal invested in ending it. To save his own skin.

"Yeah," he heard the low voice at his ear, and other voices too. "The kid's right. Hey, Chief? How about a beer? Let the kid go and let's have a beer."

The chief didn't like that. James couldn't tell if Sammy heard anything: Sammy just stood there, swaying toward his enemy. Getting ready to make his move.

The chief looked around, then back at Sammy. He reached down into his workboot and pulled out something that flashed silver, whether against Sammy or against the now unenthusiastic crowd, James never knew, because when they saw that, the men around surged into the fight, and Sammy was swallowed up.

Two men moved to hold on to the chief. The man whose arm had been across James's chest left him, to stand or fall there, as other men joined in to pull off the men holding the chief. James heard the sound of breaking glass behind him, smelled the thick, sharp aroma of whiskey; out of the corner of his eye he saw a hand holding up the neck of a broken glass bottle, holding it like a weapon. The room filled with sound—voices and furniture and a rumbling, growling undertone; the room filled with a mass of confused bodies. James slid between legs and hips to grab his brother. He hauled Sammy behind him, out the door. Running, he hauled Sammy down the dark street, away.

It was dark out there, with only one streetlight at the corner, and only little thin lines of light from behind the windows. It was dark and Sammy was just dragging along beside James, and that was wrong. James pulled his brother into an alley. He pulled him back into the dark narrow space, behind a few metal garbage cans that clattered as Sammy stumbled into them. There, they both sank down onto the ground.

The wall was behind James. He leaned his back against it. Sammy was right up next to him. He could hear Sammy breathing and feel the length of his brother's body. It didn't matter if he couldn't see, as long as he could hear and feel. After a couple of minutes, when Sammy's breathing had gotten quieter, and his own had too, James said his brother's name into the darkness. "Sammy?"

No answer. Maybe Sammy couldn't speak, maybe his jaw had been busted, or his windpipe—but his breathing was okay—maybe his brains had been knocked sideways, if that could happen—and James thought: He could have murdered Francis Verricker if he'd had the man there. For what he'd done to them.

Ripples ran along the body next to him, and choking sounds came from it. James turned to Sammy, not getting up—he couldn't have stood up right then if his life depended on it. But his life didn't depend on it. Which was wonderful to know.

"Some fight, hunh?" Sammy's voice, choked with laughter, asked him.

Before James could think of a suitable answer, Sammy burst into tears, choking over them. "I hurt," he wailed softly. "James? I hurt."

James kept an arm around Sammy, thinking. Thinking what to do next. He didn't know where they were. He didn't know what time it was. He didn't know what to do.

Sammy's tears were as sudden and brief as the laughter. By the time James realized what happened, he knew that his brother was asleep—with James's arm around him and his head heavy against James's chest. Sammy was sound asleep, his face still washed with his own tears and his own blood.

CHAPTER 14

James couldn't sleep. He sat there, his back to a shingled wall, his legs drawn up, the weight of his sleeping brother against his chest. His eyes adjusted to the dark, but the dark was so complete he could only see his own body, and Sammy's; beyond that, nothing, just the sense of close walls. It was like a cave, but reversed. The outside was the darkness and where he and Sammy were was a small area of visibility.

Street noises, TVs and rock music, came down the alley to him and kept him awake, then the sound of sirens at a distance, growing closer. He couldn't see out into the street, so he had to deduce information from sounds, and the play of flashing lights into the alley. He guessed, from the sounds, that the police had come to settle the fight. He guessed, from a later siren, one that wailed higher and longer than the police, that an ambulance had been called. Lights flashed red, white, blue, and then yellow, too, down into the alley. They'd gotten out just in time. James thought about getting up and going out, to ask the police for help—but didn't have the strength to move, didn't want to wake Sammy, didn't know whether they'd be held somehow responsible and put into cells, as instigators or vagrants. The law, he knew, could be implacable. He didn't know where, under the law, he and his brother would be placed. He wondered—his mind wandering against the sounds of raised voices and commands called out, of protest and denial—who had called the police. Probably the bartender, especially if he was also Al the owner. Like a rat deserting the sinking sailors.

James would have laughed at that thought, only it was the most he could do to smile to himself. Besides, he might wake up Sammy—who must be exhausted to sleep through this commotion. In the silence that fell after the street emptied, James's memories kept him awake.

He stared at the darkness he couldn't see into, and remembered. The remarkable thing was that he had noticed and registered so much, even while he had felt as if he wasn't functioning at all. While he had been mindlessly getting through the moments, not doing anything, his brain had been storing up pictures. The more minutes that passed by, the more time that lay between him and what had happened, the more vivid his memory grew. He saw faces, saw their expressions—saw in memory Alex's boyish face and the way the opened blue eyes and opened mouth expressed fear when Chief turned to him, the knife blade shining. Hands grabbed for the chief's arm as the memory continued, and James hoped it wasn't Alex the ambulance had come for. He heard that voice low in his ear again, saying he should just lay low, reminding him that Frankie never got caught up into this kind of trap—Yeah, he'd just baited it and set it, James thought. His memory heard Sammy's breathing, heavy—hard work, breathing; a cry of pain—he saw Sammy getting up from the floor to go for the big man again.

His brother, James thought—almost drowning under a feeling that rolled up from inside him, and rolled over him, rolling him over—Sammy. Sammy might be foolish, but he had courage. He had more courage than any other man in that place. Sammy had stood up to the chief in their conversation, while James had been silly with fear. Sammy had stood up to him and stayed standing up, no matter what. James knew it was because of Sammy that he had himself stood up, at least to some extent, against the man: because he was standing with Sammy. He wanted to wrap his other arm around his brother—he was so grateful to him—and proud of him. He didn't envy Sammy, but he admired him. And loved him, he thought; mostly loved him.

The darkness might be lying thick all around them, but they were all right for now. In the morning, they'd go back to the bus station, however long away morning lay. Until then, James would sit and watch.

Fear remembered was somehow stronger than fear being felt. That kept him awake and almost shivering, even though the night wasn't cold. The street might just as well not have been out there, so thick was the silence. Not even an occasional car motor broke the silence. Not even a bit of light as distant and unilluminating as a star broke the darkness.

James sat the time through, knowing that, being time, being measured into hours, minutes, and seconds, it would tick its way by. Nothing would slow it down, nothing would speed it up. If he could just wait it through, the night would pass by.

The first he knew of dawn wasn't light. There was almost no sky visible where he sat, and it wasn't dawn yet anyway. The first he knew was a lightening of the air. The air lightened—he could see mortar lines on the brick wall he faced; the air lay lighter on his eyeballs. It wasn't what you'd call light—just sight returned to him. But his heart lightened, as if there had really been a question about whether morning would come that day, as if he hadn't known for sure what the end of the night would be.

James spoke his brother's name and brushed the yellow hair with his fingers, to wake Sammy. Sammy raised his head and leaned back against the wall, his eyes closed. James spoke his name and told him it was time to get up. Sammy's mouth moved as if he were answering, although his swollen lips didn't open, and no words came out.

James almost smiled. Getting Sammy awake had always been a long job. "Let's go," he said, his voice patient, not urgent. It wasn't even the crack of dawn yet, so there wasn't much danger of meeting up with anybody on the streets. "Sammy?"

Sammy's face looked pretty bad, looked horrible in fact. They'd have to get him washed up, somehow, or everybody who saw him would run screaming. The rest of him wasn't any too presentable either, James thought—and his arm. His left arm. The lower part of it was swollen out as if a balloon had been inflated inside the skin.

James couldn't imagine what had gone on inside that arm to make it look like that. No wonder Sammy, who never complained, said he hurt. James wouldn't have been surprised to see sharp splintered ends of bones sticking out from that arm.

He put his two hands on his brother's upper left arm, just in case, trying to keep the whole arm still. Sammy didn't like that, and his eyelids flew up.

"James," Sammy said. The puzzled, angry hazel eyes focused on him. "You look terrible."

James leaned back, still gently restraining Sammy's left arm. "Do I? But nobody even touched me, except the once. I didn't think there was any blood—"

"Your face is dead white—and your eyes . . . you feel all right?"

"I didn't sleep. I was pretty frightened."

"Yeah," Sammy said. He closed his eyes, and smiled to himself, causing the crusted blood around his lower lip to crack. "We didn't last too long in there, did we. But you know what?" the eyes opened, and Sammy pulled himself up to sit straighter. James let go of the arm. "He must have been *something*, our father. I mean, however bad he was, he went his own way.

Nobody could make him do anything. So whatever else you have to say about him, you have to admit that."

James didn't argue. Instead, he asked, "You better look at your arm. The left. Does it hurt?"

Sammy stared. "Cripes, James, what happened?"

"How would I know? I'm not a doctor," James answered. "I think we ought to get going, though. Can you remember the way?"

"A'course."

They both stood up. James's muscles, in his legs, his back and shoulders, and his neck, too, his neck was the worst—protested. Hurt. "Maybe we should put a sling around that arm, just in case."

"Where would we get a sling?" Sammy was just holding his arm in front of him, like a swollen wing, and staring at it.

"Your sweater?"

"I left it in there."

"Then mine." James made his protesting muscles remove the sweater. He tied the arms around Sammy's neck to make a sling.

The light had been growing, and they could see the narrow, filthy alley clearly. The street dirt had been added onto by garbage dirt—slimy green vegetable leaves and oily patches of tomato—like colors spread on an artist's palette—dark brown coffee grounds, and an occasional white bone fallen free. If James could have seen the place where they had holed up, he'd never have gone into it. "Let's get out of here," he told Sammy.

"Stinks, doesn't it," Sammy agreed, cheerful. "I'd never live in a city."

"I would. It isn't all like this," James reminded him. "I think. Can you slow down? I'm really stiff and—I'm okay, I just can't hustle. Cities are all right if you're not poor, I bet. Exciting."

"Because of all the things you can buy?"

James shook his head. He didn't really have the strength for talking, not even to try to argue with Sammy about what exactly he'd meant. He'd meant: all the different buildings and what was in them, all the different faces and their lives. But he was too exhausted to talk, too physically at the end of his strength to do more than put one foot in front of the other, keeping step with his brother. As long as Sammy set the rhythm, and didn't try to hurry it up, James could keep going.

He sensed the trees of the park around him, tasted their presence in the air, but his eyes were fixed on his own feet. That helped them to keep moving. Being so frightened really took it out of you, he thought. He sensed Sammy looking over at him, now and then. He wondered if Sammy was thinking of stopping and taking a rest; but James wouldn't let him do that. Sammy had to get to a doctor; but James didn't want to tell his brother that, didn't want to worry him about that.

"Thanks, James," Sammy said. "For getting me out of it."

"Hunh?" James grunted.

"I knew I could count on you to think of something," Sammy said. "You were terrific."

"You weren't counting on me," James protested. Asked.

"No. But I knew I could," Sammy insisted. He was grinning again, James could hear it. Nothing kept Sammy down. "That was really smart, the way you stopped him. I'd have just kept on until he broke my neck, or smashed my leg, or something. But you scared them. Or slit my throat," he remembered. "Boy, were we in over our heads. We were lucky to get out of there. James? Thanks, and you'll make a great lawyer."

"I'm not so sure about that," James answered, his voice wispy. His sneakers just kept moving, left ahead then right, then left again, keeping step with Sammy's sneakers.

"You will, you'll be a great lawyer. You'll make pots of money, and—"

"No," James said. "About being a lawyer."

"But why not? What'll you do instead?"

"Can we talk later?" James asked. "Please?"

Sammy didn't even make James talk any more to the extent of agreeing with him. James felt his brother looking at him again, and they just kept on moving.

At the bus station, they went right to the men's room. Sammy took one look at himself in the mirror and burst out laughing. "Back from the wars, hunh?" He studied himself in the mirror. "Did we win or lose, James?"

"We survived," James told him. He registered only his own pale face before he left Sammy there, while he called Mr. Lingerle in Easton and said they were catching the eight o'clock bus, which would arrive at eleven thirty in Easton, and asked the man to call Dr. Landros to meet them at her office, and reassured the concerned voice that they were okay, only Sammy needed a doctor, and yes, they really were okay, he'd explain later.

Sammy didn't say a word on the bus. James thought he'd like to fall asleep, but he couldn't, with the bouncing and the frequent halts in little towns, with the red lights and uneven acceleration. At Annapolis, he thought with relief that there was only an hour and a half to go, then another hour and a half to home. "You okay?" he asked Sammy.

"He's here," Sammy said, looking out the window. "Get up, we've got to get off. Cn you get up?"

"Sure," James said, forcing himself up. He didn't remember a minute of the ride, and didn't wonder who was there. He just followed Sammy.

It was when he put his hand out to hold on to the metal railing beside the steps down from the bus that he heard—it sounded like bones grinding, deep inside the cavity of his chest. The grinding noise echoed the way a sounding bell echoes through air, only without music. It sounded inside his chest, in his ears, his head. His legs gave way under him, and he would have fallen down the steps except Sammy caught him. *He* was Mr. Lingerle, come to meet them. He took James's other arm.

"What's wrong?" he asked, but moving to the Volkswagen. "What happened?"

"Tired," James said. Sammy first, then he'd ask the doctor what would make that horrible grinding noise, as if bones were rubbing up against one another.

"There's a hospital here," Mr. Lingerle suggested, but James said no. He didn't know how they'd pay a hospital, and he could work off any fees for Dr. Landros.

"Are you okay?" he asked Sammy, who leaned back in the rear seat.

"Neither of you are okay," Mr. Lingerle announced. He was angry. James had never seen him angry. Mr. Lingerle's anger was quiet. "You told me you'd be all right, you told me not to worry," Mr. Lingerle said.

James leaned his head back against the seat and closed his eyes.

"I'm sorry," Sammy's voice came from the back. "It's my fault."

"And what about your grandmother—"

"I know," Sammy said. "We'll settle it all later. We will. It's great to see you, anyway."

Then James did fall asleep.

He woke up outside the doctor's office. Dr. Landros didn't say a word to scold them. She just took them back into an examining room and untied the makeshift sling. She was just telling Sammy, and the other two, that it was hematoma, explaining that the swelling was just that, swelling, nothing broken, when Gram burst into the room.

Sammy didn't wait for whatever it was Gram opened her mouth to say. "It's my fault. Really it is," Sammy said to her, not waiting for whatever she wanted to say.

Gram didn't answer him. She looked at Dr. Landros, who was wearing old slacks and a baggy sweater. "What kind of a doctor are you?" Gram asked. Gram didn't look any much different from the doctor, in her baggy shirt with her hair wild and curly. Neither of them looked too respectable.

"A woman doctor," Dr. Landros answered.

"Don't be stupid," Gram snapped. "It says out there obstetrics."

"Gram," James said, but it came out a whisper and she ignored him, too.

"Former internist, present general practitioner, fully licensed by the state of Maryland," Dr. Landros said, turning her attention to James. "And what damage have you done to yourself?" she asked.

"I heard something—grinding," he said. "Like in my chest. Just when I lifted my arm, and it's kind of hard to breathe deeply and—"

"Take off your shirt," Dr. Landros ordered.

"These are my grandsons," Gram explained to the doctor. She was apologizing.

"I don't blame you," Dr. Landros answered. "You can give them an earful when I'm through here. Does that hurt?" she asked James, her strong fingers pressing on his chest.

Yes, it did.

Four days later, James sat in French class, sat up straight and stiff because of the thick tape his chest was strapped around with, from armpits down to his navel. The X-rays showed two broken ribs. Dr. Landros had strapped him herself, while Gram watched, right there in the emergency room up at Salisbury. Gram hadn't asked James what happened, not then; neither had Dr. Landros. The only bright spot of the long afternoon had been watching the two women watching each other not ask any questions. They put the bicycle Gram had ridden to the doctor's into the back of Dr. Landros's car, with the fishing rods and tackle boxes. "You rode a bike?" James asked. "Maybeth was worried," Gram said. James believed that, but he didn't believe for a minute that was all. He'd smiled dopily, and snoozed, almost the whole next day through. Finally caught up on sleep, he went back to school Tuesday. There was nobody at school to tell about what had happened, so he just kept his torso stiff and went through his life as usual.

They'd almost finished with the French reports. Celie's report, and her pronunciation, had been the best so far, although James knew his had been about as good. Better in content but not so good in grammar and accent. The rest were just about what you'd expect. It was Andy Walker's he was listening to now.

James listened with his eyes on his own desk. Usually, he looked at the speaker and thought of questions to ask. There was always time for questions, and they were allowed to be in English, although the oral report, like the written, had to be given in French. James listened to Andy with his body straight but his head down. If he hadn't been strapped up, his whole body would have been hunched over.

Because Andy Walker had just taken the ideas and translated them into simple sentences. Some of them weren't even sentences, because he'd neglected to put an *est* in somewhere, or any kind of verb. Andy hadn't thought about the ideas, or connected them, or anything. James bet Andy hadn't even read the Camus essay. But that wasn't what was making him feel so terrible. James spoke sternly to himself: He'd already known how little he liked what he'd done, so why was he griping now?

He just wanted this to be over, and behind him. He closed his eyes, trying not to hear. He'd never felt so bad before, listening to Andy drop James's ideas one by one, like a kid dropping mudballs onto the ground. Andy didn't even know what the ideas were, not that they were necessarily so good, but that they deserved some attention, some respect. Ashamed, that's what James was feeling. He'd let this happen to his own ideas. He knew ideas didn't have feelings, weren't people, couldn't know what he'd done to them—but he was ashamed before his own ideas.

The ideas didn't know, couldn't know—but that didn't help any, because James knew. He'd thought he could stand it and then forget about it, knowing he'd never do it again. But now he didn't think he could do that. He had to do it, and he couldn't. Personally, he was a dork, a wimp, and he could live with that, he guessed; but his ideas were something else.

Except, there was nothing he could do.

Except, of course, there was. He saw suddenly and clearly what there was for him to do. Except he didn't have the courage. Although Sammy would say he did. Then maybe he did.

When Mr. Norton asked if there were any questions anyone wanted to ask Andy, James raised his hand. His was the only hand up. Since Andy hadn't said much of anything, there wasn't much of anything for anyone to ask questions about. Mr. Norton called on James.

"I wanted to ask Andy," James told the teacher, "if he thought Camus had based his essay on the myth that says Sisyphus was punished for defying the gods when he brought water to Corinth."

"You mean Camus's interpretation of the myth," Andy said. He hadn't expected James to ask any questions.

"The myth he bases the essay on, yes," James clarified it, making himself look at Andy. "Do you think that's the one?"

"I'd say so," Andy said, saying nothing.

James nodded his head, then raised his hand again. Mr. Norton called on him again.

"Or, do you think it was based on the story about Sisyphus wrestling Death, and winning, so the underworld was empty, so the gods punished him for that?"

"You know," Andy said, sounding surprised, "I think that's probably it. Instead."

James nodded his head. Andy was trying to sound surprised at a new idea—another old student trick—but he was really surprised at James asking questions. James raised his hand yet again. Mr. Norton called on him again, but with a strange expression on his face. James could bet that Mr. Norton could guess what his next question would be—after all, the teacher had read the essay.

"Or do you think it's the story about Sisyphus being allowed to come back from the dead to get back at his wife and then refusing to go back down into the underworld because life was so good. Do you think that's what they're punishing him for?"

Andy hesitated over his answer to that question. He was trying to figure out how to answer it without giving himself away.

"I never heard that one," he said. He wasn't looking any too pleased with James. Mr. Norton wasn't looking any too pleased with James either, although he was also looking puzzled. When James raised his hand again, Mr. Norton hesitated. A lot of people in the class, restless, ready to let Andy off the hook, turned to stare at James. He ignored them all, even Celie.

"What do you think Camus means when he says there's no fate that can't be surmounted by scorn?" James asked Andy. He didn't bother trying to make his face look innocent. Andy wasn't an idiot; he knew what James was up to. He was nervous, James could see, but scaring Andy Walker wasn't what James was after. If Andy wanted James not to ask questions, then he should have used James's ideas with a little respect. But Andy hadn't, any more that he'd used respect in making a date with Celie Anderson. James waited for Andy's answer. He knew Andy couldn't answer.

"Well, it's pretty much just what Camus says. It's pretty simple. I don't have any trouble with it." Andy tried to turn the tables on James, trying to make it sound like James was turning something simple and clear into something complicated and difficult. "It just means—you should scorn your fate. You know, not let it get you down."

Mr. Norton knew for sure, now. He looked at Andy. "I think that's about all the questions we have time for," he said, and James could see Andy relaxing. "Except I have one. Do you agree with Camus's conclusion?"

Andy nodded his head, looking the teacher in the eye the way any practiced liar knows to do.

"So you agree that Sisyphus must be imagined to be unhappy." Mr. Norton spaced out the first syllable of that last word. James knew why: because Camus's last sentence said just the opposite.

"Well, sure," Andy said, watching the teacher's face. Then he decided to go on, trying to distract the teacher, smoke-screening, derailing. "I really like Camus. I'm going to read some more of him this summer. I'm glad I chose this essay because it was so—*magnifique*."

That last piece of falsehood got Mr. Norton. He slammed both hands down on his desk, stood up leaning on them; he balled his hands up into fists and leaned on his knuckles. If he hadn't been so angry, it would have been funny. But he was angry, and his voice swelled up with it. "You're lying, Andrew Walker. You've cheated on this assignment and now you're trying to bull your way out of it."

"No, sir—" Andy started to say, but Mr. Norton didn't let him get words out.

"My only trouble is that you so obviously don't have the knowledge to do this by yourself. That's the only thing that's slowing me down at all."

"It's not true," Andy talked right back. The school was pretty strict about cheating, and he was frightened. The A-track courses, you could get thrown out of them if you cheated, which made a difference to your whole school career. And sports, too—you could be suspended from a team for cheating. "I didn't. Just because I'm not a brain, like some people—I didn't claim to really understand this essay, it's awfully hard, you know—and because I'm not one of your pets. I know I'm not, but you can't say I'm cheating just because you don't like me."

James could have admired the way Andy was trying everything. Mr. Norton just stood there, steaming angry and getting angrier.

"You're lying," he said.

"You can't say that without proof." Andy got aggressive. "You have no proof."

Mr. Norton didn't say anything. Andy was right, of course.

James raised his hand, but Mr. Norton didn't see him. So James just spoke out: "I gave him the notes. It was me."

He didn't want to raise his hand, he didn't want to speak up, but there was nothing for it, if he was going to not let Andy do this to his ideas. He hadn't realized when he started this that he'd have to finish it this way, but this was the only way to finish it. The kids around him made noises, but he didn't know what they signified. He was looking at Mr. Norton, who had turned his head to look at James.

"I read the essay and gave Andy my notes," he said.

"Did he pay you?"

"No."

"Did he threaten you?"

"No."

"Then why—"

James wasn't having anything to do with Andy Walker. He just talked to the teacher. "It doesn't matter why, because it's what I did."

Mr. Norton looked like he had no idea what to do. He dismissed everybody else in the class—and the other kids moved out of there pretty fast. Mr. Norton brought James and Andy to stand in front of his desk. "I'm going to report this," he said.

"Thanks a lot," Andy said. He looked at James, to include him in the sarcasm.

James just looked back. He figured Andy might try to get him, to beat him up or something, and he might succeed; but Andy couldn't scare him this way. Andy wasn't anything like as dangerous as those men, for one thing. James had seen worse than the expression in Andy's eyes. Andy and his friends and everyone else might lie in wait to beat up on James—which scared him, he couldn't kid himself about that. But other than that, since they already thought he was a total dork, what harm could they do? Pain hurt, but shame hurt worse, deeper.

When he couldn't make James look away, Andy turned around and sulked out of the room. He slammed a fist into the door frame as he went by it.

Mr. Norton sat down and studied James. "I have to report this."

"I know," James told him.

"Has he been cheating off you all year?" Mr. Norton asked. "I've thought so, but—" He waited.

James didn't say anything.

"Kids," the teacher said; then, "You're right not to say, I guess.

I'm not arguing with you." James didn't say anything, but he could appreciate Mr. Norton's predicament. The teacher couldn't punish Andy without including James. There was all the difference in the world between them, but they had to be treated the same.

"I find this extremely depressing," Mr. Norton said.

"Think of it as absurd," James advised him, getting a smile from the round face as he left the classroom. James gave himself the same advice, entering the hall.

It was going to be bad, whatever the trouble was he was in. Just how bad he didn't know, James thought, hoping it wouldn't be too bad. Knowing he shouldn't be hoping for anything. He moved stiffly along. He needed to stop in at his locker before the next class. Anyway, it wasn't as if he could lose popularity by this move. And if they threw him out of A-track French, he could earn his way back in, he was pretty sure of that. His record was clean up until now, that should count for something. His record would be clean from now on: That was the kind of student he was, the kind of person.

Celie Anderson was hanging around in the hall. Probably, Andy had taken out his feelings on her. James was sorry about that. He turned his torso, just to nod his head at her. He couldn't just turn his head, because of his ribs.

She was looking at him, her eyes big and filled up with emotion. She approached him, so he waited. "You shouldn't have—"

At those words, James stopped being cool, stopped not caring. He wished she hadn't waited, to yell at him. It was no good being pretty on the outside if your inside was all ugly that way. He wished hers wasn't that way, because—because her hair brushed against her cheek? he asked himself, sarcastic. Because she's pretty? He didn't want to hear whatever it was Celie Anderson planned to say.

"Don't say it, okay?" he asked.

"No, it's not okay," she told him. She sounded firm, not angry. James was surprised she insisted on talking to him. "You shouldn't have helped Andy. He always tries to slip through things, everybody knows that. I thought you were better than that."

"No you didn't," James reminded her. "You didn't think about me at all."

When she blushed, a faint pink color spread up her cheeks and her eyelids went down to hide her eyes. Her eyelashes were so long they almost touched her skin.

"I'm sorry," James said, because you didn't say the truth at someone, right out like that.

"No, you're right," she said, surprising him again. Maybe she just hadn't realized what she was doing. "Anyway," she changed the subject, "I wanted to ask you after your report, if you'd say that your book was more of a fairy tale than mine, even though mine was much more like a fairy tale."

That was more than enough apology for James. "Yes, I would," he answered. He wanted to just say yes, yes, for a while, to her, because—he'd been so afraid of what she might have been like inside herself, he was so glad to find out she wasn't.

"I'd have been misled by Saint-Exupery's style," she said. They were walking along the hallway together, somehow. James could barely think. "I was fooled by it. Style does that, in writing. Like looks, or appearance things in people."

"Agreed," James croaked out. He gave himself a mental shake, to get his mind back again, working. Do you think about things? he wanted to ask her; I never thought you had ideas, too, along with—but he knew how insulting that would sound.

"I guess you have to be careful if it's a stylish writer," she said. "I've read it, *The Hunchback*, so I could really see what you meant. I read it in English," she added, as if not to seem too smart. Was she afraid of being smart? James wondered. "Esmeralda really is much more like a fairy-tale character than the Little Prince is."

"Not her. It's Quasimodo I was thinking of," James argued.

"You're kidding. Do you really think that?" James nodded, because he did, and she looked up at him, smiling a little. "I'm tempted to say you're just identifying with Quasimodo—but that's not true, I bet. Do you ever have any ordinary ideas, the kind most of us come up with, James?"

He had her interest now, and he couldn't believe it, but he had to go to his locker so the conversation was over. He turned away.

Celie turned with him, holding her books close up against her chest.

"What's the matter with you? You're moving pretty funny."

"Just my ribs are strapped." James liked the way that sounded.

"What happened? Were you in a car wreck?"

"A fight."

"You don't look like the kind of person who fights. Where was this?"

"In Baltimore."

"What were you doing in a fight in Baltimore?"

She looked like she was about to laugh. He didn't understand girls: She actually looked like she liked the idea of him being in a fight.

James took out the books he needed. "It wasn't me, really, it was my brother. I was on the outskirts of the action. My little brother—" he closed the locker door and turned back to Celie Anderson, who was leaning up against a locker just looking at him; Celie Anderson waiting for him so they could walk on together. "Sammy was the center of it. He was—he was really something."

"You like him a lot?" she asked.

"Yeah, sure," James said. "Don't you?"

"What, like him? I don't even know him." James knew she was teasing him, and he liked that, too. "I asked because—I don't like my sister too much. But she's older."

"I've got an older sister. She's something too," James said. He'd like to hear about Celie's sister.

"Maybe you've just got a better family life," Celie told him.

If she knew, James thought, not saying anything. He knew, although he didn't know why, that she was finding him interesting. He knew that she liked what he'd done in French class. He began to hope that they might be friends. Probably, she wouldn't ever like him as a boyfriend, but friendship was what he wanted anyway. To be friends with her. Anyway, he thought, looking over at her profile, her hair brushing against her cheek as she walked beside him, that was what he wanted first.

That evening, he told Gram. They were having spaghetti made with fresh sausage from Tydings's grocery store and tomatoes from Gram's shelves. He told his family just the facts, or mostly the facts. "They'll probably call you in for a conference," he concluded. "I'm sorry for the trouble."

Gram nodded. She hadn't said anything, just listened hard. Nobody had said anything, except Sammy who'd enjoyed hearing what James had done. "Good-o," Sammy had said, when James explained about the questions he'd asked Andy. Maybeth watched James's face as he confessed the trouble he was in, but she didn't seem to see anything to worry about.

It was Gram who had cause to be worried, James knew. "I can imagine what Dicey will say," James said, to tell Gram that he could understand how she must see it.

"And she'd be right," Gram said. "Your grandfather," she looked at the children sitting at her table, "he was always one for ideas. That's one of the things I first liked about him, when we were courting. He seemed so attached to ideas—it was as if he was attached to bigger things than other people. Because ideas are bigger. But instead of tools, what happened was, he got to turning them into weapons."

James could see what she meant, and he nodded his agreement, looking straight into her straight glance. He heard the warning and he'd be careful.

"It'll be on your record?" Gram asked him.

"Permanently," he said. There was nothing he could do about that. He didn't know how much it would matter. But it was better than having the shame permanently on his back.

"Well, it's what Ophelia says. We know what we are, but we know not what we will be," Gram said.

That, James knew, was the end of it, whatever might get said in the conference, whatever Dicey might say. That was the end of it for Gram—she'd told him what she thought, and warned him. She trusted him to listen and to take warning. He wished there were words to tell her he had listened and heard; but she probably already knew, anyway, or could make a good guess; he could trust her, he knew.

"Ophelia," Sammy said. "That's Shakespeare."

"You get a little smarter every day," Gram told him. "And show-offier."

"I didn't say I'd read it," Sammy argued.

"No, you didn't," Gram agreed.

"He wrote that song about full fathom five," Maybeth explained to Gram.

"Just the words," Sammy corrected.

"Oh," Maybeth said, not minding being corrected.

"I've never heard of this Camus," Gram asked James. Well, it would be interesting to hear what she thought of it, James thought.

"I'll get a copy for you. I'd like to sing with the chorus next year, instead of playing baseball. Is that okay with you, Maybeth?" She might not want him around, and he thought he should give her a chance to say so.

"Yes. Yes, please." Maybeth wanted him around, there was no question. "We need tenors."

"What about me?" Sammy asked. "I can sing tenor."

"You're playing tennis," James reminded his brother.

"But I like to sing," Sammy protested.

"Tennis," James announced firmly. "You've got to. Because you're going to be very good at it. But mostly because"—he looked around the table, feeling fine, never mind the disciplinary question hanging over him—"Tillermans can do anything. Anything they want to. Even sports. Right, Gram?"

She knew he was joking. "Right you are. Anything they want. For good or ill—and it's been both, in my experience."

"Not me," Sammy said. His face was only slightly swollen but the bruises were still discoloring his flesh; he still looked pretty bad. "I can't."

Sammy just didn't know much about himself yet, James thought. "Don't be stupid," he advised.

"You ought to make up your mind what you think of me."

But James knew what he thought of his brother. How could Sammy not know that?

"And you can't stop me from singing in chorus either. You can't keep me from doing what I want. I'm a Tillerman too."

Sammy didn't even hear the contradictions in what he was saying, James thought. He wondered if the trouble was that Sammy didn't know what he thought of himself. James could sympathize with that.

CHAPTER 15

Sammy felt okay about things as long as the marks were on his face—the tender swellings, the big splotchy yellowed bruises—and on his body, too, with that arm that didn't hurt at all but looked pretty bad. He liked the excitement. Not at home, where they didn't pay much attention once they knew he was all right, but at school. The teachers and girls were sympathetic; the boys were envious. It made Sammy feel good about things: He was the kind of guy who got involved in a brawl, and didn't mind the danger or the getting hurt. He told Custer all about the fight. "You should have heard my brother. It was this real ruckus, and everybody in there was afraid of this guy, Chief they called him, who was lambasting me, and somebody had James pinned against the bar, and James just talked like . . ." Sammy couldn't think of anyone else who ever had talked like that. "He was just so cool-headed, and smart, and—he saved my skin."

"Wow," Custer said, as he had throughout the story. "I don't believe you really did that."

"I did," Sammy answered him. Feeling good.

But when, all too quickly, the hematoma subsided and his bruises faded away, Sammy didn't feel so terrific. He knew he could have gotten himself really hurt. He knew he'd been pretty stupid.

Sammy didn't know what to think: He knew he'd been stupid

and he knew he'd been brave and he didn't know where the one ended and the other began. He envied James, because broken bones were more real than bruises, even if they didn't show; and James always knew what to think because he was practically a genius, or something.

Sammy knew what the trouble was—he needed something to do. Crabbing, gardening, they were jobs he did but they didn't—they weren't *doing* something, not like tennis was. Tennis, you tried, you pushed yourself as hard as you could, you worked up a sweat. The other things, you worked and you sweated, but you didn't keep getting better at them. But Sammy didn't see how he was going to get any tennis in, not until practically the end of the summer. Mina was off on a European tour with the chorus from her college. She'd be back, but by that time Sammy would be so rusty he wouldn't be able to play against her. He could take tennis for his sport next year. But that was a whole summer away. He was tired of always having to wait for things. Always having not to have what he wanted. Even as he was thinking that, he knew it wasn't true—it wasn't even half true, and Sammy didn't know what he was doing having thoughts like that anyway. Sammy didn't know what the trouble was with him.

Rather than think about himself, Sammy concentrated on getting the summer organized. A couple of weekends before school got out, he invited Robin over after school on Friday, to introduce the kid to what the work would be like. They rode out on the bus together, then walked up the driveway to have a snack before taking the boat out. Robin didn't say anything much, just the polite things like the gingerbread was good and yes, please, he would like more milk. They didn't stay long in the kitchen. The sky was hanging low, as if it might rain, so they hustled on down to the dock.

Robin fastened himself into a life preserver and kept quiet

while Sammy got the boat ready. Sammy rocked the heavy motor forward, freed the catch, then lowered it gently into place. He pumped up gas from the five-gallon container. He cast off the bowline, and then, with the stern line loose in his hand, pulled on the starter until the motor caught. He threw the stern line over the dock, where they could pick it up easily when they returned, shifted into forward, and they chugged on off into the bay. Heading out.

Robin sat up in the bow, in the little triangular seat with orange life jackets jammed under it, on top of the anchor. He had his feet neatly side by side. After a few minutes in the open, he put on the sweater Sammy had made him borrow. Sammy didn't say a word. The boat cut through the tops of the little waves.

Sammy headed south. He had baited three traps that morning, and the metal cages were lined across the floor at his feet, with their plastic-bottle floats inside. He thought they'd just set three traps, just to give Robin the idea. He didn't plan to keep anything they might catch. Gram was making fried chicken for dinner, with her special gravy to go over the rice, the green beans they'd canned last year mixed in with tomatoes they'd put up, and chocolate cake for dessert. It was the meal Sammy had asked her to cook. It was Sammy's favorite meal.

For a while, Sammy just drove the boat along. It didn't matter where they set the traps—he didn't expect to catch any crabs, not this early in the season. Then he waved Robin back to the stern and put the tiller into the boy's hands. He sat in the center seat, to be handy in case Robin got into trouble. Robin kept them going straight for a while. Then he tried to make turns. It took him a few tries to get used to the backward way the steering worked. While he was making mistakes, the boat swooped sideways under Sammy, pushing him this way and that on the seat as Robin saw that he was going in the opposite direction to that which he'd intended, and overcorrected. They moved gradually toward the shore, and the details of the shoreline came into focus.

Sammy watched Robin making the usual mistakes, and watched the rim of growth that went right up to the low shelf of land, scrubs, and trees. He saw the way the water ate away under the trees at the very edge. It was a process that took only a few years once it got started. First the water would find a place to eat away at the bank, then it would gradually uncover the root system of the tree, as if the water were some kind of archaeologist, gently uncovering treasure buried within the earth. After a while, when the water had undermined enough, a little overhanging ledge of dirt was formed, which crumbled downward, and the process of erosion began again. The sides of the bay were filled with trees that had been felled in this gentle fashion. Snags, they were called.

All along the shoreline, snags lay half in, half out of the water. Some of them had lost all their branches and were beginning the final steps of decomposition. All had that bleached gray-brown color of dead wood soaked in salty water. They could be dangerous to boats, so when Robin came too close to the shore Sammy just pointed toward open water. He was pulled sideways by Robin's sudden response. When he'd regained his balance, he indicated with a gesture of his hand that Robin should speed up, and he was pushed forward onto the crab traps by the sudden burst of speed. He was laughing as he regained his seat, but Robin's face was serious, concentrating.

Sammy leaned forward. He had to yell to be heard over the motor. "Slow down, really a lot. I'll show you how to drop a trap."

Robin obeyed, handling the accelerator much too delicately now, overcorrecting again. Sammy took one of the traps, pulled out the float, and freed the feet of lightweight line that connected the float to the trap. When the boat was finally moving slowly enough, he caught Robin's eye and showed him how to stand up against the side of the boat, with the float in your right hand and the trap hanging closed from your left. As Robin watched, he dropped the trap into the water and immediately hurled the float out over the little gray waves. The line drifted out behind the float, to be pulled down by the descending trap.

The motor choked, sputtered, and died. The silence that fell over them was filled with water sounds, waves and wind. "I'm sorry," Robin said. "What did I do wrong?"

"Nothing. You just cut the speed too low. It happens. It's not serious. We'll just start the engine again. It works like a lawnmower."

"What if it won't start?"

"Then we'll row." The oars lay under the seats, out of the way but accessible.

"I don't know how to row."

"It's not hard." It sounded like Robin was trying to avoid being at the tiller. "How about if you drop the next two traps?"

They shifted seats. Robin's hands were clumsy, as Sammy had thought they would be, this first time handling the equipment. He didn't start the motor until Robin had unsnarled the line and stood in the right position.

"You have to be careful to toss the float out, to keep the line away from the propeller blades," Sammy warned Robin.

Robin nodded. "Because it could cut them," he explained.

"Not so much that as because the line could get tangled up in the blades and then the motor wouldn't work. It takes a while to free the prop when it's snarled."

"What about the boat, how would you keep it from drifting out to sea or something?"

The kid didn't know anything about the bay if he thought it

would be easy to get swept away to sea from Crisfield. It was possible, but it wouldn't happen easily. Robin was more anxious about this than Sammy had realized.

"We'd drop anchor," he explained. "The anchor's under the life preservers," he said, answering Robin's next question before the boy even thought to ask.

When Sammy looked up to check Robin's position, he saw the brown eyes looking at him with something he had to name admiration. He turned a wide circle to head back to where the float bobbled on waves that flowed by, up and down, under it. Sammy didn't mind being admired.

"Now," he called. The trap dropped, sinking rapidly into invisibility. Robin tossed the float well out and away. He bent down without being told, to get the third trap ready, and Sammy thought to himself that it might take a day or two to show him how to do things, but Robin was going to work out all right.

With all three traps set, Sammy cut the motor and let the boat drift along parallel to the distant shore. Robin watched the floats, which seemed to grow gradually smaller and smaller. "Don't you lose them?" he asked.

"Nope." Sammy looked at the gray water, then let his eyes go up to the gray sky. On the earth side, white wisps blew loose from the massed gray clouds. If you could cut through those clouds, the sun would be shining, on the sky side.

Sammy thought the wind was rising, just a little. But they only had time for a couple of runs along the line of traps anyway; he just wanted to give Robin the feel of pulling up the traps and hanging around in the boat, a feeling for the way the work went. Sammy leaned back against the bulwarks, letting his feet rest against the opposite side of the boat. The boat floated under him. The muggy air blanketed him. At the moment, he couldn't think of anything he'd change about the whole world.

"My mom says," Robin remarked, "that even considering your family you're still unusually self-reliant. She really likes you."

Sammy smiled: He'd thought so; he hoped so. He lay back, lazy. His body was tuned to the movements of the boat; his eyes automatically watched the sky he knew almost exactly how far they were from shore and where he'd head in case of a squall or any trouble—he guessed you could say he was self-sufficient.

"Dad says you've got a crush on her," Robin talked on.

Sammy made his face a mask. He didn't want his face giving anything away, even though he wasn't sure what there was for his face to keep secret. He kept his eyes on the water's surface.

"He says," Robin laughed, "he doesn't blame you, he has a crush on her himself."

Sammy wasn't interested in any of that. He sat up, bringing his feet down with a thud. "Mothers, parents—sometimes it looks like they like their kids' friends when the friends are the way they want their kids to be. The way they wish their kids were."

Hearing himself, he didn't think he'd made much sense, but Robin followed his thought. "Did yours?" Robin asked.

"What?"

"Is that what your mother did too?"

"No," Sammy said. He'd never thought about comparing his mother to other mothers. He wondered if that was because he knew how bad she'd look, compared to other mothers. "She didn't do the usual things. She wasn't like most people."

"What was she like?"

Sammy never talked about Momma; he almost never really thought about her; he just remembered. But floating along in the boat, he wanted to say something. "She played with me, she was fun. Her hair was long and soft—it kind of shone." He remembered that. Remembering that hurt, but it was a good kind of pain. "I was pretty little when she died, but I think now," he thought aloud, "she was the kind of person who might be too gentle. You know?" The kind of person who needed taking care of—he couldn't stop himself from thinking—and his father was the kind of man who didn't take care of things. And Sammy—he'd made Momma take care of him. Which couldn't have helped her out any. "She played with me," he insisted. "We had fun. She liked me."

"We play Scrabble a lot and she always beats me," Robin said. "But I don't mind, and I'm getting better, too."

"She liked me exactly the way I am," Sammy said. "Or was." He guessed, thinking back, Momma had done that, liked people just the way they were instead of wishing they were someone else. Including his father. "But she really wasn't like other people."

"Because she was sick?" Robin guessed.

Sammy didn't correct him, and maybe that was why, anyway.

"They say that mothers have a special feeling for their sons. Do you think that's true?"

Sammy didn't remember that. But how would he know? Momma hadn't been normal anyway. It wasn't normal to just abandon your kids, even though you loved them, and then go die in a hospital for crazy people. It didn't make any difference to how Sammy felt whether it was normal or not, but it wasn't normal.

"Because my mom might have another baby if they can afford it," Robin continued. "And it might be a girl."

"Yes, it might," Sammy agreed. He started to laugh at the obviousness of that. Robin joined in. They were thinking along the same lines, he and Robin. Sammy could feel that, and he liked it. Maybe Robin was going to be a friend. "My father never married her," he said. And wished right away he'd kept his mouth shut.

But Robin surprised him. "Sometimes I wished my father hadn't. They just got divorced anyway, which is about the same as never being married. Only it's worse, maybe."

"Maybe," Sammy agreed, thinking about this new angle. "You can't lose what you never had. Anyway, you got another one."

"He made her cry," Robin said. He was looking out over the water now; it made him ashamed that his father made his mother cry. "She used to cry a lot and he'd never—care."

Sammy didn't much like the sound of Robin's father, who didn't try to visit his own son, anyway, and he knew about his son, he knew where his son was. "Anyway, she doesn't cry now, does she?"

"If she did, Dad would care," Robin told him. "Did yours ever?"

"I don't remember, so maybe she didn't. She used to sing some awfully sad songs, I remember that." It was time to start the motor, but Sammy was reluctant to stop the talking. He knew he had to, they'd have lots of time for talking, all summer. And besides, all this remembering hurt him; it hurt him to love Momma and to wonder: if his father had been different, if she didn't need to go crazy and die, if there had been someone there taking care of her, instead of someone there needing to be taken care of. Sammy had never thought before how complicated it might have been.

He tried to explain to Robin about pulling up the traps, how you had to almost jerk up at first, to close the doors and trap the crab that might be inside. On the floor of the bay, he explained, the four doors lay flat open, and a long quick pull on the line from above closed them before the crab could escape. "We probably won't get any, this time of year. This summer we'll be crabbing with a trotline, but I didn't want to bait one just for an hour. This is a kind of practice."

"I'll need practice, because I've never done anything like it," Robin said. "Dad said so. He said I should plan to watch carefully and take directions."

Sammy, smiling away inside of his head at Robin's little-kid seriousness, gave him directions as he brought the boat back to the first float and approached it at the lowest possible speed. Robin leaned out to grab the line just under the water. "Got it," Robin said, straightening up and pulling his arm way back, then hauling the line in as fast as he could while Sammy turned the boat in a slow circle to keep the line clear of the propeller.

"Empty," Robin said. He held the dripping trap out over the water. "But it felt heavy."

"Just drop it in again," Sammy directed, speaking loudly to be heard over the motor. "And—" He was about to say toss the float wide, but he saw that Robin remembered. He kept his mouth shut.

The other two traps were empty too. Sammy didn't mind. Robin didn't mind.

The clouds that were moving in a mass over them had turned darker. The lower layer now blew thick, white, like whitecaps upside down. Instead of letting the boat drift, Sammy set the anchor. He showed Robin how to do it, how to pull back on the anchor line to be sure the two broad steel teeth were lodged in the bay floor. The anchor caught, hard and fast, and he checked to be sure the line was well wrapped around the cleat at the bow. He explained to Robin that the waves were getting choppier and the sky didn't look too good.

"It's okay for us to be out still, isn't it?" Robin asked, trying not to sound frightened.

"Sure," Sammy reassured him. "I've been out in lots worse." He had, too.

The boat rocked now, its floor slapping down onto the sides of waves that passed beneath them. The wind was chilly. Sammy didn't wait too long. It wasn't the time of year for squalls, he thought, but it wouldn't be too smart to get themselves soaked with rain. He started the motor after only a few minutes, then told Robin to sit at it, ready to shift into gear when he had the anchor loose.

The trouble was, the anchor wouldn't come up. It was stuck on something and Sammy couldn't pull it free. If it had been Jeff or James in the boat, he could have tried approaching the anchor from a different angle; but Robin wouldn't know how to work the tethered boat around, wouldn't know how to hold it against the wind and waves, wouldn't know how to try running the boat up over the line to pull the anchor loose, wouldn't know to cut the motor immediately so that the line wouldn't wrap around the propeller. If they changed places, Sammy thought, that wouldn't be any better because Robin wouldn't know how to play on the anchor line, feeling the right direction to pull in, if they could find it.

The waves weren't really getting that much higher, he told himself. The wind really wasn't rising so fast. He knew that. But he felt as if wind and waves were building, every second.

He jerked on the line, pulling with all his weight.

Nothing happened.

He jerked again. He leaned out over the water and tried pulling straight up.

He couldn't budge it. They were caught there, trapped.

Robin was watching him. He didn't know what to do and the kid was watching him, like Sammy had the answers to everything. He wondered how long it would be, anyway, until somebody figured out that something had happened, and found a boat to come looking for them. In this weather—which wasn't bad yet, not at all, but might get worse.

Sammy wasn't thinking clearly, he knew that. Ideas fell around in his mind, like a castle you'd built out of wooden blocks, then kicked down. Ideas fell with a thump all over his mind and he couldn't do any more than listen to them hitting the ground.

He reached down and uncleated the anchor line, tossing it overboard. He'd hear about that, but he couldn't think of anything else to do to free their boat. The anchor line sank under the waves.

As soon as he nodded to Robin, who shifted into forward with the motor racing at a speed that almost tumbled Sammy out of the boat, the wind seemed to slow down. The waves seemed to subside.

Maybe it wasn't so bad after all. But it had seemed bad, dangerous. He thought now that things were okay. But he honestly hadn't thought that before. It was an honest mistake. But what would he say to Gram and James about the anchor?

Sammy moved back to the motor, and Robin hauled up the traps, one empty, two empty. When he had the traps on board, while Sammy drove the boat in a wide circle, Robin wound the line around the float and jammed it back into the traps, just the way they had been on the way out. Robin was having a good time anyway.

The final trap had a crab in it. Robin turned around to face Sammy, his face almost split in half by his smile. "Look. Look at this, Sammy. I caught one."

Inside the metal grid of the trap the crab looked huge. It was probably six-and-a-half or seven inches from point to point.

"You almost never get one that big this early," Sammy congratulated him.

The crab's shell was browned with living through the winter. It glared out from the metal box, which swung at the end of the line Robin held. Its high round eyes looked like they personally hated Robin and Sammy.

"I caught it!" Robin yelled. "I caught a crab! My first time!"

Sammy could remember how that felt. He could remember why Robin was so excited. The crab tried to move its big front claws, to raise them out and threaten its captors, but the cage was too small. Its eyes glared and spittle appeared at its mouth. The claws pushed against the sides of the trap, as if the crab was trying to bend them.

Sammy felt for that crab, which was pretty funny considering the number of crabs he had plopped down into bushel baskets, or plopped down into steaming water, or plopped down into his mouth for that matter.

"Open the door and let it go," he called forward. "We've got to get back, and pretty fast." The wind *was* rising. Robin was having trouble keeping balance as the boat bucked under them.

"I can't keep it?"

Sammy shook his head. Robin wanted to ask again, but Sammy shook his head again. Robin obeyed. He shook the trap out over the water until the downside door opened. The big crab, almost as if he didn't trust this trick either, clung for a minute, one of his pincers locked around a strand of metal. Then the boat dipped down into the trough of a wave and water splashed up onto the crab, which let go and fell free.

Robin returned to the middle seat and Sammy opened the throttle. The nose of the boat rose up as they bounced their way home. The wind was against them, the waves were against them, and heavy spray splashed up wildly. Spray rained down over them, cold and wet. Robin's hair strung down along the side of his face. Sammy's cheeks stung and his left shoulder was soaked. It was almost dangerous out there, and they looked at one another to laugh out loud together at the wildness of it.

CHAPTER 16

Sammy leaned his elbows on the table and rested his chin on the palm of a hand. He yawned. After the confusion of the afternoon, of feelings and thoughts, of weather and people, it was good to sit in his own kitchen, warm, dry, his stomach full. He saw that Maybeth hadn't taken more than a couple of bites of her cake. "Can I finish that?" he asked her. She passed the plate over to him.

Sammy wasn't hungry. In fact, he was full, but he wanted the taste of chocolate in his mouth. James was eating away at his second big piece of cake as if he were still really hungry—maybe he was. Maybe James was the kind of person nothing was enough to satisfy, nothing filled up. Eating lazily, his chin still resting on his hand, Sammy felt sorry for James—because you'd always be hungry, for all kinds of things, for friends and grades and other things to do. You'd always be seeing what might be coming up next and not what was there now.

Sammy saw what was there now, and he was satisfied. Yeah, but that was why James would always do better than other people. James would always be moving forward, looking at new ideas; he'd keep on discovering things, while Sammy—

Sammy dropped his fork down on his plate. He'd already swallowed the bite that was too much, the one that turned full into stuffed. He felt heavy and overfed, and as if he'd never be able to move from the table. He envied James his unfillable appetite.

And his brains, too, the way they kept him out of trouble or got him out of trouble. The chocolate taste in Sammy's mouth was too sweet now, and bitter. He got up to pour himself a little more milk, to wash it away. Robin had gone home and it was time to tell them about the anchor. He stood at the counter and looked at his grandmother. They'd give him an earful, he knew that. He dove into trouble like going off the dock. "I lost the anchor this afternoon."

His grandmother looked at him and he looked right back at her, ready to get angry back. But she didn't say anything. Maybeth didn't even raise her head. It was James who jumped in. "You lost the anchor?" James sounded as if he couldn't believe what he'd heard.

Sammy nodded his head.

"How could you do something like that?"

Sammy shrugged. There was nothing to say. If James had asked *how* it had happened, that was a question he could answer. But James didn't want to know that—that was one of the few things in the world James wasn't curious to know, because all James wanted was to feel superior.

"Anchors aren't free," James pointed out.

Sammy nodded.

Gram wasn't angry after all. She was looking at him as if she were thinking hard. "I set it," Sammy explained to her, "to show Robin how and because drifting makes him nervous, and there was a wind." He tried to explain how the anchor had to be left behind, not trying to pretend he hadn't made any mistakes. He wasn't trying to convince them he thought he had done something right. When he finished he sat down again.

James was pretty disgusted with him and Gram was

disappointed. The only one who didn't have anything to say was Maybeth. She'd been pretty quiet, too, all through dinner, but then Maybeth was like Robin in that way, shy, needing to be taken care of. Sometimes, Sammy thought, it was better to be gotten mad at. Sometimes, he stared at Maybeth's head with its soft, shining golden curls, sometimes he could understand why his father had just taken off.

"How are you going to earn the money to replace it without the anchor to have in the boat so you can go out crabbing?" James asked, being logical.

James didn't need to say that; Sammy could think of that all by himself without anybody telling him. He'd already thought of that difficulty.

"We'll replace it," Gram told James. "You'll have to reimburse us," she told Sammy.

As if Sammy didn't already know that. As if he wasn't planning to.

"You should have waited for a calm day, anyway," James pointed out. "You didn't have to go out this afternoon. You knew Robin didn't know anything about boats. Or taken someone else along with you," he suggested.

Yeah, but it was too late now.

"Or tied a life preserver to the line. Then we could have gone back and had a chance of recovering the anchor," James went on.

"Or one of the bailers, which are easy to replace," Gram suggested.

Sammy couldn't say anything because everything they were saying was right. But he wished they'd stop talking at him. What was done was done. He was sorry. He'd said he was sorry. There wasn't anything else he could do. So why did they have to keep blaming him? They were acting as if he were the kind of person who didn't care what he did, or always went around losing anchors and things. It made him angry and he wished they would just let the subject go.

"Anyway, who could I take?" he defended himself. "You weren't around," he reminded James.

Nobody had any answer to that. Suddenly, nobody had anything to say.

Sammy had said something wrong, something awfully wrong, and Gram and James knew what, but he didn't. If they didn't tell him, how was he supposed to know? How was he supposed to guess, without being told? And then, the way they were looking at him—like he should know, like they couldn't believe he didn't know. They were blaming him now for not knowing. It made him angry, even though he maybe ought to know whatever it was he didn't.

Sammy just looked around the table, feeling helpless, and wrong, and angry, and sorry for whatever it was. He looked at Gram, who didn't look any too pleased with him. He looked at James, who looked like Sammy had done something incredibly stupid. He looked at Maybeth, at the top of her bent head.

"May I be excused, please?" Maybeth asked, her voice soft.

"Yes, of course," Gram said.

Without raising her face, Maybeth left the table, left the room. She moved so gently, Sammy wasn't sure whether she had gone upstairs or not. "What's wrong with Maybeth?" he asked his brother.

James just shook his head at Sammy.

"You haven't helped her one bit, young man," Gram said to Sammy.

"What did I do? I didn't do anything. It's only an anchor," he reminded her.

Gram just shook her head at Sammy. "And this business, going off to Baltimore to get in a brawl about your father."

"That wasn't why—" Sammy started to say, but she cut him off.

"I don't know why you couldn't just ask me. And now your sister—maybe I'm just not used to having someone around who cares about dances, maybe that's why I'm feeling so inadequate."

Sammy wanted to tell Gram that she wasn't inadequate, but he didn't know whether to say anything to her or not.

"What's the problem with the dance?" James asked. "She has that green dress to wear, is there something wrong with it?"

"The problem is, she doesn't have a date," Gram said, pronouncing the word "date" as if it were something in a foreign language, a foreign language she didn't like.

"But she's popular," James said. "She's sure to be asked."

"Why does she need a date?" Sammy asked his grandmother.

"Don't ask me. She says she does, because of the kind of dance it is, some sort of beginners' prom. Don't ask me to explain—I can't make sense out of it myself. A couple of boys did ask her, but they weren't boys she wanted to go with, so now she's not going at all."

That all sounded pretty clear to Sammy. Maybeth had made her decision. It had nothing to do with him.

"And I think I shouldn't have told Dicey she could take that job in Annapolis," Gram said. "I'm not sure it's good for her always to be trading off housework and babysitting for her living quarters, even if she can learn ships' carpentry there."

"It's what Dicey wants," Sammy said. He'd rather have had Dicey around for himself, too, but that wasn't going to happen. "Dicey is going to school most of the year, which is what you want her to do," he reminded his grandmother.

"I know," she said, "and I don't know about that, either."

"We could use her around here," James said.

"And that can't be good for the girl," Gram said. "I wish I knew."

"Yeah," James said, meaning something more than what Sammy could figure out. Gram could figure it out, because she gave James one of her quick smiles. They'd left Sammy out, left him behind.

"Then, the way you two never even asked me," Gram said.

James looked at Sammy, but Sammy didn't know what she was talking about either.

"Asked you what, Gram?" James asked.

"And I'd guess you were right not to," Gram went on. "Because I only know what he wanted me to know. He was like that."

"Our father," Sammy told James. "Asked her about our father she means."

"I'd have told you he was a charmer, and I'd have been misleading you—but you never asked."

Sammy looked at James: Neither of them had ever thought she'd feel that way.

"Sammy was afraid you'd think we thought you weren't doing a good job," James explained.

"And James wanted to do it himself," Sammy added. "Well, that's true," he told his brother.

"We didn't want to worry you," James said.

"That's the only reason why," Sammy echoed.

"Ah," Gram said, and she laughed. "I see."

Sammy laughed too, with James, but he was laughing for more than the reason of Gram's joke. He was laughing because he guessed his father hadn't wanted them to know anything about him. They only found out what the man wanted other people to know. They hadn't found out anything, and they'd worried Gram, and the whole thing had been a mistake. Sammy, for one, was finished with this father business.

"I can get a newspaper route again, to pay for the anchor," Sammy offered.

"There's no need for that," Gram stopped that suggestion dead. "We need you around here." She looked at him then, making up her mind.

"Maybeth thought she was going to work with you this summer. The anchor business is settled, but—she was counting on it, that's my guess."

"But I never said she was," Sammy protested.

Gram didn't say anything.

"Maybeth never said so," Sammy protested.

"Yes, she did," Gram corrected him.

She had, yes, but it wasn't anything exactly. Nothing like, Can I be the one to work with you, giving Sammy a chance to say exactly yes or exactly no.

"But—" Sammy tried to think of something. He knew there was a reason.

"But I didn't know," he said. That was true. He was sorry, and he thought maybe he should have known, but he hadn't.

"I didn't say you did," Gram said, as if that was even worse.

James got up and started clearing the dishes. Sammy couldn't move. He felt—terrible. If he had known, if he'd paid enough attention to notice, he'd have asked Maybeth. He should have noticed. He was sorry he hadn't. He was nothing but sorry these days, it felt like.

"It's too late now, isn't it?" he asked. He didn't know why he asked, since he already knew the answer. Maybeth would have liked to help out, to be helping out. She wouldn't have figured out, either, that Sammy had just forgotten about her. And he didn't know why he had. He didn't even know why he hadn't done something he hadn't done.

Sammy wanted to get up from the table and—and go outside

into the night, maybe ride his bike fast and dangerously in the dark. He felt so bad, though, that he didn't even have the energy to get up from the table and wash dishes.

Maybe he'd just let James wash the dishes by himself, since James was so perfect. Maybe, since he got everything going wrong, he'd just plan to be that way. Maybe that was just the way he was and there wasn't anything he could do about that. And maybe he didn't even want to.

Sammy got up from the table, then, and set his chair neatly, precisely, back into place. He didn't say a word. He just walked out the door, across the porch, down the steps, and away.

Sammy lay on the dock, out at the end of the wooden platform. In a while he'd go back inside, he guessed, but he didn't know what he'd say to them, if he'd say anything. He was flat on his back, his legs dangling down from the knees. He had his eyes open, staring up at the darkness overhead, staring into it.

A rising wind was breaking up the cloud cover, blowing it away over the land, blowing it east to the ocean. As the clouds separated they revealed the night sky waiting behind them. The dark wind filled his ears, blowing over above him. Beneath him, waves rushed up to the shore, slapping against the sides of the little boat. Beyond all of it, in distant silences, he could catch glimpses of black fields of space, scattered with stars.

Each star was a sun, and who was to say what planets whirled around their suns out there. The clouds broke up, blew away, and the whole endless starry landscape of space opened up before him. There might be life out there. The same logic that pointed out what a strange and singular event the coming of life to earth was—using that argument to say combinations of circumstance couldn't happen again—had to admit that strange and singular things were not impossible. What had happened once could happen again. Not in the same way, probably. Even people—who were pretty much the same stuff, made out of the same stuff to the same basic design—people never exactly duplicated one another. Sammy let his mind wander out there, moving among the possibilities the stars might offer. A kind of explorer, a kind of pioneer, adventurer—he'd like that.

You couldn't just go out into space because you wanted to, though. If he wanted to do that, he'd have to learn to be more like James. You'd have to be able to do things *and* have ideas. He wouldn't mind learning from James, anyway. James, at least, when he did things, like that French report he'd told them about, he went ahead and did something to correct it.

But Sammy couldn't think of anything to do to correct the things he'd done. The anchor was gone, lost. You couldn't find things you'd lost overboard. The bottom shifted, mud and sand moved constantly, covering up anything that fell in; and then, it was almost impossible to pinpoint any particular spot on the water, because there were no stable landmarks. You couldn't mark anything by a wave. A wave just moved on away; it was just part of a moving pattern.

There wasn't anything he could do about Maybeth, either. He'd already asked Robin. He was sorry, so sorry it squeezed at his heart, but he couldn't think of any way to fix things up. Sammy sat up to swing his legs over the dark water. He couldn't see anything except the massed shadowy shapes of things. Even with his eyes accustomed to the dark, he couldn't pick out much of anything.

When he heard somebody walking along the dock, he knew it was James. Maybeth wouldn't be coming down to find him; Maybeth never pressed a person. Gram's bare feet would have moved soundlessly, imperceptible under the sounds of wind and waves. These were sneakers he heard, at the ends of cautious legs which moved slowly because of the blindness of dark. Sammy wished James had left him alone out here.

James sat down. Sammy waited.

"From here," James said, "the stars look close together, the sky looks crowded. It looks like you could just step from star to star, doesn't it? I know that's not true, but it really looks that way."

Sammy didn't say anything. Old James couldn't even see something as ordinary as the night sky without starting to think about it. James was—always so unexpected.

"Do you ever wonder . . . ?" James's voice drifted off.

Sammy waited, then asked, "Wonder what?"

"Oh, about how things look not being the same as how they are. That difference. It makes everything so complicated and hard to figure out. Do you ever wonder about that?"

No, Sammy hadn't. He wasn't sure he wanted to. "Not yet," he said.

Their voices didn't blow away on the wind. Because they were sitting side by side on the narrow dock, their voices just floated between them, back and forth.

"Besides," Sammy pointed out, "they don't always." Which made things even more complicated.

"Anyway," James said. "I was wondering how you feel. How *are* you feeling, Sammy?"

For a minute, Sammy didn't answer anything, because he was wondering how James knew to ask that question. Then he said what was true. "Bad. About—everything. About myself, too. And angry."

"Yeah, I know."

Sammy couldn't see how that was true. "You don't even know how to get angry."

"Not that, but—feeling trapped, trapped in someone you don't want to be—and it isn't what you're like, but everybody keeps you there, so—you figure you might as well really be that person."

Sammy turned his head to stare at James's profile. If he looked, he could see his brother, even in this dark light. That idea pleased him and he wanted to tell it to James. "It's like a dark light out here."

"Do you mean literally or metaphysically?" James wondered.

Sammy had no idea and it didn't matter. "I'm really sorry about Maybeth and the crabbing. I should have known. She's like Momma, isn't she? And someone like Momma you shouldn't ever—" He didn't have to finish that sentence. Because they were Maybeth's family, he suggested, "Why don't you take her to that dance? She wouldn't mind going with her brother, she's not the kind of girl who'd mind that. You know? And then she'd have someone to go with."

"I've never been to a dance. I don't know how to dance. I'd be a disaster as a date," James said.

"Okay then, we'll both take her." Sammy knew how to dance, and he liked it. Both of them would be even more fun; that was something nobody ever did, both of them being Maybeth's dates. Sammy thought it was a great idea.

James didn't. "You can't be serious."

"Why not? I can't take her on my own because I'm not old enough and if anyone recognized me they might send me home, and she'd be left alone, but if we both did—"

"It's not a bad idea. Not in itself. It's a pretty good idea, in fact. But I'd be incredibly out of place. I'll hate it," James admitted.

"I won't. And you might not. Maybeth can teach you how to dance—she's really good. And think of all those eighth and ninth grade girls, looking up to you as the older man."

"I'll probably embarrass you."

Sammy laughed. "Nothing embarrasses me."

"I envy you," his brother said.

Sammy couldn't believe that. He wondered what James was really thinking about, that would make him say that, and he wondered why James was agreeing to go to a dance. Even if it was one with only underclassmen he was going to for the sake of his little sister, it was still a dance. Sammy guessed, wondering, "James, you haven't ever been out on a date, have you?"

"A date with a girl?"

"Don't be stupid."

"Hey," James joked, "nobody's supposed to say that to me."

He was avoiding the question—Sammy could figure that out. He let James avoid it. He guessed, wanting to avoid it answered the question.

Over to the east, over the black, choppy water, the moon had risen, to begin the journey across the sky. Sammy could see how you would think the moon, with its cold, sad face looking down, was a chariot, pulled by pale horses, driven by a goddess. The silver light glimmered on the tops of the waves. Sammy thought, It would be something to stand on the moon and see the earth. He wondered if the earth shone. "Could you look it up in a book to see if the earth shines, from the moon?" he asked James.

"I guess. They took pictures, the astronauts, so I guess you could. I didn't know Mr. Norton was Robin's father."

"He isn't. He's a stepfather. Robin likes him better than his real father, it sounds like, when he talks, but he doesn't seem to know that."

"Yeah. He seems kind of young. Robin."

"Didn't you like him?"

"I liked him fine," James said. "He's just—sort of pale, quiet—I dunno, he sort of reminds me of myself a little, kind of wimpy."

"Wimpy?" James wimpy? If James hadn't sounded serious, Sammy would have laughed.

"You know, the way he didn't say much and tried to agree with everyone."

"Nobody thinks you're wimpy, James." Sammy tried to explain: "You're weird—different—because you always—think so much about things and I never know what you're going to be thinking, but—"

"Wimpy," James said. "A dork. That's what people think."

"Stuck-up, maybe." Sammy could see how people might think his brother acted superior.

"You just don't know, Sammy."

Maybe he didn't. But even if he found out, he wouldn't agree. He knew better, and he would know better than the people who only knew James at school. He *knew* James.

"Anyway, why didn't you tell me who Robin's father was?"

"I didn't know if you'd want me to know. You didn't say anything about what happened after. What is going to happen?"

"They made him flunk me for the last marking period, which includes the exam. It'll make my year's grade a low B, at worst, but that's only a sophomore grade so it's not all that serious. I hope."

Sammy didn't know anything about how colleges and scholarships looked at grades, but he hoped so too. "He had to flunk Andy Walker, too."

"Mr. Norton didn't mind doing that I bet. And Andy won't get a C for the year, so he won't be able to take French III either."

"Serves him right. But how do you know what he'll get?"

"I know the grades he's been getting all year."

"How would you know that?"

"You can see, when they hand the papers back."

"But why would you care about what other people get?" Sammy wondered.

James took a while answering that question. "No good reason," he finally said. "You're right, Sammy, there's no good reason for that."

"One good thing," Sammy pointed out, "you won't have to study for the exam."

"Yes, I will," James said. "I'd like to get a perfect A on that one.

"But why?"

"Because I can."

James was so right about some things, it was almost depressing. And he was so wrong about others—Sammy couldn't tell what to think about James. He wished he knew for sure, but he guessed he couldn't; but it wasn't the kind of thing he was comfortable with, not being sure. He wondered if getting older meant just getting less and less sure about more and more things. "James," he started to ask, but James was already talking.

"Do you remember," James said, so cautiously that Sammy listened carefully, "how we'd go out, all three of us, us and Jeff, crabbing?"

Sammy had caught on and finished the idea before James had half-finished asking it. "And we could split the money three ways, with us getting two-thirds of it, which is almost as good as all. It's lots more than half. I didn't even think of that, James. Let me be the one to ask her, okay? I get to do that. Because—why didn't I think of it? I'm really stupid sometimes."

"Yeah," James agreed. Sammy punched at him, for saying that; not hard though, because of his ribs. "Well, you are," James said.

James looked at his brother, close beside him. He could see that Sammy was glad to have a solution, genuinely glad. Sammy's gladness spread out from him like light, almost visible. James hoped, thinking back over the spring, that Sammy would forget about their father. He didn't want Sammy to be troubled, as he had been troubled, by this question of the man they'd never find.

Sammy wasn't the kind of person to worry at a question though. He was a doer, not a worrier. As long as he had something to do. "Let's build you a backboard," James said, the idea just shooting into his mind and out of his mouth. He didn't know where the idea came from. "That way, with a backboard to play against, you can practice your tennis even while Mina's traveling in Europe with her choir. So you don't have to get rusty, or whatever it is that happens when you don't practice." James thought he could figure out how to build a backboard. He could read up on what it was supposed to be like. "We could use the barn wall," he said, "That should work." They'd have to figure out how to level the ground, and how to start earning and saving some money for the materials they'd need to buy. When Sammy had something to do, like playing tennis, he was easier on himself; and that would give Sammy a better chance of keeping what was so good about him while he was growing up. "Do you want to?" James asked, doubting now because Sammy hadn't said anything. Thinking about it a second time, James wasn't so sure he wanted to make a backboard. The more he thought about it, the more hard work he knew it would take. It wasn't the kind of thing he was good at, hard work.

Sammy looked at his brother. Did James think he didn't want a backboard? How could James even think he wouldn't want one? How could James not know that was about the best idea Sammy had heard in . . . in ever. Poor old James—he didn't know enough about other people. Sammy hoped that James would be able to forget about their father, gone like that anchor was gone, gone and done with. Sammy figured he himself would have done a lot of fighting with their father, and he wouldn't have liked the man much. Except sometimes he thought they would have gotten along just fine, and that was just as bad. He had less of a father than any of the rest of them, because their father hadn't ever even seen Sammy, and that was a lonely feeling. If Sammy had known him, though, it probably would mean only that he knew who he didn't want to be like. Which he already knew a lot about. Without a father, it was like being lost without a map: Sammy pictured that, being lost in the stars and no map to guide him. But the picture was exciting, not frightening; it was an adventure. Sammy didn't mind adventures. Not even if they were like flying blind and alone, and wondering what he was going to do next. That was the kind of thing that bothered James, but it didn't bother him. And if James had something to think about, the chances were pretty good he wouldn't waste time being bothered. A backboard was a kind of tennis court, and they weren't easy to build. It would take a lot of planning, and learning about things neither of them knew anything about. James would enjoy that. It was just like James to have such a good idea, but Sammy hadn't known that James understood how he felt about tennis.

There was, however, one thing he needed to get straight with his brother. "Once we start on the work—we'll have to clear away the bushes and flatten the barn wall, maybe rebuild it—you're going to want to quit. I'm not going to let you, once we start. I'm going to stay on your back. I'll make you work more than you want to, make you work hard." Sammy could do that—he could make James do more than he wanted to, or thought he could. Sammy knew that about himself and about James.

"I think that'll probably be good for me," James admitted.

"And I'm still going to sing in the chorus, too," Sammy said. "You can't stop me."

"Who says I want to?" James demanded. "I never said you couldn't."

"That way, we can keep an eye on Maybeth," Sammy pointed out.

"Keep an eye on her?"

"She's awfully pretty, James." Sammy didn't want to say outright that he didn't want anyone like their father moving in on Maybeth and making a mess of her life. He didn't know how James would take that.

"I can't see myself battling off her boyfriends," James said.

"I can do that part. What I can't do is know who should be fought off, or when she needs to just make up her own mind. But between the two of us—" Alone he'd probably make a mess of it, Sammy thought. James wasn't saying anything. He wondered what James was thinking.

"We'd probably be smart to do that," James said. "I'll try," he said, giving his word. His brother's word was good enough for Sammy.